Extreme Cuisine

Kit Sloane

DURBAN HOUSE

Extreme Cuisine

Printed in the United States of America.

For information address:
Durban House Publishing Company, Inc.
7502 Greenville Avenue, Suite 500, Dallas, Texas 75231

Library of Congress Cataloging-in-Publication Data
Sloane, Kit, 1940 –

Extreme Cuisine / Kit Sloane

Library of Congress Control Number: 2004115673

p. cm.

ISBN 1-930754-68-X

First Edition

10 9 8 7 6 5 4 3 2 1

Visit our Web site at
http://www.durbanhouse.com

Cloquet hated reality
but realized it was still
the only place to
get a good steak.

—Woody Allen

William Styron has said that writers have "loneliness as a companion for life." I respectfully disagree. I owe great debts of gratitude and acknowledgement to Steve and the rest of my remarkable family; to Suzette and Frank Stephenson, star chef proprietors of the *Boar's Breath* restaurant in Middletown, California, for letting me look behind fictional kitchen doors; to Celli Martin for her sharp eyes and wicked imagination; to G. Miki Hayden for her counsel, insights and splendid wit; and to John Lewis for the inspiration.

The line that Carlos Estrella repeats onscreen, "A true love is complete in every moment it exists," is extracted from the brilliant novel *The Serial Killer's Diet Book* by Kevin Mark Postupak, and reprinted with the kind permission of Durban House Publishing.

Chapter I

GOLD COLORED WALLS surrounded her on three sides. The window to the right looked out on busy Sunset Boulevard. The noise of the constant flow of traffic, the headlights and taillights glittering in the night, was dimmed to nothing by the double-panes of glass. Jazz music from invisible speakers was kept low. Wooden fans hanging from the high ceiling rotated slowly, moving the fragrant garlic-scented air gently though the room.

The restaurant, housed in the corner of an old downtown building, was an art director's dream, the perfect background for its fabled "California cuisine." The room was simply but expensively furnished—the dark woods, the white table linens, the heavy flatware. No flowers. Lots of candlelight. The wood burning brick oven in the corner illuminated discreetly by overhead lights, a stage set for the artistry of the chef.

Margot O'Banion looked across the table at Max. He smiled at her, obviously pleased at her reaction to the ambiance of the restaurant.

Max Skull toyed with his slice of baguette in the dish of extra virgin cold pressed olive oil with a small pool of dark Balsamic vinegar in its center. "Whadaya think?"

It's wonderful." Margot smiled, glancing around at the tables of animated patrons, smoothing the black silk of her skirt over her knees.

It was so unlike Max to bring her here. Everyone who was anyone agreed that Café Estrellado, with Carlos Gustavo Estrella as owner and chef, was *the* place to go. She felt a little nervous. Max always said he hated high profile places like this, restaurants that got as much news coverage as any desperate search for world peace. And this chef's face had adorned more magazine covers than that of any slim model's.

She glimpsed Carlos Estrella through the throng, tall and handsome—really movie-star handsome, she thought—his high bright white chef's hat a beacon to his patrons, as he bent over the sizzling pans flung onto the immense stove. She could hear the swish of olive oil hitting the hot metal—did he use all stainless?—of the sauté pans. Any smoke from these kitcheny maneuvers billowed discreetly up an invisible vent.

Café Estrellado was rumored to be booked months in advance. People from all over the United States—heavens, all over the *world*—made their reservations by FAX and email. People determined the dates of their vacations and business trips to Los Angeles around the confirmation of these reservations. Had Max booked months ago? He'd never said a thing. But he wouldn't. Max didn't think anything beyond the next day's film shoot was worth considering.

"I've got something for you, babe," he said. His hand appeared from beneath the table top, depositing a small black satin box between the heavy silverplated hotel ware, the kind you never saw anymore, ready for her entrée.

Margot stared down at the box. Her life, a flash of her lifestyle, single and contented, blazing across her mind's eye.

"Max?" She felt her voice waver, but her eyes still focused on the small satin box. Oh God, he hadn't, had he? He wasn't asking, was he?

"Margot, babe," Max's hand slid across the table covering hers. She looked up catching the humor dancing in his dark eyes. "It's not what you're thinking. I swear, I'd never surprise you like that…well, not without warning you."

Nodding and feeling a warm blush starting over her face, she took the box and opened its top, the silky satin cool in her fingers. The gleam of a dark, smooth stone nestled in the creamy interior. Taking it between her fingers, she lifted up a ring, the large, smooth stone…was it a ruby?…set in gold, feeling cold and heavy to her touch.

"For you, kiddo." Max took the ring from her, sliding in onto the ring finger of her right hand. "It matches your hair."

"It's beautiful," she said. "It's perfect."

His hand closed over it, her fingers clasping his. "It's our twentieth. You know, since Luis was born. Luis is going to be twenty this summer. I wanted you to have this. Found it at Justine's on Melrose. It's called a cabochon cut or something like that. That means it doesn't have edges, you know, facets. I know you don't like glitter."

Margot's mouth went dry. Sentence after sentence formed in her head as a large white oval plate materialized in front of her. She sat back, Max's hand releasing her newly ringed finger.

"It's Chef Estrella's special *Spiced, Smoked, and Grilled Pork Loin with Tomatillo and Chayote Salsa and Soft Polenta,*" the waiter said. "Enjoy."

Chapter II

THE AIR SMELLED OF FRESH PAINT. Max's living room resembled a morgue, Margot thought, with the plastic tarps covering all the furniture and the floor. She reached for the envelope she'd stuffed in the pocket of her jeans, her new ring catching on the denim. Her curly mane of dark red hair was pulled back in a pony tail, but she'd still managed to streak it here and there with the golden yellow paint they were using on the walls.

"Guess what, Max. Loretta Rose is coming!"

"Where?" Max looked around, paint roller in hand, the ladder he was on shaking at the sudden movement.

She glanced at him, his black hair mixed with gray, tall, handsome and lanky in old jeans and a paint splattered t-shirt. She smiled. She loved the way Max looked. She loved it that she had to look up at him. Tall herself, it was nice to be with someone even taller. Max was a gorgeous man and, thankfully, unaware of his beauty. His ego was huge, but only about his undeniable filmmaking talent.

Margot shook her head. "She's coming here, Max. Here to L.A.. Don't looked so shocked. I invited her years ago."

"Jeeze," Max said. Margot tried not to smile. "Hey, don't look at me like that. You know what she's like. She's a man hater."

Margot rolled her eyes. Max was terrified of Loretta Rose Cinefucco. She knew that. Most men were. Loretta Rose was nothing if not formidable. Beauty and strength of personality were her major attractions, but the combination could still, unfortunately, be off-putting to some people. Loretta Rose didn't care.

"Just because she didn't come on to you."

"You're right." He chuckled. "She didn't. Well, maybe she has better taste than I thought."

"Anyway, she says she's sick of her brothers fighting all the time," she read on. "She refuses to work for either of them anymore. She's out of the wine-making business."

Loretta Rose was one of a few women winemakers anywhere and she'd been *good*, darned good. Margot peered at the flamboyant scrawl that chased itself across the piece of stationery.

"She says she wants to get into the restaurant business down here."

Max made a harrumphing noise. "Yeah? Like waitres-sing? I sure don't see her as a waitress. She'd be sarcastic and surly."

"Not waitressing, Max. I think she wants to be a chef."

"Well, good luck on that idea. Most new restaurants go under in three months. What does Loretta Rose know about cooking, anyway?"

Margot shrugged. "Oh, all those wine people are food fanatics. You know that. Food and wine go together—you love one, you love the other. She's probably a fantastic cook. Though," she added, peering down at the piece of paper, "she doesn't say what she's going to be doing exactly, restaurant-wise. Maybe she'll just buy one or something. I don't know."

Max was still scowling. "So what's going to happen with Cinefucco Cellars and the other guy's winery, the competing one? Those brothers of hers won't last a week without her to keep them apart. Damn, they hate each other. She's the only thing that's kept them from fratricide. Not to say that I didn't like them both. They're great guys, just kind of *controlling*. You know."

Margot raised an eyebrow, remembering the personalities. "Yes, well, not any more, apparently. Let's see here, Loretta Rose says they've bought her out. That must mean a lot of money. So financing a new restaurant doesn't sound as though it would be a problem."

"You're kidding," Max said. "It costs millions to open one, at least, a good one."

"Well, maybe she got millions. You know what those wineries are worth."

Max grunted. "Those brothers wouldn't give her her fair share no matter what. She's frickin *leaving* them. They'd burn the money she's owed before giving it to her. No, she'll have to have backers, people with tons of money who'll support whatever she wants to get into. It's kinda like making a movie. First and most important, except for getting me to direct it, of course, is the financial backing. That's why Arcturus studios keeps old Colin Peabody as producer, *my* producer, around when they probably can't stand him either. Colin may be a horse's ass, but man, can he drum up the big bucks. So Loretta Rose will need a financier, if she's serious about this."

"How did you learn all this restaurant lore?"

"I listen, babe. I listen to the movers and shakers. Hell, I'm making a damned movie about the kitchen culture, after all. You oughta understand. You're editing it. And cooking is a helluva curious business. Big money if you do it right and get lucky. Hell, half the studio execs probably have invested their extra bucks in the fanciest restaurants in town. The mob's probably in it, too, for all I know. Anyway, the restaurant business is a risky enterprise, but you can make money if you get the right combination going—the biggest name for your chef, the best decor. It's not just about an over-priced meal. It's a mixture of art and entertainment. It's like making a movie!"

"Well, I'm sure Loretta Rose knows about those things. I'm sure she's thought of all that. The wine business isn't exactly an easy business, either."

"Yeah, that's for sure. Man, can you imagine that scene between the brothers when she took off? The whole farewell scene could probably be stuck, as is, in a Scorsese film rated 'R' for profanity and violence." He made a face, stepping away from the wall he was painting, inspecting the golden color it was turning.

Margot had picked out the paint. It was the same color as the walls at Café Estrellado. She hoped Max wouldn't notice the similarity. But it was a blessed change from the unrelenting white that was Max's favorite.

Max loved white. And it wasn't as though the white he chose for his house was one of the whites that had a fancy name and some drops of another color to liven them up. Max preferred white that was pure, unfancy *white*, the white that she'd only seen before on refrigerators. His house was covered in it, literally, inside and out. But now its austere quality was beginning to soften under the paint brushes and rollers. No longer did she feel as though she'd entered a mausoleum when she stepped inside. She might even get to like it here. Maybe.

She shook her head. Max who was so sensitive about how

everything appeared in his films, micro-managing every part of the art production, driving his production designers crazy. But this white, white house had remained the same no matter how she teased him about it. Goodness, she thought, he couldn't be color blind, could he?

"I suppose you'll want to paint the bedroom next, won't you?" he said.

"Yes, the bedroom and everything else. I'll wait, though, till Loretta Rose gets to town. I want her opinion. I'll bet she's great on colors. She has exquisite taste."

"She looked good in that wedding dress when she almost got married," he admitted.

"You liked it because it was white."

Max smiled wickedly. "It wasn't really white. I liked it because she looked totally magnificent in the thing. I didn't know brides were allowed to look like that."

Margot raised her eyebrows. Replacing the letter in the envelope, she stuffed it back in her pocket and reached for the sticky paintbrush.

Max looked thoughtful. "Do you think she's with some guy by now?"

"You mean romantically?"

"Yeah. Whadaya think?"

"I don't know. Last time we saw her, she was especially uninterested in romance."

"I know. Can you blame her? But I was thinking...we've got this great guy consulting on *Extreme Cuisine*. He's making the whole restaurant schtick come alive for us. He's really into food and he's just about her age, too. What do you think?"

Margot stopped, the paint brush dripping into the can. "I'm

amazed you would ever think of fixing someone up, much less fixing Loretta Rose up. It's very romantic, a side of you I've never seen."

"Oh, come on, babe. I'm a romantic fool. You know that. But, yeah, well, it's just a thought. You know, since both of them are into food and stuff. Anyway, don't you agree, it's good to keep Loretta Rose occupied? We don't want her running around loose." He laughed heartily. "So I just thought of this guy."

"What is he doing for you?"

"Well, you know the storyline's about a restaurant and its prima donna chef, a guy who gets more publicity than our movies, like the honcho at the place I took you to. So, I know a lot about a lot of things but I sure don't know how restaurants actually work. I needed to feel what it's really like doing that kind of macho chef stuff, so this guy's our consultant."

"Is *that* why you took me to Café Estrellado? You were researching?"

"Well, not entirely. I knew you wanted to go and it seemed a good place to deck you out in jewelry. Anyway, I'm always researching, you know that. And that powerhouse chef, Carlos Estrella—the guy who made our dinner—is gonna let us use his actual chi-chi kitchen for a couple day's location shoot, too. So I was just looking around there that night. This consultant I'm telling you about comes in almost every day now. He's terrific. Hell, I oughta write a story about *him*. Anyway, it's changed the way I've been thinking about the movie and you know how hard it is for me to deviate from my perfect storytelling. You just know this guy is *good*."

Margot nodded, still distracted by the idea of Max as matchmaker. *Extreme Cuisine,* Max's new film, was nearly half finished. He'd cast the film with several well thought of Latino actors who'd never gotten a real starring role in anything before. Times were finally changing. The film industry was actually acknowledging the rise of the Latino culture and these veteran actors were suddenly looking hot and commercial. Every success these days seemed to be about timing, *and* politics and money, of course. Max's Latino actors were lucky enough to be working now when it was considered an advantage to actually keep your given name. And many of the bit parts were Latino kitchen workers moonlighting from local restaurants. Max loved *authentic*.

As usual, the studio had gone ballistic about Max using non-actors, even in secondary roles. But good old Max had won them over. In another life, he'd have been an outstanding casting director. Wasn't it John Huston who'd said if you cast it right, you didn't have to direct?

Max dabbed at a corner of the wall with a dripping brush. "Thanks to this guy, I'm making one hell of a great picture. I mean *great*. It's gonna give people their first chance to see behind the kitchen door. Hey, good title. Maybe I shoulda titled it that."

"I give up. What's this paragon of cuisine virtue's name?" she asked.

"Name's Robert Madrid. Heard of him?"

"You mean Robert Madrid, *The Late Night Chef* on TV?"

Max made a face. "Yeah. I mean, that's probably not his *real* name. It's too cool to be real."

"But, Max, he's famous. I mean really famous. We all watch Robert Madrid every chance we get."

"What? You mean you and Sophie and Ivy sit around and watch a goddamn cook on the tube?"

Margot ignored his tone. "Everyone does. Robert Madrid is

changing the state of cooking."

"All those food people say they're doing that."

"Well, he's doing it and on *television,* too, like Julia Child did. He's gorgeous, and he's really famous."

"You already said that. Anyway, I'm famous, too."

"Right, you're famous, but can you cook?"

Max seemed to consider her question seriously, swiping the wall with another roller full of paint. "Well, maybe you're right. He sure sounds like a good cook. Gives lots of good advice—insider stuff. Stuff that's making the story sizzle. And he's got those bit part actors of mine actually acting like real chefs."

"They are real chefs."

He stared at her, looking absolutely horrified. "Real chefs? No, my guys are the real kitchen slaves, the sous chefs and line cooks. The ones who do all the work. The powers-behind-the-throne kind of workers. My God, Margot, real chefs are generally totally nuts. You know that. If I'd hired a genuine major chef kind of person, I'd have had a meat cleaver through my skull after the first take. I wouldn't even hire one of their *chefs de cuisine*—you know the people who do the actual cooking while the big name chef is off signing autographs at some bookstore during dinner. Anyway, our budget couldn't have managed the salaries they'd want, either. No, old Robert knows what I want and he's getting it for me. He doesn't seem too full of himself, either."

"Not like some people I know."

Max shrugged. "So I have an ego. Big deal. Anyway, your culinary hero wants to become an actor, but that's no problem."

"Why not?"

Max shrugged again. "Because he's *not* going to become *my* actor. He can act all he wants on someone else's time. Hell, you

already said he's big on TV. Maybe I should watch his show…
Anyway, I just need his cooking expertise. So, want me to tell him
about Loretta Rose? We could have a party or something. Get
them together."

"Hold on," Margot said. "I don't even know when she's
arriving. Loretta Rose is typically vague on details. Still, it might be
fun to have a party—after we've painted everything—to welcome
her when she gets here." She paused. "And invite Robert Madrid.
I'd love to meet him. Do you think he's a strong enough character
for Loretta Rose…"

"Good point. You know I really like the woman, but she is a
bit much. You've got to admit that."

Margot didn't admit that. Loretta Rose was just Loretta
Rose. So she'd had the nerve to call off her wedding in front of
two hundred guests and the would-be groom. Margot thought
that was a brilliantly brave move, especially in view of what had
happened.

"Hey, babe." Max waved a paintbrush at the nearly completed
wall. "You know, this place is beginning to look just like that
fancy place we ate in. Did you do that on purpose? Anyway, this
chatter about culinary *ambience* is making me hungry. Let's call
it a day and get something to eat. We've painted six square miles
already."

LATER, AFTER A LARGE PLATE OF PASTA and her half of the red wine,
Margot agreed that it was foolish to drive back to the apartment
she shared on Melrose with her housemates, Sophie and Ivy. She

could do a sleep over, he said, grabbing her playfully as they did the dishes.

After all, their son, Luis, was away in his sophomore year at college. Dear Luis, who, to their mutual distress, was majoring in theater arts. Margot sighed. Their business was such a hard business. But with two successful parents who'd "made it," did Luis think it was an automatic? Margot sighed again. Of course, they'd help where they could, but that kind of help was problematic at best, often backfiring. It was going to be up to Luis, Luis and his magical gene pool, as Max noted.

But lately, even with the comings and goings of her housemates, the old apartment was unnaturally quiet. She found herself spending more and more time at Max's, in Max's igloo. Not that she ever minded spending time with him…. She left a phone message at the apartment that she would be at Max's overnight and took his hand as she trailed him up the curving staircase to the master bedroom.

Margot stood in the doorway and looked around the vast white room. She suppressed a shudder. Of course, over the years, she'd been able to make some inroads in the stark decor. There were the pictures of her and Luis; the pillows she'd made from the colorful fabrics they'd bought in Guatemala; the deep rose down comforter she'd insisted Max buy. The rest of the room, however, was still white and the master bathroom adjoining was the same. Max's silly huge house, so large that it took up the entire lot. It hardly had a garden. It didn't even have a swimming pool. It was all *rooms,* rooms and rooms and rooms. All white, all huge. And he loved it.

"You're figuring out what color to paint it, aren't you?" Max's arm circled her waist.

"Apricot," she said. Yes, apricot—a nice hue between coral and gold. It would be just right.

Max checked his email from his laptop on his bureau while she showered. He was under the comforter rereading the current script when she climbed in beside him.

"Whadaya think?" He pointed to the page he'd been reading.

It was covered with his notes in different colored inks. They'd filmed this particular scene the other day. Margot had just been working on it in the editing room.

"It works very well," she said. "I think you got it just right."

"That's my girl," he said. "We can go over it tomorrow, okay?"

She nodded and yawned as he reached out to turn out the light. She scrunched down to curl around him—Max was always wonderfully warm—and was asleep, immediately.

IT WAS A FUNNY, SCRATCHY SOUND that awakened Margot out of whatever interesting dream she'd been having. Still wrapped around Max, she waited, ears pricking, for the noise to be repeated. There it was again.

"Max," she whispered. "Max, do your hear that?"

"Whaa?" he mumbled. Then he rolled over, instantly awake. "Whadaya hear, babe?"

"There's someone in the house. I know there is. It sounds like they're coming up the stairs. Be careful."

Max slipped out of bed and crept toward the bedroom door, grabbing a flashlight from the bureau and holding it like a throttling weapon over his head.

Margot wondered whether she should get up and hide behind something and then watched, wide-eyed through the darkness, as his naked shape materialized in a faint shadow against the pale wall. He stopped by the door. She cringed in anticipation as he flung it open to the corridor.

There was a blood curdling yell from the hallway and Margot joined in the noise with a loud shriek as Max shouted back and threw up his arms in alarm looking like a cartoon animal that has been accidentally electrocuted.

"Max! Max!" Margot flung off the bed covers, and ran to his side.

Margot followed his gaze and stared into the hallway in amazement. There in the dim glow of the night light stood a nearly familiar apparition, a vision in slim black jeans and black leather jacket, the tousled dark curls frothing about her head.

"Hey, you guys," said Loretta Rose Cinefucco, dropping her bag to the floor. "Cool it, will you. You're gonna wake the dead."

Chapter III

MARGOT LOOKED AROUND THE BUTCHER BLOCK TABLE at the three of them. A teapot sat in the middle, each of them was holding a steaming mug. Max wore jeans and a T-shirt he'd hastily put on after confronting Loretta Rose at the bedroom door. The fact they'd all been shrieking at each other had probably diverted her from seeing that Max was naked. Or more likely, Margot thought, Loretta Rose hadn't noticed and wouldn't have cared anyway.

Margot was decently clad in Max's bathrobe and Loretta Rose looked her usual casually elegant self in the all-black outfit matching her thick, black curls, her pale face with the huge dark eyes suggesting someone famous whose name you couldn't quite remember. Loretta Rose couldn't help it, she always looked stunning, no matter what the circumstance.

"So how did you find us, Loretta Rose?" Max asked.

"I called Margot's apartment from the road. One of your roommates—the Ivy one you told me about—said you were over here. I thought it was too late to call you guys. Didn't want to wake you up or anything." Loretta Rose smiled an ingenuous smile.

"Gee, I can't believe you don't even have a swimming pool, Max. I mean, there isn't even a garden." She looked around the kitchen where they perched on stools sipping hot tea. "This is Hollywood, isn't it? I thought you'd have a big pool and stuff like that. This house is huge, though. Who built it?"

"Actually, Loretta Rose, this isn't Hollywood, it's West L.A. And I bought the house from Nareem Abjar," Max said. "He was a helluva big guy."

"The basketball player? Well, that explains some things." Loretta Rose waggled her finger at him. "But not the lack of a garden. That's really a crime. All this *house*. Really, Max, the place really needs *something* besides acres of walls and a roof. Maybe I could putter around a bit out there by that gigantic garage you have. There's gotta be a couple feet of dirt to play with at the edges. You need some vines. Trust me on this."

"Sure," Max said. "Go ahead. Maybe you could whip up a nice Cabernet while you're at it."

She nodded. "Why don't you hire someone to do some landscaping?"

"As you saw, there's not much to work with," he said.

"So dump the garage." Loretta Rose sipped her tea. "You know, dynamite the thing. Southern Californians aren't supposed to have garages, anyway."

There was a pause. "And how did you get around to the back?" Max asked.

"I was looking for a way to break into this shrine. I just crept around the edges. And then I came back and, wow, I tried the front door. It was unlocked. It was the last place I tried, too. Surprised me. Boy, you really ought to watch that, Max. You never know who might be ambling by feeling bored, with nothing to do but check out the inside of your house, though, frankly, it's not the most inviting-looking house on the block. I thought you Southern Californians liked *colors,* Mediterranean colors, nice warm colors."

"You sure saw a lot in the dark." Max's eyes narrowed. "Why didn't you just ring the doorbell?"

"Oh, I saw that armed response sign you've got out in front and wanted to see what would happen if I walked in. Well, *nothing* happened, did it? You oughta check out those guys who are supposed to be protecting you."

Max yawned. "That sign—it's just a sign. It was out there when I bought the place."

"So, whatcha working on these days, Max?" Loretta Rose helped herself to more tea. "Got another great movie for me to go to and say I know you?"

"Yup, another great flick is in the works," he said. "Well, it better be great. Monolith, the holding company that owns Arcturus is breathing down our necks for a *big* commercial hit. Again. But I'm doing a food flick. Well, I tell them, everyone likes food, don't they? So maybe this is the right film to keep the wolves at bay, whatever that means. They gave in and greenlighted us. I think they're afraid of me. Say, Loretta Rose, this flick's right up your alley, too, or your *new* alley, I guess. It's called *Extreme Cuisine."* His smile broadened.

"What's it about?"

"What do you think it's about? Food."

"You're doing a movie about *food?* That sounds electrifying."

"It's not just about *food,"* he said. "It's about people, the *stars* who make the food. These people are true eccentrics, Loretta

Rose. I mean *really* eccentric. They're 'on' all the time. They work twenty-hour days. They work *all* the time. They create amazing recipes and hide them and hoard them and sometimes sell them for thousands and thousands of dollars. They would cheerfully murder their competition. In fact, in my 'food' flick, one of them does just that. Hey, babe," he said turning to Margot, "I've gotta scene you're gonna love. Want you to check it out tomorrow and tell me what you think."

Loretta Rose smiled. "Are you doing it digital?"

"If I wanted my films to look like that, I suppose I could do it that way."

"But lots of directors use digital now," Loretta Rose went on, unfazed. "They say no one can tell the difference."

Margot shook her head, marveling at the woman—Loretta Rose was fearless. She wondered what her house-mate, Sophie Bellakov, would make of this friend of hers. Sophie was the other fearless woman she knew.

"But I don't *care* what other people do," Max said. "I like film. I like canisters of it. I like reels and reels of it. I like the way it feels. I like the way it smells. I'm a celluloid kind of guy. Other people can do what they want. There's room for all of us. I just know what I like. Call me a traditionalist."

"Okay, you're a traditionalist. Well, I'm with you on the cuisine part of your movie. It drives our lives. I've heard of people flying cross country to take in a new chef's brand of fusion food. It's hilarious. Or is yours a serious movie?"

"Serious? You mean did I write something with no actor in it over twenty-years old, about someone with a serious problem who has an epiphany, comes to a new awakening and it's all done with voiceovers and a great, roiling theme song?"

She grinned. "Yeah, something like that. That's the sort of thing that's so popular now."

"Jeeze, you sound like the jerks from Monolith. Well, no, I'm not doing that. I'm doing cooking as theater."

"Theater?"

"Yeah, as a show. That's what great restaurants provide. Think about it. They provide an evening of theater *and* you get to eat it. Speaking of, do you know Robert Madrid?" Max asked.

"Robert Madrid? You mean *the* Robert Madrid, *The Late Night Chef*?" Loretta Rose's eyes widened.

Margot laughed.

"Yeah, yeah, the same Robert Madrid," Max said. "So, why are all you guys sitting around watching late night TV? What's the world coming to? You oughta be out on dates. Well, Margot shouldn't, but you should."

"Come on, Max. What about Robert Madrid?" Loretta Rose said.

"Oh, he's consulting on the new flick for me. Nice guy. Single."

"Cool." Loretta Rose grinned. "So am I. Single, I mean. Still."

"You guys probably have a lot in common."

Loretta Rose looked thoughtful. "Well, yeah, but he's a *star*, a genuine celebrity. I'm just breaking into the food business."

"You're a famous ex-winemaker. That counts," Max said, pushing his tea away. "So Margot's right when she says you're gonna open a restaurant or something?"

"Yeah, I did write you that, didn't I? But new restaurants are so problematic. Nearly all of them fail. Robert Madrid must have told you that. I don't want to risk the whole restaurant bit yet.

I don't want to give my incredibly non-supportive brothers the satisfaction of seeing me fail right off the bat."

"What happened when you told them you wanted out of the wine scene?" Margot asked.

"If my saintly brothers had been carrying little guns, I think they would have shot me dead. Of course, the way they work, they'd have ended up shooting each other instead." She smiled at the thought. "The way they carried on you'd have thought I was abandoning two orphaned kiddies. But I'm thirty-eight years old and they're old as the hills. I've done enough for them. Let them find another winemaker. They used me like a slave. Of course, I'm the best and they know that, even if they constantly put my talents down. I don't care now. I'm out of there."

"But how did you decide on the restaurant business?" Max asked. "Talk about going from the frying pan into the et cetera."

"The food business seemed kind of a natural progression. I'll use my wine reputation and eventually slip into a new spot."

"Tough business."

"Yeah, but I've got something going that will ease me in."

"What?" Margot asked.

"Well, you know how it takes a ton of money to start up a restaurant. Believe me, what my brothers grudgingly gave me as my third of the family winery wouldn't float a leaky boat. But I've got a good deal going now. Someone rich and powerful found me a foodie job to start me off. It'll give me a good basis for whatever I go into next. You might know the guy—Colin Peabody? He said he works around here somewhere."

Max's face froze. Margot felt hers doing the same. She was speechless. Colin Peabody backing Loretta Rose? *Their* Colin Peabody? Oh, no.

Max sputtered to life, "You're *what*? You've got him doing *what*? Backing you? Backing you for what? Jeeze, do you know anything about Colin Peabody?"

"Sure, I do. I haven't said yes yet, either. He has big bucks, that's all. That's what I need and he got me this job…"

"Loretta Rose, Colin Peabody is my producer. He's producing my flick."

Loretta Rose nodded, her tangle of black curls bouncing. "I told you you'd know him."

"Jeeze, Loretta Rose, why are you hanging around with someone like him?"

"I'm not 'hanging around' with anyone, Max. Colin Peabody's a wealthy man and he's an admirer of my wines from my old, former screwed up life. He's also a major food junkie. He came up to the winery a month or so ago and wanted to meet. We chatted about this and that, and I told him how I wanted to leave the wine business and that I liked the idea of a restaurant, and he got all excited and suggested my coming down here and here I am."

"But what are you going to be doing that involves *him*?" Margot said. "He's a movie producer."

"I'm starting off by being part of the studio commissary— isn't that what you call the place where you guys eat? I'm going to be working there till we get all the restaurant details sorted out, *if* I go along with his plans. After all, there are *other* rich people in the world."

"But what are you going to be doing at the commissary?"

Max's voice sounded patient, but Margot knew he wasn't.

Loretta Rose reached for a cookie. "Managing. I'll be managing something called the executive dining room. You know, the honchos. They have their own little special room, just for them and their friends. Colin calls it the 'Boy's Club.' He says they're really into wine. I'll start there and then we'll see…"

"You mean you'll be working for the Estrellas? They've run the commissary, including the executive dining room, for twenty years."

"Colin didn't say anything about working for anybody. Who are the Estrellas?"

"Their whole family's in the restaurant business.They start off cooking at the commissary and then move on to the exec's dining room and then they take off from there. Rafael Estrella is the chef for the exec's club now. I'm pretty sure his mom's the overall commissary manager. The Estrella family has a monopoly on the great restaurants in the city, starting with Carlos at Café Estrellado."

Loretta Rose blinked. "Are you talking about Carlos Gustavo Estrella, *the* Carlos Estrella, the one who's on all the foodie magazine covers? That's *his* family at the commissary?"

"You know about Café Estrellado, too?" Margot asked.

Loretta Rose gave her a withering glance. "Margot, *everyone* knows about Café Estrellado. You're sure it isn't another Estrella family at the commissary, Max?"

"No," he said shaking his head. "It was Rafael Estrella who got us the reservations at his brother's hot place. Believe me, you need a major 'in' to get a table there. Rafael did it for me."

"So he's a brother to that big honcho? Jeeze, what am I getting into now. I'm sick of brothers. Just tell me the Estrellas all get along okay?"

"Can't tell you that, Loretta Rose. Rafael didn't look totally thrilled when I mentioned we were going to his bro's place."

"Really? Oh hell. But, I don't think I'll actually be working for them anyway. They must have already quit because Colin said *I'd* be in charge of the private dining room. Hey, there isn't gonna be a conflict there, is there?"

Max frowned. "Well, I'm sure we're talking about the same place. It's the exec's little hideaway, their posh club. Jeeze, they probably have a private handshake for all I know. Anyway, it's the only private area around. Maybe the Estrella's are dividing up the commissary work these days. They're probably tired of doing the whole job. Rafael must be ready to move on to his own place. Don't worry. Guess I'm just outta the gossip loop. But do you really want to cook for those people, Loretta Rose? Everyone hates the executives."

"Of course they do, but up-tight people still have to eat and drink. Anyway it's just a jumping off place for me while I figure out my next move. I sure hope I'm not barging in on somebody else's position though. But Colin made it sound okay…"

"What did you think of him?" Margot asked.

"Old Colin? A bit of a slime, isn't he?" She yawned widely disclosing her perfectly even, white teeth. "But a good businessman, right? I mean look at what he does for you, Max. You work for him and you wouldn't work for just anyone, would you?" She yawned again. "Anyway, I'm used to slimy businessmen. You've met my brothers. And as I keep telling you, I haven't told Colin he can finance whatever I do *next*. He just helped me get this job. I want to see what's going on around town before I make any decision on what's next."

She got up from the table and reached for her duffel. "So where do you want me to sleep tonight? Here I hope. You must have tons of rooms. And I'm sorry to cut the evening short, but it's after midnight and you guys have to get up early, don't you?

Anyway, that drive down here wore me out. I'm not as young as I used to be."

"Yeah, right, Loretta Rose." Max chuckled. "You're a shadow of your former self."

"Thanks Max. I know a compliment when I hear one. Just lead me to a bed. Hey, and don't worry about old Colin Peabody. I can deal with him. Don't forget, I've had a lot of experience with grabby people like him. I just want his money."

They went up the curving stairway, Loretta Rose pausing to comment favorably on the paint job in progress. She was left in one of Max's four guest rooms and Margot promised to wake her early. Max would be off to the studio, but she didn't have to get to her editing room until later. That's what assistants were for, she told Loretta Rose. They could have breakfast together and she'd show her the way to the Melrose apartment. Loretta Rose could have Luis's room until she found her own place.

Back under the covers, she whispered to Max. "What do you think about all this?"

"She's as beautiful and flaky as ever."

"No, I meant about her working with Colin."

"Oh, *that.* Jeeze, I know what you're thinking, babe," he replied. "That is a frickin recipe for disaster. And, you know, I haven't heard word one about the Estrellas leaving the commissary. Damn, we'll just have to hope that Colin behaves and doesn't have a hidden agenda on the commissary deal."

"But Colin *always* has hidden agendas."

"Yeah, babe, I know. That's why we don't like him. He probably wants her to poison someone for him. But that's one weird deal—the exec's dining room. You don't suppose he fired the Estrella family or something, do you? You know, forced them out, the old dead cats on the doorstep, that sort of thing. I can't imagine him just moving Loretta Rose in on that tight family, having her be in charge of Raphael. Hell, *he's* in charge. Talk about resentment…" He paused, looking up at the ceiling. "But I also think Colin would do almost anything to make room for her. He's always had a crush on the woman."

"He has a crush on the wine she made. Remember when he wanted me to steal that special bottle from the winery?"

"Yeah, well, clue the woman in. He's bad business, babe."

Margot pushed herself up on her elbow looking down at Max, his eyes closed, an innocent smile on his lips. "Fine help I'll be," she said. "I'm the wimp here and the eternal optimist. I always hope that Colin won't turn out to be the way he always turns out to be."

"Well said, babe." Max turned out the light. "Maybe we'll get lucky and Monolith finally *will* take over Arcturus and Colin will finally get fired. Hell, the trouble is I'd probably be fired then, too. Hell. But go to sleep now. We'll figure it out tomorrow. Jeeze. Loretta Rose. She has no idea what she's in for."

Chapter IV

AFTER A QUICK BREAKFAST, Loretta Rose followed Margot's car through the congested city streets across town to the Melrose apartment. They were lucky to find two parking places within walking distance and Margot got her friend settled in Luis's sunny room with its rock posters and athletic regalia still intact.

"Come to the studio with me. We'll have lunch in the commissary," she said. "I just have to look at that scene Max mentioned last might. It'll only take a minute. You can help."

"Help? Help Max?" Loretta Rose seemed astounded at the idea.

"He just wants a reaction to whatever he's filmed."

"Cool. I'll give him my reaction. I'll tell all my friends I was Max Skull's advisor. That oughta do something for my dwindling image."

The studio lot was bustling this time of the morning, but Margot pulled right into a parking space, a sign with her name on it on the curb. This was her space—her favorite, and the most practical, symbol of success in the business.

The editing office was deserted. Her assistants gone. Margot wasn't concerned. She'd worked with both people before. They were pros. They'd be busy doing something, moving the project forward. Neither of these people wasted time.

The footage in question was sitting on her desk in a shiny steel container. She lifted the lid and smelled the familiar, faint chemical smell of processed film. Maybe Max was right. There was something almost magical and exhilarating about miles of unviewed film. It always made her feel that the possibilities were endless. She never felt this way when working digitally on the bank of computers behind her.

She fed the film into the sprockets of the old Moviola machine and leaned forward, flicking the on switch as she adjusted the speed of the strip. The machine whirred and she focused intently as the film advanced.

It was a long shot, the master shot that would be Max's— and later her—reference point for the scene. Everything else, the close-ups, the different angles, everything would key off this one camera angle.

Now she viewed the scene, getting herself oriented visually. The set was an ultra-modern restaurant kitchen, the camera angle so wide she could see the corners of the set. Or was it a set? No, Max said they'd been working on location last week. The 'edge' she was viewing must be the wall to another room.

The scene began. Margot tried to concentrate. Loretta Rose was leaning so close over her shoulder she could smell the citrusy shampoo her friend used. She brushed away a black curl that didn't belong to her.

"So where are the actors…" Loretta Rose asked and then stopped talking as a shadow fell across the kitchen floor.

The actor, Martín Alisandro, a lean Latino actor in his fifties, was wearing a business suit and dragging a man's body across the vinyl floor—an unconscious man, or was it a dummy? The face was lowered and unrecognizable, the body's heels trailing limply over the shiny tiles.

"Why isn't there any sound?" the voice asked at her ear.

"They put that in later. Just watch. He said this is the murder scene."

Alisandro released the body to the floor as he reached for the handle on a huge stainless steel door set into the kitchen's wall.

"Oh, no!" Loretta Rose whispered. "I think that's a meat locker. I bet he's gonna stash that body in the meat locker. What a way to go. I just hope the guy's dead. Otherwise, think of *freezing* to death. Oh, this is totally gross. I love it!"

Margot put the machine on pause and waited until Loretta Rose's verbal critique was ended. She nearly smiled. If Max wanted to know if the murder scene was filmed realistically enough, she had an answer in the affirmative for him from one viewer.

"Turn it back on!"

She flicked the switch and they watched as the massive door was pulled open revealing a dark, nearly black interior. No, it wasn't totally dark. Artful lighting and camera work hinted at various amorphous objects hanging from its ceiling.

"Those must be carcasses," Loretta Rose murmured.

They had filmed the scene "cold." The usual color was washed into a sepia-like version of black and white. The "cold" was accentuated by the superbly filmed exhalations of the murderer—she'd have to get close-ups of the vapors—the clouds of his breath becoming a trail of puffs in the air as he laboriously pulled the body across the floor, over to the threshold of the freezer. Now he was inside, still viewed from long range, and they could see him arranging the body into a sitting posture against the freezer's wall. The murderer pulled the man's arms around his knees as though to keep the victim warm. A nice macabre touch.

The scene stopped abruptly after Martín Alisandro straightened up and shutting the heavy door firmly on his victim, turned and grinned into the camera.

"Wow." Loretta Rose stood back as Margot rewound and removed the film. "Cool movie," she said. "But what was that all about?"

"Goodness, I have no idea. It's all out of context for me at this point. Max just said it's the murder scene."

"Could someone do that? I mean stick a person in a fridge like that and just let them freeze to death?"

"My firsthand knowledge on the subject is slim, but if Max wrote it in, I guess it could be done. Nasty, isn't it?"

"I'm shivering and we're not even there."

"Good. I'll tell Max we believed the shot. Right?"

"Absolutely. Max sure has a strange imagination, doesn't he? Why would he put a murder in a food flick, anyway?"

Margot shook her head and put the reel back in its container. "I'll give you a copy of the script. Let's go eat."

They walked down a wide corridor and through the doors into the commissary. Aside from a slightly foodie scent, it was possible to think this was any large, very large, restaurant. The massive room was able to feed hundreds of people at a time. It was, in fact, a cafeteria that was artfully decorated to look semi-intimate. The designer had used high-backed burgundy leather-like booths that provided some privacy, and had arranged the room as spaces within spaces, not the long family-style tables that

Margot found so intimidating at other studios.

All in all, it was a pleasant enough place to eat. And, thanks to the expertise of the Estrella family, the food was better than most restaurants serving a much smaller clientele. Several tables had people hunched over cups of coffee, sandwiches and salads, with briefcases spilling papers and files and newspapers spread out in front of them.

"Nice space," Loretta Rose said. "So where's the exec's fancy hideaway?"

"Over there." Margot pointed to a polished wooden double door, closed now.

"What's it like inside?

"I have no idea. I've never been inside. I'm not a studio executive."

"Well, I know that. I thought Colin Peabody might have invited you to lunch or something."

"Well, he's not really an executive either. I don't understand how he's involved in all this."

"So he has friends. Somehow he's convinced them that only he can pick out their wines, or something. Maybe he does stand-up comedy during dinner. Come on. Let's take a peek."

They walked across the carpeting of the communal dining area. The coffee sippers didn't even raise their heads. Stopping, Loretta Rose turned the bright brass doorknob and pushed open the heavy walnut door nearly slamming it into a person in a whirring electric wheelchair who nodded and continued on out.

Margot held the door open till he'd passed—wasn't that Elliot Ferrigan? He'd been on that crew up in Berkeley a decade ago. He was an attractive man in a craggy sort of way, she thought, with thick graying hair and a full, neatly trimmed beard.

"Elliot?"

The chair stopped.

"Margot O'Banion Lake," he said. "How the heck have you been?"

They shook hands and Margot introduced Loretta Rose. "Loretta Rose will be managing the executive dining room soon," she said.

"Well, good luck to you," Elliot said. "It can't be an easy job."

"She wants to learn more about the L. A. restaurant culture."

Elliot grinned. "I don't know if I'd call it *culture,* but it certainly is a phenomenon." He looked at Loretta Rose, his head cocked to one side. "You're a winemaker, aren't you? I've read about you and I certainly wouldn't forget your face."

"I *was* a winemaker," she answered. "It was time for me to move on."

"Hey, I understand. Moving on is my speciality. Still working with Skull, are you, Margot?" She nodded as he glanced at his watch and whistled. "I'm late, ladies. Great to have seen you both," he said and wheeled away.

"He seems nice," Loretta Rose said. They stepped inside the executive dining room. "Look at this." Loretta Rose touched Margot's arm. "We're in frickin Versailles."

Margot nodded. There were definite similarities to a French palace in here; the pale green damask draperies, the flocked wallpapers, the ornate moldings, the not-too-subtle use of gilt paint, the outrageously elegant carpet they stood on, the huge oval mahogany table in its center. Well, if you couldn't get a decent 17th century palace facsimile created in Hollywood, where could you?

The room had the hushed quality of a seldom-visited museum. Still, there was that faint smell of food and, as she watched, a nearly invisible door cut into the fancy wall, slowly opened. Out stepped a man wearing the classic high chef's hat, his white smock pristine.

"Can I help you?" he asked.

Margot hesitated. She'd seen him before, of course. It was one of the Estrella family. He'd stopped by their table the one time she and Max had managed to have lunch together at the same time. Beside her she saw Loretta Rose smiling as the man's eyes gravitated toward her. Uh oh, but this person was either going to be the boss, or vice versa.

"Mr. Estrella?" Margot said taking a step forward. "I'm Margot O'Banion. My friend and I were just looking around. I'm afraid we've wandered into hallowed ground here."

The man's solemn expression lightened. "Hey, you're Max Skull's friend, right? I remember. Nice to meet you. Call me Raphael. So how was dinner at my brother's famous restaurant?"

"Perfect," she answered. "Thanks for helping Max get those reservations."

"No problem."

Margot turned to Loretta Rose. "This is our friend Loretta Rose Cinefucco..." Margot watched as Rafael Estrella's eyes narrowed. The welcoming smile faded.

"Ms. Cinefucco." Raphael offered his hand which looked dark and elegant against the blinding white of his chef's smock. "Colin Peabody told me about you."

Beside her, she felt Loretta Rose holding her breath. She wanted to nudge her in the ribs, anything to get this awkward conversation moving along.

"Will we be working together?" Loretta Rose finally asked.

Rafael smiled. "Of course we can work together. That is if you want to help us find a place and open it for us. We've been fired. Oh, I'm sorry, that's politically incorrect to say these days, isn't it. We've been *downsized*. After twenty plus years working our tails off here, the Estrella family is now deemed irrelevant."

"The whole family?" Loretta Rose's voice dropped. "But you run the commissary, too, don't you?"

"Yes, we did. All of us. Well, the ones that are left here. My oldest brother, Carlos, has his famous restaurant. Here there's me and a bunch of my crazy cousins. My mother manages the whole place, including this fancy dining room for the big guys of the studio and I still work here, for the short term, as executive chef. My mother, Louisa. Have you met her?"

Margot shook her head. "I believe I've seen her."

"You'd remember if you met her," Rafael said. "Mother's the director. She directs us all. She's particularly concerned about me these days what with our leaving here so quickly."

"I thought Colin Peabody said you're opening your own place."

"No, my brother Carlos is going to open another restaurant. This time he's working on a new concept, what I would call a *gringo* diner. He is calling it the Starlight Café. I won't be cooking for him. I don't do meatloaf."

"Will you work with him at Café Estrellado?" Margot asked. "That's a wonderful restaurant."

"No. Carlos and I have what you might call artistic differences."

"I know all about feuding," Loretta Rose said. "I'm sorry. Well, I guess I've really barged in here, haven't I? I've created one of those 'situations.' I'm so sorry. I don't know what to say."

Suddenly Rafael Estrella's expression changed. "I realize you don't know what has gone down here."

And Margot thought he was actually *seeing* Loretta Rose, at last. Loretta Rose in all her chagrined beauty. She was difficult not to see and admire. Margot was surprised it had taken him this long, due partly, she was sure, to his intense anger over the situation. That damned Colin Peabody.

"You don't have to leave here right away, do you?" Loretta Rose asked. "If you stayed, it would sure be a help to me."

Raphael looked away. "Much as I'd like to help you out, Ms. Rose, I don't think that would be the best situation, do you?"

"Let's go," Margot said. "I think you should have a talk with Colin."

Loretta Rose nodded and looked at Raphael. "Nice to meet you. I'm sorry about…"

Raphael raised a hand. "Things happen."

"Shit," Loretta Rose said as the door shut behind them. She said it loud enough that two diners looked up briefly before returning to their papers. "What do I do now? That glorious looking guy is ready to kill me."

"You can't really blame him," Margot said.

"Thanks a lot." Loretta Rose clenched her fists. "Damn. I left the most *impossible* situation up north. I came down here in good faith. Colin *assured* me everything was all ready for me. I didn't know I was gonna be responsible for the downsizing of an entire *clan*."

As they turned away, Margot saw Rafael Estrella hurrying down the corridor. He'd removed his chef's hat, his white smock was open to an "I-heart-New-York" T-shirt tucked into jeans, a thin gold chain around his neck. Without the chef's hat, he looked younger, still as handsome but less formidable.

"Hey, Ms. Rose," he said. "Look, I want to apologize for my attitude back there. This wasn't some deal you thought up to get us out of here. You didn't even know we were here, right? And, hey, it was time for me to move on. I've got a heavy backer now, someone who wants to finance me in a new place. And I'm going to do that, but first I've gotta get my name known. You know, ease in through the front door, be already famous with an eager clientele."

"How are you going to do that?" Loretta Rose asked.

"Oh, I'm going to be on TV," he said. "That's where the reputation part comes from. I'm gonna become a household word, *then* people will flock to my restaurant, my own restaurant. You see, I'm gonna help my brother Roberto on his show. You know, Robert Madrid, *The Late Night Chef.*"

He nodded cordially and left.

Margot and Loretta Rose exchanged a look.

"He's Carlos Estrella's *and* Robert Madrid's *brother*?" Loretta Rose said, eyes wide and admiring. "Wow!"

"But he's too young for you," Margot said. "He can't be more than twenty-five."

"Yeah, I guess so. Well, whatever. They may hate me, but I'm becoming a big fan of the Estrella family."

MARGOT LEFT LORETTA ROSE OFF at a local realtor's office to look for an apartment. She returned from the studio at six to find Loretta Rose full of news, chatting with her housemates, Ivy Knight and Sophie Bellakov. Loretta Rose had found a furnished studio apartment not far from Margot's and could move in immediately.

"It's great," she told them. "Old and Hollywoody-looking and clean. It even has a patio with a little fountain."

After dinner, the four women curled up on the living room furniture in front of the TV. They were in their pajamas, ranging from Sophie's flannels with the dancing teddy bears, to Ivy's diminutive red Chinese silk pair and Loretta Rose's plaid granny gown. Margot wore her usual t-shirt, a giveaway advertising some forgettable movie, and blue cotton pajama bottoms with her cloud-patterned fuzzy slippers. The scene did rather resemble a college dorm party, Margot thought.

She shared the sofa with Sophie who was a fabulous pale golden hue after her three weeks as an assistant art director on location in Mexico. And Margot was glad to note that instead of grating on each other, Sophie and Loretta Rose seemed to find each other delightful company. Privately she thought both women must admire themselves in the other.

Loretta Rose told them that Colin Peabody had assured her, emotional outbursts from any of the Estrella family aside, the executive dining room of the Arcturus commissary was hers. Rafael Estrella was exaggerating his plight. Most of the family had grown tired of their work at the studio and were ready to move on. The main commissary kitchen would be run by four cousins who had learned at the Estrella family's knees. Rafael was just young and ambitious and you know how young people are…

"I listened to that one with a huge grain of salt," Loretta Rose said. "And he said I can start working right away, going over the menus, etc. The executives are expecting great things from me, if only in the short term."

"So who do you believe?" Ivy asked. Ivy was in a hit TV comedy series and not privy to all the standard studio gossip.

"I, for one, don't believe anything Colin Peabody says or is reported to have said," Sophie replied. "I've done enough studio work to hear the rumors."

"The part I don't get," said Loretta Rose, "is why he's such a honcho if he's such a creep."

"Because he's a good producer," Ivy said.

"Good counts more than ethical in our business," Sophie added. "Sad but true. He's an old timer by current Hollywood standards. Colin's from the old school. He has some ins with the big guys. They'll never fire him. Not as long as he convinces Max Skull to keep making films for Arcturus. He's just unethical."

Loretta Rose shrugged.

Margot could guess what her friend from the wine country was thinking. Being unethical was not just a city dweller's vice. "I really don't know how you'll be comfortable having him back you in a new business…" she said.

"I may not have to be." Loretta Rose smiled a fox smile. "Someone actually called here an hour ago and approached me about financing a real place of my own."

"Already? Who?"

"I shouldn't say anything yet," she said. "You understand. It's kind of tricky what with kind of promising Colin that if I came down here… And now there's this other person, who seems a lot nicer to work with, who enters the picture so fast. You know…"

Well, Margot did and she didn't. This was a circumspect businesslike side of her friend she hadn't encountered before.

"You haven't signed anything with Colin then?"

"Hell, no. I'm not an idiot," Loretta Rose said, reaching for the popcorn.

Amory, Margot's large black cat, was stretched out across the sofa's middle cushion. Ivy had made a gigantic bowl of popcorn which was being passed around and back again. Margot looked at her friends. They were all single women, way, way beyond their twenties. Professionally successful, none of them, besides herself, had a serious relationship going. Goodness, next they'd be doing each other's hair and trading nail polish colors. Would they still be sitting here in front of the television in twenty years—herself, too? Oh no. Maybe Max was right....

"Jeeze." Sophie ran her magenta fingernails through the cat's sleek fur. "Look at us. We're like a bunch of old hens."

"That's what Max says," Loretta Rose said, her eyes glued to a cable promotion for a biceps building machine.

"He said *what* about us?" Sophie asked.

"He just said it was weird for all of us to be sitting home on a Saturday night watching *The Late Night Chef* week after week. There may be some truth to it," Margot said.

"Oh come off it, Margot. Max is an idiot when it comes to all of us. He can analyze to his heart's content but he'll never understand us." Sophie's eyes narrowed. "But, you know, ever since he gave you that 'friendship' ring or whatever you guys call it, you've been acting married. You don't need to agree with him all the time."

"I don't agree with Max all the time."

Was she acting that way? She and Max had been together for years now. They hadn't seriously discussed the possibility of living together, much less the possibility of marriage. Of course, now that Luis was away at college... But neither of them wanted to change their comfortable lifestyles and work relationships. She twisted the ring with its glowing dark stone around her finger. Still...this gift. It was so unlike Max to give her something like this.

The familiar theme music erupted from the TV and four pairs of eyes turned to the opening credits for *The Late Night Chef Show*. They'd all watched it before—as Max was fond of pointing out—but never with as much interest as tonight.

Robert Madrid, with his movie-star good looks, smiled into the camera. He introduced the menu for the evening and began working at the counter, a ceiling mirror showing his well-manicured hands deftly chopping and stirring. All the while his warm voice was discussing the ingredients, and bantering with his audience.

Loretta Rose smiled. "My, my."

"You're getting a date with *him?*" Ivy said. "I've always just thought of Robert Madrid as this foxy wizard chef on TV. I didn't even know he was a local and now you're going to meet him?"

"He's one of the Estrella family," Sophie said. "You know, the restaurant people. The people Loretta Rose got fired so she could take over their jobs."

Loretta Rose hooted with laughter.

"Well, Max says he's really nice, too," Margot said. "He looks nice, don't you think?"

"Who cares about nice."

They quieted down as Robert Madrid began final preparations for a traditional *Dia De Los Muertos* dining experience. Loretta Rose grabbed a notebook and began taking down details of the menu.

Following the last commercial, *The Late Night Chef* approached the camera, his handsome face with its crown of thick dark hair neatly slicked back—the new retro hair look from the 30s—nearly filling the screen. "My dear friends," he said. "Tomorrow night starts a new format for us on this program. Tomorrow, there will be two of us, two chefs. You will meet my brother Rafael Estrella, former chef to the stars. He has left his position with Arcturus Studio commissary..."

"Oh God, don't remind me." Loretta Rose raised a hand to her forehead. "But it's great news if that's really what he's going to be doing next. It's not like Rafael'll be out on the street."

"...and Rafael will be at my side, the two of us turning out menus to keep you thinking about or, perhaps, *dreaming about,* all night long." He smiled, his improbably white teeth gleaming in the studio lights. "*Buenas noches,* my friends."

The Late Night Chef 's flashing logo of crossed skillets apparently aflame—Margot noted the famous name of the pan's manufacturer prominently displayed...hmm, good product placement—faded to black.

"Well, we all *adore* Robert, of course," said Ivy. "What's not to adore? But I, for one, can't wait to see this little brother of his. What did he say his name was?"

Loretta Rose stood up and stretched. "His name's Rafael Estrella. You'll like him," she said. "Margot and I met him this afternoon."

Margot nodded. "He's very...ah...fiery. Wouldn't you say, Loretta Rose?"

"Yeah. Feisty, even. Actually he was mad as hell, but he apologized nicely after our little conversation." She shrugged. "I'll tell you one thing. I wouldn't have apologized if I'd been him, since I seem to have taken over his job."

"Taken over his job? What are you talking about?" Ivy said,

concentrating on the closing credits.

"You know, like a corporate raider or something," Loretta Rose said. "Whatever old Colin did to get me the job at the executive dining room, it wasn't very diplomatic."

"But what's he angry about? I could understand if he didn't have this great opportunity on TV." Sophie said. "Here he'll be on a popular TV show making heaven's knows how much *dinero* now instead of slaving for those uptight studio execs—the way you'll be doing."

"I know." Loretta Rose made a face. "Sometimes I really wonder... I mean I just wish I'd known *whose* bodies I was going to be walking over to get my new job. But, as far as the clientele goes, after dealing with my two idiot brothers, any ego-crazed movie exec is gonna be a walk in the park."

"Fair enough, Loretta Rose." Sophie stretched lazily, her long arms waving gracefully at the ceiling. "But how about using us as your proving grounds. I want to see how good a cook you really are."

"Why not?" Loretta Rose said. "Tomorrow night, Robert Madrid's famous *Dia De Los Muertos* menu, right over there on your very own dining room table."

Chapter V

"Café Estrellado West," Max whispered in her ear. "That's what it looks like."

He was standing in the middle of his spacious living room taking in the surrounding walls. Three were a pale gold now, the fourth one a darker tone. Two weeks earlier Max had given in and hired a team of house painters. The painters had been quiet and professional and non-judgmental, she'd noted, going room to room turning the chilly atmosphere of the house into a more congenial one, nearly homelike.

She didn't care if Max teased her about the changes the painters had made. He might even learn to like living in a house that didn't resemble a walk-in freezer. It wouldn't hurt him to enjoy something in his life besides filmmaking.

"You look good in here. Do you know that?" he said.

Margot gave him a look. But when she glanced down at her sage green, clinging silk dress and pictured herself with her flaming hair against the walls, she decided he was right. Good heavens, was that the reason she'd chosen the wall paint and this dress? She decided not to analyze her choices.

Tonight was Max's party. Ostensibly it had been planned to introduce Loretta Rose to Robert Madrid. But since the twosome had been seeing each other since Max had invited her to visit the set, the party had become simply that, a party.

Margot had never seen so many people in the house at one time. Max's usual idea of entertaining was to have his production people over for beer and pizza in the kitchen, all the while talking business, business, business. He'd never entertained formally here before, to her knowledge. It was a pleasant crowd tonight, too. Max had not invited his producer, the erstwhile Colin Peabody, or any of the actors. He hadn't invited anyone, he told her proudly, whose egos were larger than their capacity for decent wine. Plus, she knew he didn't want to be bothered by Colin's dire predictions of what would happen if *Extreme Cuisine* didn't, as he put it, knock the socks off the powers-that-be. Colin was getting worried about producing the bottom line for the parent corporation and it showed. Margot didn't want to think about that either.

The film was progressing. Loretta Rose was in her new apartment. She'd begun her job in the executive dining room and, apparently, spent every night dating Robert Madrid. Now the man, looking even better than he did on TV, if that was possible, was chatting with Max across the room while Loretta Rose helped the caterers set up the buffet.

Loretta Rose was in charge of the party. It was a given that catering for the heavyweights' affairs—and Max was definitely one of the studio's heavyweights—went hand-in-hand with being the executive dining room's chef/sommelier/manager. It seemed a bit peculiar, Margot thought, to have a date when you were working a party, but Loretta Rose was her usual unfazed self.

And, busy as she was, Loretta Rose appeared to be having a wonderful time in L.A. Once she was convinced that she hadn't actually put the Estrella family out on the street, she'd relaxed and concentrated on her new job. As Colin had promised, she oversaw the executive dining room menu and the special gastronomic needs of its hotshot clientele and, as she said rolling her eyes skyward, believe me, some of these needs were *special*. She didn't do much of the actual cooking, but she supervised each and every meal. The chefs and sous chefs were hand picked by her, filling the places vacated by those workers, all family members, who had followed the Estrella family away from the studio.

According to Loretta Rose, there actually had been a civilized turnover, handled more or less cordially on the Estrella family's part before they'd fanned out to join this or that restaurant. Their name was their claim to fame and chefs were picking up the cousins right and left, knowing they were well-trained and well-connected. Word had it that the mother was already *chef de cuisine* at Carlo's new diner.

And Colin's stake in all this? No one was quite sure, but he had made a point of mentioning to Max how glad he would be to turn over the exec's wine list to Loretta Rose "at the appropriate time." He said the time it took to keep the wine list *au current* was exacting and demanding. He offered no comment when Max suggested he quit doing it.

And the first thing Loretta Rose had done was review the list, the list Colin Peabody was so proud of doing. The man's a terrible wine snob, she'd whispered to Margot. She waited until he was out of town on business and completely revamped the wine cellar. And that, she said, she'd done in half an hour. She knew wine. Colin probably wouldn't even notice the changes. He'd take the credit for any positive changes, anyway. She didn't care.

Now Margot watched Loretta Rose as she emerged from the dining room. The woman didn't look as though she'd been working furiously behind the scenes with the kitchen help. She looked fresh and quite glorious. Loretta Rose shut the door behind her and was immediately holding court. Wearing a slip of a black dress, her dark hair coiled on top of her head, she was listening to one of Max's guests, a sudden and attentive supplicant, smiling at some inner amusement. Seeing Margot watching, she nodded and glided away from the disappointed man.

"So what's happening?" Loretta Rose said. "Great wine." She took a sip from Margot's glass.

"Did you choose it?"

Loretta Rose smiled. "Of course."

"How are you and Robert getting along?"

"He's interesting." She lowered her voice. "I mean he's *really* interesting. He already suggested I guest on his show!"

"Wow! Really? But what would you do on it?" Margot visualized the scene from *Bridget Jones's Diary* where Bridget's dowdy mother runs off with the flamboyant infomercial star, becoming his front man with her hair bleached an improbable shade….

"What *are* you thinking about, Margot?"

Margot shook her head, the fantasy vanishing under her friend's gaze. "How stunning you'd be on television," she said.

"Well, anyone can be stunning, but, duhh, woman, I can also cook. Robert knows I can cook. *That's* why he asked me." She frowned. "You aren't thinking that he expects me to just stand there handing him utensils, are you? You know, like that poor lady who does the letters on that game show?"

"Of course not," she said. "So, how is it working out with Colin?"

"Oh, Colin." She laughed. "Old, *silly* Colin. For-tunately other aspects of his various 'careers' are keeping him busy and out from underfoot. Now I know Colin Peabody isn't one of your favorites. Still, I think he's smart and he's a good businessman. I just wouldn't ever take advice from him. I'm sure you wouldn't either."

Margot sighed. "Where does Colin find the time for all his miscellaneous endeavors? He's supposed to be producing movies, for heaven's sake."

"Oh, Colin's into everything. I think he fancies himself a Renaissance man. Over the years he somehow oozed his way into micro-managing that fancy dining room. I don't think anyone minds. He adores wine, of course, but he's just your typical restaurant owner wannabe. I mean, he likes the *idea* of being this great restaurateur, but in reality, he'd hate it, all the work and long hours. He'd never make it. So he lives vicariously though us who do make it, or try to make it. Frankly, I think the Estrella's are better off far away from him. I will be, too, as soon as I figure out my next step."

She nodded. "Max says Carlos Estrella's new diner got a great review in the Times."

"Yeah. We should go there," Loretta Rose said. "I want to make sure the family isn't holding a grudge. I'll be cat food if that family decides to blackball me in the industry. I'll make Robert take me. I can meet the mama. That'll make me legit. I mean, did I know I was going head-to-head with the mafia of restaurateurs? The Estrella family rules. They could make life very hard for me in L.A. if they wanted. It's a good thing Robert likes me."

"So he's really an Estrella?"

"The same. Robert just uses the Madrid name for TV."

"I wondered about that."

"Yeah it's a show biz thing. Say, there is *one* hilarious thing I could tell you about old Colin…" Loretta Rose quickly scanned the room making sure no one was in hearing distance. Margot stepped closer. She loved hearing gossip about someone she didn't like.

"Well," Loretta Rose went on, "I was at his house picking up some forms for the dining room and, guess what? I'll bet you half his furnishings are straight from the studio property department. I saw a tag he'd forgotten to remove from this priceless looking chest of drawers. He's got all the best antiques. I think he must have just lifted them off the sets. It's really awful of him. He has more than enough money to buy anything he wants. Jeeze, think of living with hot furniture."

Margot raised an eyebrow. Nothing Colin Peabody did surprised her.

The party continued. By Hollywood's tabloid paper standards it was a sedate one. And Max was right, it was more fun without actors. When actors were present, there were always these intense competitions, the who was talking to who bit, the subtle litmus tests for who was doing what and where it ranked on the success scale and the inscrutable *agendas*. Tonight the guests were a crowd who took their behind the scenes professions seriously, but weren't constantly on the make, business-wise. They networked among themselves. They didn't rely on catching the eye of someone like Colin Peabody…or Max.

By midnight the house was quiet. The catering staff was busy, silently cleaning up though there wasn't much of a mess.

Loretta Rose ran a tight ship. The food had been delicious. Loretta Rose had done herself proud.

Margot and Max sat in front of the fireplace with Loretta Rose and Robert Madrid, sipping the last of their wine. They certainly made an attractive couple. Margot tried not to appear *too* interested.

Max kept nudging her. "See," he whispered. "I told you so. I told you they would like each other. They're two peas from the same pod."

Margot raised an eyebrow, but cliché aside, Max was right, at least from the physical aspect. Wouldn't that be something if they'd actually found "the one" for Loretta Rose?

"You certainly have an interesting family," she said to Robert.

"Yes, they are something, aren't they? I'm so much the elder brother that I can speak of them, well, more subjectively than most siblings. I'm ten years older than Carlos and fifteen years older than Rafael. He's the baby in the family. Have you met our famous mother?"

"Not yet. Raphael did mention her."

"Well, when you do, you'll understand why the Estrellas are successes. Mother is the equivalent of Max here. She's the director. And a very successful one, too."

"And the producer," Max said. He laughed loudly at his little joke as the rest of them groaned good-naturedly. "So don't you have the restaurant bug, Robert? I thought it ran in the family."

"Doesn't work for me," the man replied. "The TV show is more than enough. I have no desire to work eighteen hour days for an enterprise that can go out of favor and out of business like that," he said snapping his fingers. "I think I was initially hired for *The Late Night Chef* because the producer thought I'd open…what?…a *Chez Roberto*? He would finance the enterprise and coast to great riches through my name. But I've told him over and over, that life is not for me."

"Who does *The Late Night Chef?*" Max asked.

"Ferrigan. Elliot Ferrigan. Know him? We have a great studio right under my brother's restaurant in the basement. It's really handy for getting supplies and equipment, as you can imagine. You ought to stop by and check it out. Kind of an intriguing space. Elliot would be pleased to show it off."

"Under Café Estrellado? Sounds interesting. Yeah, Elliot used to do films. He was pretty good."

"I guess not that good if he ended up directing me on TV. You know what they say about television directors."

Max shrugged. "There've been some great ones. Funny though, they usually segue up to film, not over to TV."

"Not everyone makes it on the big screen, Max. You know that."

Max shrugged. "Hell, lots of the cable companies make better movies than the studios. Should piss me off, but it doesn't. They're geared more toward individuality, like me." His face brightened at the thought.

"Well, Elliot does a good job for the show and he's been fair to me. Maybe he can coerce Raphael into letting him back *him,* now that Raf's in the mix. Raphael's younger. He's got more energy. Maybe he wouldn't mind taking orders from rich people who think they know about food, the kind who drink half a bottle of hundred dollar wine and make a big show of sending it back as inferior. Who needs that kind of grief? I take the responsibility as Raphael's elder brother to tell him not to do this. It's not worth it, slaving for other people to make large amounts of money."

"I couldn't do it," Max said. "I hate eighteen hour days. I *do* eighteen hour days but I hate 'em."

Robert nodded. "Time to head for home." He stood up, exchanging a quick glance with Loretta Rose. She unwound her long legs off the sofa and stood up, leaning casually against him. Margot didn't have to look at Max to know what he was thinking now. She could *feel* his self-satisfied smirk.

"Great party, Max," Loretta Rose said leaning forward to kiss him on the cheek.

"Thanks to you," he replied, unexpectedly gracious for Max.

"Call you tomorrow Margot," she added. "Will you be here or…?"

"I'll be at the apartment," she said. "I have to get to the studio early."

As if on cue, everyone smothered a yawn. Late night festivities just didn't fit into a professional life that often began at dawn, at least they didn't fit into her life. As for Max, well, she was surprised he'd managed to stay awake till now.

She kissed him lightly and followed the tall couple out into the night. With a wave and a grin, Loretta Rose ducked into what must be Robert Madrid's car, low and dark, and she watched the taillights slow at the corner and make a graceful turn left. Interesting. She knew Loretta Rose's new apartment was to the right.

She drove back to her apartment, undressed and climbed into bed. The apartment was quiet. Both her housemates were already asleep. They were in the business, too.

THE BLEEPING OF THE TELEPHONE AWAKENED HER ABRUPTLY. She sat up. The green digital numbers said 6:11. Too early for a dreary winter morning. She moved her black cat aside and grabbed the phone.

"Margot? It's Loretta Rose. Come down here." The usual husky, low voice rasped in her ear.

"Where? Where are you? Why are you calling so early?"

"Get down to the commissary," she said. "Keep out of the main dining room. Take the kitchen entrance. It says "staff" on the door. I need you." Loretta Rose hung up. Margot still had the phone clamped to her ear, her eyes widening.

It took her half an hour to dress and race through the still quiet streets to the Arcturus Studio complex. She parked in her assigned space and ran inside. Skirting the corridor to the sound stages, she turned and entered the wing where the commissary was located. Following Loretta Rose's orders, she bypassed the main double doors and opened one marked "staff." Stepping into a narrow hallway, she saw a solid gray door at its end.

Opening it, she nearly ran into her friend. Loretta Rose was standing there, waiting, looking frozen in stone. She was dressed in dark trousers and her pristine white chef's smock, her smooth olive-skinned face looking pale and pinched. She put a hand out toward Margot. Margot took it—it was ice cold and the grip was strong—and allowed herself to be pulled into the kitchen.

"Loretta Ros…" she began.

"Shh. Just come with me," she said. She gave a yank and Margot nearly stumbled as they passed through another door into what must be the pantry of the main kitchen. It was filled with shelves holding every sort of canned food and basic essential ingredients; huge jars of olives, tall gleaming tins of olive oils and stacks of herbs and spices in quart-sized containers.

Loretta Rose released her hand and moved across the room to a bank of shiny stainless steel doors. The doors nearly filled the wall space, floor to ceiling. She turned, her eyes narrowed. "Ready?" she asked, her voice low.

Bemused, Margot nodded, Loretta Rose reached out and grabbing one of the handles, pulled open the door. A wave of cold, slightly chemical smelling air filled the room. "Well, get over here."

Margot walked to Loretta Rose's side and stared into the dark, frigid space.

"Wait." Loretta Rose reached to a wall switch and the interior of the huge refrigerator or freezer—Margot wasn't sure which— was illuminated by a soft yellow glow. "See?"

Margot leaned forward into the chill. Hanging from hooks were large slabs of meat, a whole side of bacon and other things of an origin she could only imagine.

"There."

She followed Loretta Rose's pointing finger. She blinked and took a step closer.

"No, don't go in. Look down there."

Margot's gaze shifted. And there, on the floor of the freezer, looking overly clothed next to the dangling carcasses, was a man's body. It was seated, the face down on knees that were pulled up to the chest, as though trying to keep warm. Margot took a step back. Still, she saw the dark jacket and gray trousers clutched by a pair of very white hands. A sickening sense of déjà vu made her clutch at the cooking island for support.

Turning, she looked at Loretta Rose. Her friend's face was nearly as white as her starched chef's coat.

"It's him," she said, nodding, her voice harsh and flat. "It's Robert, Robert Madrid. He's sitting in a meat locker and he's dead. Cold and dead. It's the murder scene, Margot. It's the scene we saw on that machine in your office. Look in there. It's right out of Max's new movie."

Chapter VI

MARGOT STARED INTO THE OPEN FREEZER, the frigid air wafting out in waves into the kitchen space. The vapors looked like the labored breathing of the actor in the film as he'd dragged the body across the floor, his exertions so artfully filmed for Max's movie. Max's murder scene. Oh God, what had they found here?

Finally she recovered her voice. "How could this happen? Are you sure it's Robert?"

"Sure? Sure of what? He's *dead,* Margot. Don't you get it?"

"But…"

"But what? Of course I checked for a pulse. I'm not an idiot. I mean, my God, I know what Bobby looks like. I just left him a few hours ago. He was okay then."

"You were at his place?"

"Yes. I'd left my car there so we could drive to Max's party together."

"That's all?"

"You mean, did we have sex or something? No, we didn't. It's a *work* day today, if you haven't noticed. Anyway, Robert's gay."

"He is?"

"Stop being so shrill, Margot. Yes, he's gay. I mean, he was gay. So what? Look at him now." Huge round tears were starting to trail down the pale cheeks.

"I'm just surprised, that's all." Margot suddenly felt like weeping, too. "You two looked like such a nice couple."

"Well, we *were* a nice couple. I like gay guys. They don't push you. You can just be yourself around them. So now you know Robert's gay and he's also *dead*. What do we do?"

"The police?"

Loretta Rose stopped frowning and stared, seeming oblivious to the tears still streaming down her face. "Oh my God, the police. I have to call them, don't I?" She wiped her nose, ran across the room to a stainless steel counter and grabbed a black phone. Margot could hear the 9-1-1 call punched in. She turned away as Loretta Rose described the horror into the receiver. It was a brief conversation.

"They'll be here pretty soon." She hung up the receiver. "What should we do till then?"

"When do people start coming in?"

"Oh, no. I forgot. Lunch. And my sous chef and his helpers should be here any moment. I'd better get out and head them off. You stay here."

Margot shook her head, shivering at the thought of staying in the awful death room by herself. Loretta Rose had shut the food locker door, but still… "There's no reason for anyone to stay in here. I'll go out front with you.

"We'll go through the exec's dining room. I'll just lock the back door. That'll keep everyone out of here."

She waited and then watched as Loretta Rose began scanning

the scarred vinyl flooring covering the walkways. Margot looked too. She looked for the telltale scuff marks that had been on the film, the scuff marks of heels being dragged over the tiles. She couldn't see a mark disturbing the surface. At least this part *wasn't* like the film they'd watched.

"What are you looking for?" she asked.

Loretta Rose stood up, frowning. "Robert's chain. He always wore this kind of thin gold chain. I teased him about it looking so eighties but he says all the family wears one. You know, it's like the one Rafael had on. They're from his grandfather in Mexico or something. But," she said, still peering into corners, "he doesn't have it on now."

"Did you look?"

"Yes, I told you I did. He's not wearing it. Let's get out of here."

Margot nodded and followed Loretta Rose to a door opening off the kitchen. Suddenly they were in the hushed splendor of the private dining room. Loretta Rose leaned against one of the damask walls. "What happened back there?"

Margot slumped next to her friend. She felt lightheaded. "It's just like Max's scene."

"You don't think he had anything to do with this, do you?"

Margot was horrified. "Max? Of course, not. It's just a terrible coincidence."

Loretta Rose nodded. "It must be coincidence." She paused. "You don't suppose we were *supposed* to see that particular scene of his before this happened, do you? You know, for some weird reason..."

"But why? Why would anyone do that? And that was weeks ago..." She thought of the terrible twisted mind that would engineer a "coincidence" like that. She looked around the clean, hushed space. "Why were you here so early?"

"I'm always here before seven. That's the only time it's quiet around the place. It's when I make sure the lunch menus are straight and the right supplies are in, and, hell, everything. You know, that's my job."

"How did Robert get in here?"

Loretta Rose's eyes were wide. "I don't know. It's not like the place is ever locked though. I dunno about the main studio door, but once you're inside the place, this room is always open. There's self-service coffee and stuff for the night owls. Anyone could come inside."

"But what was Robert *doing* here?"

"How the hell do I know? Getting stuck in a freezer, I guess. I don't think he was trying out for a frickin movie role." She took a deep breath. "Sorry. I really don't get it. There's an emergency alarm button inside the door in case something like this happens. It's supposed to open the door from the inside, too. The button hasn't been activated. Did you see that light over the door? It would have been glowing red if he'd pushed the alarm."

Margot nodded. She hadn't seen any red light on. "You don't think he did it on purpose?"

"Suicide? Freeze himself to death. Oh God, no. Why would he do that? It's some incredible accident. That's what it is. But did you see what else?" Loretta Rose's voice dropped. "He's wearing the same stuff he wore to the party last night. I mean, he never changed. He must have left me off and then come here for some weird reason."

"You mean like an assignation?"

Loretta Rose gave her a despairing look. "Holy smokes,

Margot. Do you mean a *sexual* assignation? In a meat freezer? Do you have to put a sexual connotation on everything?"

Margot was taken aback, but put her friend's anger down to shock and stress. "Of course not. I don't do that. But you have to admit his being here so early seems awfully strange."

Margot followed her into the executive dining room. Halfway across the thick ornate carpet she paused. A paper was lying wedged against the table leg of the oval mahogany table. Aside from two empty coffee cups on the table, the paper was the only item out of place in the quiet room. Picking it up, she stuffed it in her purse and hurried to catch up with Loretta Rose.

"Oh, God," Loretta Rose said. "We're doomed. Colin's gonna kill me. You know how superstitious film people are. They'll think the whole place is hexed. We'll never get our fancy executive boys to eat here again after they hear what happened."

They exited the room as the main commissary door was flung open revealing an official-looking contingent of people. The early morning coffee drinkers looked up in interest. The new arrivals stood just inside the door. They were looking around the quiet space with sharp, solemn expressions on their faces. Margot recognized the studio security people. There were also two firemen in full fire fighting regalia, two paramedics in rescue gear, and three Los Angeles police officers in their navy blue uniforms. She and Loretta Rose walked toward them.

"Are you going to tell them about that piece of Max's film we saw?"

"I don't know what to do," Margot said.

TEN MINUTES LATER Margot was still being questioned. She leaned against the back of a booth while a policeman asked her about this and that, jotting her answers down in a black notebook. She'd been at a party Mr. Madrid had attended? Had she noticed excessive drinking? Margot nodded yes and no. None of the party-goers had been drinking hard at Max's. He nodded and closing his notebook, walked away.

The kitchen staff arrived in a group and had been stopped before entering the kitchen. Now they were seated at a table looking as shaken and shocked as she felt.

She looked longingly at the exit doors when Colin Peabody strode in, buttoning the buttons of his suit jacket, his expression perplexed, little frown lines furrowing his round cherubic face. Margot knew his innocent looks were deceiving. Colin was tough as nails. Max refused to play handball with him, saying he was a damned poor loser.

"What is happening in here?" Colin's voice was pure big studio producer, the words drowning out the low murmurs of inquiry.

Margot watched him dig his hands into the pockets of his impeccably tailored dark jacket. He seemed to be daring someone to answer.

Heads turned, but no one responded. Frowning, he walked over to her. "What is this, Margot?" he asked. "What is going on here?"

She took a breath as as she noted the carefully coiffed, thinning hair on top of his very pink scalp.

"There's a body in the kitchen freezer, Colin. I think it's called a food locker."

She saw Colin appraise her words as though he were waiting

for a United Nations translation that would cause them to make sense. "A body," he finally said.

She nodded, feeling the beginnings of a headache creeping across her temples. "A body. Loretta Rose found him. It's Robert Madrid, you know *The…*"

"*…The Late Night Chef?* What? You mean *Bobby's* in there? He's dead?" Colin's pink face went several shades lighter.

"I'm afraid so."

"What was Bobby doing in the kitchen?"

"I have no idea."

"Was it his heart?"

"I don't know. I think he froze to death. He looked frozen. Loretta Rose found him. She called me. I saw him all curled up in there."

"Curled up? What do you mean 'curled up'? Was he murdered?"

Margot cringed at his loud voice blurting out the dreadful word. Heads turned.

"What?" She realized she was whispering. "I don't think so, Colin. I think it was some kind of kitchen accident."

"Good heavens," he said. "It's just like in the film—Max's murder scene. Have you viewed that murder scene?"

"Shh, Colin. I haven't mentioned the scene to the authorities. It's just an awful coincidence, anyway."

"You mean some of that life imitating art foolishness?" he asked. "I hope you're right. But I don't see how we can keep that information out of the papers."

Oh no, Margot thought, looking at the man. She could almost see the wheels turning in his head.

Colin continued to stare at the people clustered about the

room and then she watched as he seemed to change his mind about what tact to take, a crafty expression making his full lips curl upward in the semblance of a smile, or maybe he was grimacing— with Colin it was hard to tell.

"This will be a blow to Max, won't it, this terrible, terrible accident?" he said. Colin seemed to have perked up considerably. "There was all that help Robert was giving him consulting on the film, too. The PR people were having a wonderful time with that aspect of the story. They just loved *The Late Night Chef* connection. They felt it would make Max's film more reachable."

"'Reachable?'"

"You know, by the masses. Arcturus needs a *massive* hit. Robert was our link to the burgeoning Latino clientele. He was going to bring in his people to the movie. Do you know the demographics of Latinos in Los Angeles?" he asked.

"*Demographics*? Really Colin, sometimes you sound like such an ass." She felt hot tears rolling down her cheeks.

"Margot, my dear. I will ignore that comment. I realize you've had a dreadful shock. It was a dreadful, shocking thing and here you are, our brave girl, having to see poor Robert and talk with the authorities, as well. You are a wonderfully strong person, Margot, and you're entitled to a few tears. He didn't leave a note, did he?"

Margot shook her head and snuffled into a Kleenex. Colin— silly old Colin. He, after all, was the one who had to go out and face the sullen studio executives whose focus was purely financial. Their cold pragmatism made Colin's narrow emotional range look positively hysterical in comparison. They could stop production in a second if they deemed it a good business idea. It would be Colin's job to convince the studio executives that what looked like a PR disaster could be turned into profit.

Colin would know what to say to the press, too. She *knew* he'd tell them about the murder scene in Max's new film. It was great publicity. And how could they keep it quiet anyway? There must be hundreds of people within a twenty mile radius who would remark on the similarity of what had happened here and what had been filmed weeks before. It was the sort of titillating news that everyone would delight in discussing.

"Feeling better?" he asked.

"I'm angry that Loretta Rose is caught up in the middle of this."

"Margot, Margot." Colin placed a warm hand on her forearm. "Loretta Rose is a big girl, quite sophisticated, too, considering she's from the country."

"Loretta Rose is from one of the leading wine families of the world, Colin. She's made a name for herself as Cinefucco Cellar's winemaker. You know that. She's mixed socially with everyone from movie stars to royalty. Country, indeed." She stared at him. "So why did the Estrella family leave, so conveniently, just as Loretta Rose arrived in town?"

"What a curious mind you have, darling. It was all pure coincidence, just coincidence and the happiest confluence of fate and serendipity. Bobby. Bobby. Really *muerto*, is he? You're not exaggerating, are you darling? I'd heard he might have a dickey heart. It was probably his heart. Too young, of course, but these things happen."

"*He's frozen solid.*" Margot sighed. Why on earth was she talking to this man? His mind was already on spinning the tragedy to advantage. "You *did* really know him?"

"But of course, dear girl. Everyone watches and knows about

The Late Night Chef, and then he was Max's trusted advisor on the new film. I had lovely talks about *haute cuisine* with him each time I visited the set. Of course, Max was always shushing us."

Margot bit her lip as the policeman who'd asked her the questions came toward them, his gaze on Colin. "You're free to leave, Ms. O'Banion," he said. "We have your telephone number if we have any more questions. Here's Detective Wilson's card in case you think of anything you might want to add to your statement. And you, sir... Who are you?" he said.

Margot made her escape. Colin wasn't going to level with her. Whatever Machiavellian plot he'd concocted concerning Loretta Rose and his grand commissary plan would go to the grave with him. She smiled seeing him frowning at the inquisitive policeman. It felt good to leave Colin to fend for himself. He wouldn't have hesitated to do the same if the situation were reversed.

Loretta Rose was standing by the entrance looking strained and uneasy, her white chef's coat hanging from a finger tip. "What were you saying to that old goat?" she whispered.

"Colin? Well, nothing. Really nothing. I can't ever get Colin to make sense. I think the man's mad. He thinks it was Robert's heart."

"I can't believe this." Loretta Rose ran a hand through her tangle of black curls, "It's incomprehensible. It's terrible. And the cops are sealing off the entire kitchen until 'further notice,' whatever that means. I can't even get in there to get my jacket. I'm out of work until they do whatever it is they're gonna do. Come on."

They stepped into the main corridor of Arcturus Studios. The hallway was crowded with people, some still in costume and makeup, attracted by the unusual comings and goings and the hints of official activity inside. They were craning their necks trying to peek into the dining area, their view blocked by a security person's broad, immovable shoulder.

Loretta Rose took Margot's arm and made a sharp left. No one tried to talk with them. Margot knew that no one in their right mind would try to strike up a conversation after seeing the expression Loretta Rose wore on her white, determined face.

As they pushed open the wide glass door leading to the parking area, a group of people appeared from around the corner, Rafael Estrella in the lead. He stopped when he saw them, nodding curtly in acknowledgement. "The police called mother." He looked toward a woman, her head lowered, being ushered up the stairs, a man and a woman grasping each of her elbows.

Rafael's mother—what had he said her name was?—suddenly looked up, straight at them, bright black eyes under thick, shapely eyebrows, zeroing in on their faces. Margot suppressed a shiver of anxiety. This woman wasn't her idea of the stereotypical old family matriarch. This mother was stylishly dressed in black trousers and a black silk shirt. Her shiny blue-black hair was pulled back tight in a braided coil at the back of her neck. Long silver earrings swayed as she turned. Shaking off a restraining hand—or was it a comforting one?—the woman walked straight up to Loretta Rose. Mrs. Estrella pointed a white shaking manicured finger in Loretta Rose's face.

"This is your fault," she said. "This is all your fault, Ms. Cinefucco. You've killed my eldest son and you're going to pay for it."

"Time to go," Margot said. She grabbed Loretta Rose and dragged her to the car. After pushing her friend into the passenger seat, she ran behind the car and jumped into the driver's seat.

She backed out swiftly, away from the white-faced Estrella family, staring after them on the sidewalk.

Margot slowed at the security gate, watching for the wave from the kiosk that meant she could drive on without setting off the alarm. Seconds later they were on the busy, four-lane street that paralleled the studio complex. She turned the car toward her apartment. At the first stop sign she glanced at Loretta Rose. Bright red circles had blossomed on her cheeks. She looked like one of those old-fashioned dolls, Margot marveled, with the rose-painted, white china faces. Loretta Rose stared straight ahead. Margot couldn't tell if she was going to faint or start howling.

"Oh, damn, Margot. What have I gotten into now?"

Margot focused on the traffic and accelerated toward the apartment.

Chapter VII

MARGOT STOOD IN THE KITCHEN waiting for the tea kettle to whistle. She was anxious to call Max and alert him to this morning's tragedy. She didn't want him to hear secondhand how his film's murder scene had improbably come to life. But first she wanted to get Loretta Rose some hot tea before her friend's condition worsened. Loretta Rose was obviously in shock. Margot was certain hot tea would help. The English swore by hot tea.

Impatient to get to the phone, she poured the kettle before the water boiled. Dipping the tea bag up and down in the cup, she thought about the terrible thing that had happened. The whole scene was so macabre and improbable. It was something out of a bad horror film. Well, it was out of *Max's* movie, too, but that was just coincidence.

She looked down. The tea was overbrewed. It was a nearly black hue that would certainly taste terrible. Adding a splash of hot water before carrying the cup into the living room, she grabbed the cell phone on her way. Loretta Rose was on the sofa, long legs stretched out in front of her, looking like death.

She took the cup and peered into the liquid. "Jeeze, Margot. A tea bag? Don't you have any real tea?" She drained the cup and made a face. "Next time I'll make it."

Margot nodded, intent on punching in Max's cell phone number. "Babe?" he answered. "What's up?"

"Max, I've got some awful news. I mean Luis is fine, don't worry. It's nothing about him. But Loretta Rose found Robert Madrid in the commissary freezer," she said, keeping her voice low. "He's dead, Max. The police are all over the place."

"Robert's *dead*? What the hell are you talking about? How can Robert be dead? Are you sure it's him?"

"Of course, I'm sure. He froze to death in a freezer."

"He froze? Jesus. Where?"

"The commissary kitchen. It was a meat locker or something. And Max, it was identical to your scene, that murder scene you shot a couple of weeks ago."

"You mean the one where Alisandro drags the body through the kitchen? But that was pretend. I made that up."

"I know, Max. But this was exactly like yours. Well, we didn't see anyone dragging anybody, but Robert's body was in the same position in the freezer. You know, on the floor, all huddled…" She heard her voice break. "Where are you?"

There was a pause. "Me? Jeeze. Well, we're down here shooting at Café Estrellado. We're doing kitchen stuff. Well, we were shooting. Damn. I wondered where all the kitchen extras went."

"Who?"

"The cooks. I mean, the chefs, the sous chefs. All those people."

"Why would they leave?"

"And all that time I was waiting around for Robert to come and help us out with the action. I *needed* him here."

"But where did all the kitchen extras go?"

"The extras?" Max said, sounding suddenly impatient, "I assume they went to the studio commissary if their dead relative was found there. They're all Estrellas, after all. Are you sure Bobby's dead?"

"Of course, we're sure."

"But what were you doing in the commissary kitchen?"

"Loretta Rose called me. She found him first. I mean she just opened the freezer and there he was. And I saw him in there, too. Max, please, I want you to come over."

"I'll see you in about an hour. Damn, what a gross and terrible thing to happen."

"I think we ran into your extras going inside the studio when we were leaving. I thought some of them were wearing makeup. What are we going to do, Max? Robert's mother was there, too, and I realize she's devastated, but... Well, Loretta Rose is here. She's pretty upset."

"You don't think the police suspect me, do you?"

"You? What are you talking about? You mean because of your silly scene? No, it was a terrible accident. No one's mentioned murder. Well, Colin did, but you know Colin. And goodness, Max, we don't even know what happened yet and I certainly didn't tell them anything about that footage." She didn't mention the glint in Colin Peabody's eye remembering Max's death scene. He'd certainly made the connection.

"So do the police suspect our friend there?"

Margot glanced at Loretta Rose. "Suspect *her*?" she whispered. "It was an accident. I mean, Robert just didn't get out of the freezer. Well, no, of course they don't suspect anyone."

"Whadaya mean 'of course they don't suspect anyone'? And who says it was an accident? No one freezes to death in a freezer. Anyway, most homicides are done by the nearest and dearest. And, let's face it, there's our Loretta Rose, right there in the middle of everything."

"Goodness, Max...."

Loretta Rose suddenly stood up from the sofa, stretching her arms up toward the ceiling. "Oh, for heaven's sake, Margot, *I'll tell him.* Give me the phone," she said, snatching it from Margot's hand.

"Max. Robert and I were not that close. We weren't lovers. Your gorgeous friend was gay. We were not a romantic item. No, I don't know if he was out or in the closet. So you're thinking we're talking a murder here? Well, I didn't shove him in a freezer. I really liked him. Someone else did the deed, if it was indeed a deed. You think maybe a family member?"

Margot couldn't hear Max's reply but Loretta Rose smiled the first smile she had seen her make since the night before. "No kidding?" she said into the phone. "Well, it's nice to know there are dozens of suspects then, if needed. Here, wanna talk to Margot?" She nodded and pushed the off button, setting the phone down with a clunk.

Margot stared.

"He had to go," Loretta Rose announced. "He'll be over later. Says if it's anyone at all, it's gotta be one of the family. He figures most relatives in most families probably hate each other. You know, like me and my brothers," she said and then started crying again. "Damn, I'm a basket case. Do you have any coffee? Real coffee?" she said. "I need a dose of heavy caffeine."

The doorbell rang. Loretta Rose looked at Margot. "I'll get it," she said. After wiping her eyes, she opened the door wide.

Margot saw Loretta Rose's shoulders tense. Standing on the small porch was the striking figure of Robert Madrid's mother. Margot sprang to her feet wondering whether to flee to her bedroom or stand her ground and support her friend. Loretta Rose took a step back as the woman leaned inside.

"My name is Louisa Estrella," she said. "I must apologize for the scene I made at the movie studio this morning. I had been thinking that if we'd been at our usual places in the commissary kitchen today, this monstrous thing would never have happened. We don't blame you, Ms. Cinefucco."

Margot watched as Loretta Rose took the woman's arm and led her to a chair by the fireplace. "This is my friend Margot O'Banion," she said. "I'll go get us some coffee."

Margot nodded at the distraught woman. Goodness, she must have had all those children as a teenager. Louisa Estrella might be in her early fifties. Her face was smooth, her figure trim and lithe in her black trousers and shirt. She looked like that wonderful Mexican painter, she thought—that unconventional woman artist...ah, yes, Frida.

"I'm so sorry for your loss," she said.

Louisa Estrella stared at her. "Yes," she said. "Robert was my eldest. He was a star, too, just as Carlos is, just as Rafael will be. My children like the spotlight. But Roberto was no fool around a kitchen. I don't understand why he was in the *freezer*. He knew about freezers." Her dark eyes brimmed with unshed tears.

Margot felt her eyes widen. "Did he have heart trouble? Someone mentioned maybe that's why he...ah... couldn't get out?"

Mrs. Estrella sat back against the chair cushions, looking tense and cautious. "There was nothing wrong with Robert." Her eyes narrowed. "One of the cousins told me that Mr. Skull has a similar scene in his movie. Is that right?"

Shocked, Margot shook her head trying to look innocent of any knowledge of the bizarre coincidence. "And he was so successful," she put in. "His television show and everything."

Louisa Estrella sat forward, shaking her head. "Yes. That television show. I asked him a thousand times to join us in the family business. He had any restaurant to choose from. We'd have given him star chef billing."

"Star chef?"

"Yes. You find the term amusing?"

"No. Not at all."

"You see, Ms. O'Banion, most people in this city wouldn't know good food if it hit them in the face. They take it for granted. They eat the food we prepare. They pay the high prices. But their palates…well, we are not gods. We can't improve on something that doesn't exist."

She paused as Loretta Rose came in carrying a tray with three steaming coffee mugs teetering on its surface. Margot watched Louisa Estrella examining her friend head to toe. "And you were seeing my son. Is that right?" she asked.

"Yes. I liked Robert very much."

"You know he was *joto,* gay. You knew that, didn't you?"

"Yes."

"He may have preferred men, if he'd found the time, but, still, he loved beautiful women." She smiled. "Now Rafael must take his place as *The Late Night Chef.*"

"Really?" Margot asked. "Rafael will take over? That's wonderful."

Louisa smiled her strained smile. "We haven't officially heard, but who else would they use? Robert *was* the program. He *was The Late Night Chef.* Rafael has been on the show. He knows what to do. It is only right that he will take Robert's place. Well," she said, putting her untasted coffee down carefully on the table top, "I must leave. I felt I should come and tell you I am sorry for shouting at you for no reason. We Estrellas are not barbarians. I must get to the new restaurant now. The patrons will act sympathetic and understanding if they have no dinner tonight, but they will not forget. They would not come again." She stood and Margot quickly went to the door and opened it. Outside along the curb a large late model Mercedes Benz was parked, its huge engine idling like a gigantic purring cat.

"I am going to find out what happened to Robert," Louise Estrella said. "The authorities will make a big show of finding out this or that, but their version of the facts may not explain what really happened. I will find out these things." She pulled a pair of sunglasses from her bag and put them on.

A youngish man in a dark suit jumped from the car and opened the passenger door for her.

"It is not easy to lose a son," she said. "I have already lost a daughter. Now with Robert gone, that is enough pain for any person. This is my nephew Benardo," she said. "He runs Chi-Chi-Chi," naming yet another famous restaurant that was the toast of the city.

The man nodded toward them, shut the door after his aunt, and ran to the driver's side. The door slammed, or actually, Margot thought, it was the costly kind of metal that *bumped* softly shut, and the car drove off.

Loretta Rose turned her large dark eyes on her. "And what in the world was that all about?"

Margot shook her head. "I just know I wouldn't want her coming after me."

HALF AN HOUR LATER, Max strode in, the door slamming behind him. "What the hell is this all about?" he said. "Police are all over the studio. Some 'accident.' And all our work at the restaurant location is a disaster. I don't have anyone who knows *anything* about frickin restaurants to tell *anyone* else what to do. The stuff we filmed today is worthless." He shook his head. "You'll never see *those* scenes, Margot. I'm gonna burn the buggers. Looks like a film student's version of chaos theory. I need Robert Madrid there. You oughta know what was going on in Robert's life, Loretta Rose. He was a helluva nice guy. What was he doing in a freezer?"

Loretta Rose sighed. "I knew Robert for a month, Max. We went out to fun places, lots of restaurants. Mostly we ate. I'm sorry, Max, I don't know a thing about his personal life."

"You knew he was gay."

"So? So what?"

"Well, nothing. But didn't he tell you other things?"

"Really, Max. You mean other *terrible* things?"

"Of course not. What kind of insular idiot do you think I am? I meant if he confided his sexual preferences to you, maybe he confided other things, things he was involved in. Enemies he had, stuff like that."

"Well, he didn't. He seemed totally involved in good food, period. His TV show. Reviewing new restaurants. He liked to gamble a bit, here and there. Nothing big. Stuff like that. He liked being on

TV. He didn't want his own restaurant. I guess in his family that makes him different."

Max nodded. "You know, I'd been rethinking the whole bit with Robert. I knew he wanted to act and hell, he had the TV show and everything and God knows he was good-looking enough and charismatic and I was thinking I *would* put him in the picture. He was gonna play this new chef's role, the star chef role with all hell breaking loose around him, all that drama, the true *art* of chaos. I wish I'd told him." He sighed. "Well, hell, what am I gonna do now?"

"What are you *trying* to do, Max?" Margot tried to make her tone circumspect. Hearing Max shouting his frustrations was not something she wanted to listen to—especially now.

He turned his dark gaze on her. "You're the film editor, Ms. O'Banion. You know the screenplay as well as I do. What am I trying to do?"

She took a breath. "You're trying to show the qualities that make these new restaurants so popular, so great. You're trying to show what it's like behind the kitchen doors. And you just happen to have filmed a sequence that played out in real time today."

"Well, that's not my fault. Don't blame me for what happened to Robert. I can't be held responsible for every strange thing that happens. There have been a lot of weird coincidences in film. And then, of course, there are the *real* nut cases out there who take fiction and make it into fact. And that's not my fault either. There's a fine line between fiction and fact, you know that. I'm not the one to blame here."

"We aren't blaming you, Max." Margot said.

"Oh, hell. I know you aren't." Max slumped on the sofa. "I'm just feeling guilty, I guess. It's damned weird knowing that stupid scene came to life. It's shook me up a little. I'm still trying to figure out what I'll tell the police when they ask about it. It's just a matter of time until someone rats on us."

"But your movie isn't even a murder mystery," Loretta Rose said.

"Of course it isn't. That scene just sorta came up. These chef people are highly ambitious and competitive. So I took one character who was a little over the top, *too* ambitious and competitive, that's all. Shit happens. But overall I am *trying* to tell a story that shows that running a restaurant is like putting on a play—it's high drama. You know? Passions run deep. And I don't know how to do this without the expertise of someone who can run a kitchen the way it's supposed to be run, because, believe me, it's a damned complicated scenario to orchestrate and now Robert's *dead*. I've got to find someone who understands the concept, the restaurant concept, the star chef concept."

There was a long pause. Margot could hear the clock ticking against the far wall. Suddenly Max sat forward. He had a gleam in his eye. Uh oh, she thought.

"Loretta Rose!" he said. "How would you like to become a movie star?"

Chapter VIII

T HE NEXT DAY Margot walked down the studio hallway toward the cutting room, her mind distracted by thoughts of Robert Madrid. She reached for the doorknob and paused, listening to voices from inside. She didn't recognize them. It certainly wasn't her assistants. The police? Could it be the police? It was possible, she supposed. But why would they want to talk to her again?

What else could they ask her? All she'd done was look inside the freezer. At the visualization, her stomach gave a lurch. Poor Robert. What had gone wrong? She wondered how Loretta Rose was holding up today. The morning papers were lamenting the loss of the popular TV figure and calling the death "suspicious."

She stood there, undecided whether to cut and run or walk inside. The sound of conversation continued beyond the door, low and conspiratorial, or was that her overactive imagination? Suddenly she heard a drawer being shut. Well, that was enough! Whoever was in there was going through her office as though it belonged to them. This couldn't be legal.

She reached for the doorknob. It would be better to confront whoever was in there now before they made a shambles of everything in the room. She opened the door and stopped, astonished, on the threshold. Two men looked at her in…what?… alarm?…guilt?

She knew them both. The tall, lanky one with the sardonic expression was Jonathan Keller, Max's first assistant director, the man he loved most to hate. Jonathan was lounging casually against the cutting bench, his gaze unperturbed by her abrupt entrance. What on earth was he doing in here? Shouldn't he be with Max at the restaurant shoot?

She also recognized the man in the wheelchair. It was Elliot Ferrigan. And certainly he had even less business being in her office than Jonathan. He didn't work here. He wasn't even with the studio. Elliot looked as though he'd been busy this early morning, too, his arms buried in the trim bins, the containers that held discarded footage. His cool gray eyes appraised her.

"What are you two doing?" she asked.

Elliot dropped whatever he had in his hands and deftly spun his wheelchair toward her. "Hi there, Margot. How have you been? And you know Jonathan Keller, of course."

"Yes, I certainly do," Margot said. "Am I interrupting something?"

"Ahh," Jonathan said. "I'm sorry. We're encroaching on your domain, aren't we?" His eyes were bright and determined. "Elliot and I are just checking up on a few things," he said. "Say, did you happen to find a locked scene from *Extreme Cuisine* sitting around here anywhere?"

Margot's apprehension vanished, replaced by anger. "What are you doing here?"

Keller and Ferrigan exchanged glances, neither of them answering.

"What was in the scene you were looking for?" she asked.

"Oh, just a clip from another of Skull's flights of fancy," Keller replied. "Thought you might have run across it. You'd remember it if you'd seen it."

"Really?" Margot said. "And what do you two want with it?"

"Hey, don't get mad at us." Ferrigan raised his hands. "Jonathan and I go back a long time. He wanted to show me something that concerns Robert Madrid. Do you know what we're talking about?"

"Of course, I do," she answered. "You're talking about the murder scene in that restaurant kitchen."

"Yes," Jonathan said. "That's the one, the film clip showing old Martín Alisandro dragging a body into a freezer. It's going to be hard for the cops to understand why life is imitating art in our film. I don't want to try and explain that to them. They might confiscate the film and stop us working on it."

"Really? Why on earth would the police want to do that?"

"Well, think about it, Margot," Elliot Ferrigan said. "It looks to us like someone is trying to make the film come alive. Anyone can see the connection. Somehow they're trying to sabotage my TV show, too."

"In what way?" she asked.

"By killing off my star. Robert Madrid won't be easy to replace."

"And tell me again what you two are doing in here?"

"What Elliot is trying to say is that certain aspects of the film story have been happening in real time." Keller eased off the bench. "The police may find this curious. We've all certainly found it curious. We just want to avoid any unnecessary probing on their part."

"So you want to destroy the clip?" Margot said. "Two hundred people, maybe more, know about that scene. It wasn't exactly filmed in a vacuum, you know. What can you guys be thinking of? If the scene disappears, that doesn't mean other people, people with less imagination than you, won't tell the world all about it. I'm surprised it's not already in the news."

Ferrigan stared at her. "If there's no physical evidence, then it's just a story, a story about a scene that was filmed and unhappily came true in real time."

"I saw the scene," she said. "It was on the Moviola." They all turned to look at the machine. It sat silent and empty. "My assistant must have put it away."

"Where?" Keller asked.

"I'll let you know when it surfaces, okay? We can all look at it together and try to figure out what it means."

Jonathan raised an eyebrow. "Okay, Margot, I'm outta here. Skull gets pissed—sorry, Margot—when I'm late. Anyway, we can't do anything more if you don't wanna cooperate. See you, Elliot. You know your way outta this hole."

He disappeared through the door. Margot could hear the click-clicking of the heels on his cowboy boots as he walked down the hall. She turned to Elliot Ferrigan. She couldn't figure out his motive for this silliness. And why didn't he take the hint and leave the way Keller had?

Ferrigan sat straight in his wheelchair, his feet resting on the foot guard. His cool appraising eyes continued to watch her.

"Yes?" she asked.

"Did you know Robert?" he asked.

"No, not well," she answered. "He was my friend's friend. We only met once."

"Too bad. He was great," Elliot Ferrigan said. "I'm trying to figure out what my star chef was doing in a freezer."

"So that's why you wanted to see the scene from the film? Did Jonathan describe the scene?"

"Yeah." He smiled wryly. "You know Jonathan loves to spread bad news. He couldn't wait to tell me about Robert's accident and how they'd already filmed the damned thing."

. "And that's really why you're here?"

"Sure. It was Jonathan's idea. God, he and I go back a long time. I guess Jonathan means well. I never know for sure."

"I'm sorry. I can't help you. I don't know what good it would do to see what Max shot. I'm sure Jonathan can describe it to you, frame for frame."

He took a last look around the room, before putting his wheelchair in motion. "See you."

Margot watched him leave. She locked the door and retrieved the reel of film from her desk drawer. Thank heavens she'd interrupted the men before they'd completely searched the room. She had a feeling that they would have done so properly and thoroughly.

Sitting at the Moviola, she fed in the leader film and once again she peered into the screen. She watched the tiny figures reenact the scene she'd witnessed yesterday in real time. The scenes were nearly identical—the same accident, the same setting, except this time Robert Madrid had done the stunt himself. She zoomed in on the body in the freezer and felt distinctly uncomfortable recognizing the same posture, even the hands placed together the same way. Flipping the switch off, she sat back, unable to watch more.

Accident? Well, accident or not, *someone* was imitating art,

Max's art. She rewound the film strip and placed it carefully in a small canister before putting it back in the drawer. There'd be a zillion copies floating around, of course, but at least she knew where this one was if she wanted to see it again. What in heaven's name were those ridiculous men thinking?

THE NEXT WEEK WAS UNEVENTFUL. The movie was still going forward. The first shock of witnessing Robert's peculiar final resting place was fading a bit from her mind. Now, back in her office, Margot went to the computer and watched the digital of the scene she'd put together the day before. There was no sound track here, nothing but images. Prominent among the actors swirling around the Café Estrellado kitchen location was Loretta Rose. Margot smiled and shook her head slightly. She wouldn't tell him, but Max was a genius. Loretta Rose was a natural. There she was gesturing with a wooden spatula at a sous chef who'd blown a recipe, her eyes sparkling with professional disdain. Margot could almost hear her distinctive voice.

While Loretta Rose semi-perfected the craft of acting, the commissary's executive dining room remained closed until further notice. The studio executives were wary of deaths on the studio grounds, especially "accidental" deaths that had ongoing investigations.

The police had packed up their equipment and left the kitchen intact, presumably with vials and bags of evidence for the crime lab. Still, film people were so superstitious, perhaps it was just the threat of bad karma that kept the lovely room closed. The commissary itself had reopened and the coffee drinkers were back in their places.

Margot had learned nothing new about the tragedy. According to the newspapers, the police were still studying the evidence. It was termed death under suspicious circumstances. Suspicious, indeed, she thought. The papers had been full of the story for a few days, but the front page coverage had dwindled as the days went on without any new facts or conjecture. Loretta Rose had been grilled, to use her description, twice at the police station, but there was nothing to connect her with the death except for knowing the victim and finding the frozen remains. Of course, for all they knew, any one of them could be a prime suspect in the officials' minds if they weren't convinced it was an accident. And if it wasn't accidental, then Max was right, *someone* had to have done the terrible deed.

The story was still a hot commodity in the entertainment papers. Colin had seen to that. He had set the studio PR vultures on the Estrella family and the stories, Margot had to admit, were nothing if not colorful. Robert Madrid's television station was planning a testimonial show and the papers were full of his connection to Max's film. In fact, she noted, they made much more of his connection to the film than there'd actually been. Colin's work again, no doubt.

Colin Peabody, meanwhile, had morphed from concerned film producer to a complaining entity lurking around the sets and location, decrying Max's decision to hire Loretta Rose on a daily basis. Now his great studio *haute cuisine* plan was on hold and what about their plans for the new restaurant? But Loretta Rose was on location at Café Estrellado. She played dumb during his phone calls. She was out of his clutches for the time being.

Margot glanced at her notes from the rushes yesterday. Yes, that's what Max had asked for. He wanted his chef character to dominate the scene. Well, Loretta Rose as head chef, *star chef,* certainly did that. It was a brilliant move. The actual actors did fine, too, but the ten—or was it even a larger number?—cooks, chefs and sous chefs, bus boys and dish washers all scurrying right and left, dancing an incredible dance while avoiding flaming sauté pans, hot oven doors, scalding water, screaming wait persons, and each other, was a great sight. They were pros. They should be, most of them carried the Estrella family genes.

Her musing was interrupted by the telephone. "Margot," the gravely voice said. It was Jonathan Keller. She waited. "Sorry about barging in the other day. We thought it was a good idea at the time. Anyway, Max wants you down at the shoot. Know where that restaurant is?"

"Café Estrellado, right?"

"Yeah, sure. Whatever it's called. Wherever Max set up shop. I don't frequent places like that except professionally. My salary can't handle those prices. See you down there."

"Thanks," she said and hung up. Old bitter Jonathan Keller, the veteran second in command, she thought. He'd never adjust to the realities of his position. And she'd better not find him inside her office again, ever.

She didn't question why Max was requesting her presence. Max never made frivolous requests. Whatever had happened to make him ask for her was either very good or very bad. He never let the gray areas of life bother him.

Chapter IX

WALKING TO THE PARKING AREA, she swore under her breath. Colin was standing by her car obviously waiting for her. There was nowhere to hide. Colin was frowning as she drew closer. He clutched at her elbow. She was trapped.

"Now you and I have known each other for many years, Margot, haven't we?" he said. "And you're where you want to be, aren't you?"

"Yes," she said.

"Well, I'm *nearly* where I want to be. The problem is, of course, that Arcturus Productions is about to go down the toilet.... no, don't laugh, I'm serious. Monolith wants direct control of Arcturus. They'll bring in their own people. No more intelligent projects like *Extreme Cuisine*. You read the trades. And if the silly studio goes, I'll probably go with them. There isn't much call these days for old failures."

"But, Colin, they're always threatening something. You know that. And you're not a failure." Oh heavens, she thought. I'm not going to have to help Colin through some late midlife crisis, am I?

"Not a failure *yet*," he said. "But you know as well as anyone that we're all old by present industry standards, if you can call ageism an industry standard. Hell's bells, Margot, you see the kids working around us. I could count on one hand the number of people at Arcturus who are over forty. They just keep us around, and I'm including Max in this, too—he must be nearly forty, isn't he?—because we've done good work for them. It's just a matter of time."

Great, Margot thought. Just what she needed to hear. Of course, hadn't Sophie said that Steve Sanders didn't get that last art director position, that some twenty-something *wunderkind* had gotten it instead? And Steve had been around forever…

"Anyway," Colin said, "I'm looking into new ventures. Everyone thinks moviemaking makes the world go round. But it doesn't. I want a new challenge, especially if I'm fired, if we're *all* fired. The poor film. Those damned execs. They've all gone totally corporate."

"Can't you explain to them how exciting Max's film is?" Margot said. "It's a great story. They liked it enough to greenlight it. People will love it, especially younger people. Really, Colin, you're starting to make me nervous with all this talk."

"You *should* be nervous. None of us are getting any younger, are we? We should *all* be nervous. I know I am."

Margot opened the car door. "Call me if you hear anything, will you?" she asked.

He nodded and walked away.

She glanced into the rearview mirror. Was she just tired, or was she really starting to look her age which was, as Colin had reminded her, just the same as Max's, the damning "nearly forty" age? Blast that man and his insecurities, anyway.

Twenty minutes later, she pulled into the parking lot reserved for Café Estrellado's patrons. The famous restaurant's minimalist facade looked ordinary and unassuming at eleven-thirty in the morning. Amazing what dramatic night lighting could create. The wide street was empty of cars and packed with large, white production vehicles, the studio's distinctive logo emblazoned on both sides. Max had gotten the hallowed premises by promising Chef Carlos Estrella that they'd be at work early and be out again before the Café Estrellado workers began their dinner preparations at one. Café Estrellado didn't cater to the luncheon crowd.

Margot parked next to a mobile sound lab truck and hurried to the entrance. Max appeared on the other side of the heavy glass. He pushed opened the door and she ducked inside. The room she remembered from their dinner was deserted, the dimmed lights up full today, the tables bare, the elegant ambiance gone. Cables lay in neat snake-like lines over the rich carpet. Café Estrellado had become a work place.

The fancy grill area with its gleaming counter was deserted, too, but the door leading to the interior kitchen gaped open and she heard muted conversation from inside. She looked at Max scowling ferociously, his lean face contorted in anger. He led her to the kitchen and then she understood. Uh oh. No one was there. The production crew was inside, of course, but she didn't see any of the talent—none of the actors, the bit players, nobody was working.

"Where is everyone?" she asked.

"Well, our friend Ms. Rose isn't here this morning. That's okay though. She went to meet Colin about the exec's dining room reopening. Something dumb like that. It's the everyone *else* who isn't here that's driving me crazy."

"But what happened?"

"The fear factor. Someone set the I.N.S. on us. Everyone took off."

"You mean those cooks don't have green cards?"

He gave her a long look. "Of course not all of them have green cards. Do you know how difficult it is to get hold of one of those these days, and how long it can take to glom onto one? Jeeze. But even the legals took off. No one trusts the I.N.S."

"If they raided here, the studio could really get in trouble."

"Well, screw them, but yeah, old Colin would have a heart attack. So we get a phone call warning us that the I.N.S. was on its way. Hell, everyone just took off. I mean they *disappeared* into the vapors. Not that I blame them. But, man, old Carlos Estrella is gonna have my ass in a sling over this if his staff doesn't return."

Margot looked around at the empty kitchen, all the equipment strewn about, as though hastily dropped, utensils scattered here and there. "So where is the I.N.S. then?"

"Yeah, well, that's the weird part. They haven't shown up. At least, I haven't seen any feds barging around."

"Who called in the warning?"

Max paused. "Oh, hell, babe, you're right. I wasn't thinking straight. Of course, the warning *created* the fear factor. That's all that was needed." He smiled grimly. "Oh great. Someone screwed up our whole day of shooting on purpose. Now who would have done something like that? Who knows we were here?"

"About two hundred people know. Maybe more." Margot looked out the door at the bustling neighborhood. "Then there are all the Café Estrellado neighbors, everyone. It's difficult to disguise a production company on location."

"Jeeze, so who have I pissed off now?"

"Colin Peabody?"

"He wouldn't stop production. He's an ass, but he's not stupid. He's just mad that he doesn't have Loretta Rose to boss around this week."

"Well, the executive dining room won't stay closed forever. He's probably afraid there'll be a time conflict."

"Who cares. Anyway, Colin knows darned well this filming won't last forever, either. After she's done here, she can decide what she wants to do next. She's a grownup. She's having fun. She needed a break after that damned business with Robert."

"Did you get any of the scene done this morning before that phone call?"

"Yeah. Actually I got most of what I was after. We can check it out later at the dailies. You can tell me what you think is worth keeping." He looked at the room crowded with pieces of equipment, the production people standing by looking bored. "Okay, group, we're outta here. I think we can finish up with two more days in the kitchen. That is, if our actors ever come back." He took her elbow and they began walking toward the door.

"Why did you ask me to come down here?"

"I wanted you to see the place. I know you see all the footage. I wanted you to see *what* we're filming. Make sure I get it all in the scenes."

She nodded. Max was right. Looking at filmed scenes was confined by the camera lens. She went through the kitchen door. This was a much fancier setup than the commissary kitchen. There was a long cobalt blue counter top stretching down the center of the room; the stacks of shining cooking utensils; banks of ovens and stove tops, coal black under the huge vents overhead. There was the back door of the brick oven from the main dining room, an ante-room with deep zinc sinks and huge, stainless steel dishwashers. There was also the hum of a heavy duty air conditioner keeping the room cool, at least for now when none of the appliances were being used. Later it would be a madhouse, she imagined, hot, noisy and congested. That was what Max wanted to convey on film.

A narrow door at the back of the kitchen caught her attention. The old wood didn't fit in with the highly efficient-looking decor surrounding it. She walked over, skirting a too-familiar looking huge stainless steel freezer door. Turning the knob, she looked into a long dim corridor that knifed through the building. Yellowing light bulbs overhead hardly made a dent in the gloom. The hall smelled musty. Curious, she walked halfway down the corridor and stopped. How bizarre. She peered through thick glass on the top half of a narrow door, the beveled glass edges reflecting like a prism. She was looking into a tiny, ornately paneled elevator. The interior looked barely big enough for two people—two *thin* people.

She stepped away, wondering where it went—down to the basement, the space Robert had said was used for taping *The Late Night Chef*? And Café Estrellado was housed in a corner of a large old building. She hadn't really noticed the exterior but remembered it had at least three or four floors. These ancient, by L.A. standards, downtown buildings had probably seen many lives through the decades. This one might have started out as an apartment building. That could be the reason for an elevator. Not that *she* would ever want to use that dilapidated-looking contraption. She'd have to ask someone how they accessed the studio basement. It would be fun to take a peek at the TV setup.

She was walking toward the kitchen door when she stopped,

listening. A sibilant whirring noise seemed to be somewhere behind her. Turning, she looked down the dimly lit corridor. As she listened, the sound stopped. The elevator? She glanced back at the elevator door. Ears still perked, but now hearing only her own breathing.

Faintly she heard, "Let's go guys," Max shouted. "Damned early, but we might as well call it a day. I want a meeting for *everyone* who's here now at three at Arcturus. You know the room."

His voice was a reassuring noise, and then, as she stepped over the door sill, she noticed the wheel marks on the dusty floor behind her. A bicycle? No, there were two lines of marks. A wheelchair? Elliot Ferrigan was stuck in a wheelchair and, after all, he was *The Late Night Chef's* director. He must use this door all the time. But surely there were easier ways to get down there than going through here. She wondered if the state agency on Access for the Disabled knew about this. They could close the building if it didn't provide proper access for someone like Ferrigan. Beyond the legality, however was the fact that the entire space could use a good vacuuming. She stepped inside the brightly lit kitchen with a sense of relief.

"Where were you, Margot?" Max looked up as the silent crew packed up the cables, cameras, lights. "Where did you disappear to?"

"Exploring. This is a big building, isn't it?"

"Yes, old L.A. But be careful. I don't know who owns what's beyond the restaurant and the TV station has that basement space."

They were nearly to her car when Loretta Rose drove up and slammed the car door shut. "Colin's acting weird."

"What's the matter now?" Margot asked.

"The studio has closed the exec's dining room forever."

"Why?" Max asked.

"Well," she said and started to grin, "apparently some of the bad boys have been gambling in there after hours. You know, doing their damned coke and gambling the family fortunes away. Someone told on them. The studio head thinks it doesn't look good, doesn't give the 'right impression' and is terrified the press will get hold of the story. That tidbit would be a bit much after Robert's death on their premises."

"Didn't you say Robert liked to gamble?"

"Well, yes, he did say that, didn't he? Well, heck. So my fancy dining room was an after hours den of iniquity. So what. Anyway, there goes that job. But it's just as well." She paused, a look of delight on her face. "So guess what? I can't believe my good luck! Looks like my financier is ready to deal on my project, my *own* project this time. It's an incredible place to start from, too. See, I'll be doing a wine bar right here, inside Café Estrellado!" She pointed to an adjacent corner of the building next to the café's entrance. "They're gonna make access to it from the main dining room, right through the wall. It'll be too cool and then there will be Carlos Estrella and all his clientele already there and who knows what this could lead to."

"That's fabulous," Margot said. "Have you told Colin you've found someone else to back you?"

Loretta Rose made a face. "I told him I have 'someone.' He wasn't pleased, to put it mildly."

"He'll probably kill you, or hell, kill your backer, when he finds out who it is," Max said. "So who is it?"

"Well, Carlos Estrella has the same financier and Carlos is acting as go-between. Apparently he's been wanting to add this wine bar to the premises and then he heard about me and, blah blah, here I am! It's all totally hush-hush for the moment, but Carlos says the guy has really worked out for him. The money's good and plentiful and he leaves you alone. I trust Carlos, not like some people I could mention. Colin can go do something else to someone else," she added, her eyes dark with pleasure at what had happened. "So, Max, how many more days do I have of being a movie star?"

"About two. We'll finish filming here and then you're free to pursue your other adventures."

Loretta Rose's good humor dissolved. "I really miss Robert," she said. "When he was alive we had all these great plans—his TV show, helping me with the new restaurant or whatever. Oh, hell." She wiped her eyes with her hand. "He'd have been sensational with the wine bar idea. So, did I miss anything this morning?"

It was Max's turn to change mood. "Just watching fifteen employees scared out of their skins take off at warp speed. Someone called and said the I.N.S. was on its way to check everyone out."

"What happened?"

"Nothing. Well, everyone left and not one official arrived." Max made a face. "Someone's idea of a joke, I guess. God, if Colin hears about this, he'll have a fit. Another day's shooting down the tubes. He's already in a semi-panic about our little movie, if you haven't noticed."

Margot nodded. She'd noticed. She didn't want to get into an agonizing "what if" conversation with Max. She was anxious enough as it was, thanks to Colin's meandering conversation hitting on every sore point he could think of.

And *Extreme Cuisine* was looking so great. It would be such a waste to shelve all their work and the artistry behind it. Of course, the studio could care less about things like that, which was the trouble in the first place. What a business. She wondered if Max knew how precarious their position was at this point, not even counting the fallout from Robert's death. He'd probably laugh at the fight between Arcturus and Monolith. He disliked both organizations. And, at this point in his career, he could find another place to get a film made. Or he could do it himself. He was always threatening to try. But, so far, he and the idiosyncratic Colin Peabody had made a good team. The studio had always greenlighted Max's every idea and Colin had stood firm behind him. But the business was changing. Heck, it was always changing. Bigger business. Less art. So what else was new. Now she felt depressed.

They said goodbye and walked to their cars. Margot waved to Max, hesitated behind the wheel and then turned toward the studio and her editing room.

Her cell phone bleeped as she pulled into her parking space.

"My dear, all is well," Colin said. "The powers that be don't want to shelve the film. Actually some do, but for the moment the general consensus at Monolith is that Arcturus Productions adds some much-needed and genuine substance to their generally venal and greedy reputation. So, it's a go with *Extreme Cuisine*. You know what that means, don't you?"

"Uhh, we keep doing what we're doing?"

Colin chuckled. "You are such a wit. A beautiful red-headed wit. I love it. Yes, it means we keep doing what we're doing. And just tell Max to make it jazzy, okay, darling?"

"Make the film 'jazzy'?"

"Exactly."

"I'll mention it to him."

"Wonderful, darling. Get him to feature as many of the Estrella family as he can in his kitchen scenes. You know, get those family extras up in front."

"I don't know if they would want to do that."

"Oh, I'm sure they would. It is their famous relative's restaurant we're filming at, after all. What a chance for more fabulous PR. Monolith is very happy about the pre-release publicity, too. Of course, we must remember poor, poor Robert. Still, we want to keep the Estrellas in the public eye, don't we? Oh, and Margot, that friend of yours, that Loretta Rose Cinefucco...well, I am *deeply* disappointed in her. Did she tell you she's jumping ship and abandoning our plans for her new restaurant idea, something about a fancy wine bar? Did she *mention* she's found somebody else to back her, after all the trouble I went to to get her set up at the commissary and I'll just bet I know who the scheming double dealer is, too. Did she happen to tell you the person's name?"

"No. she didn't, Colin. See you later." Margot hung up. Even with his good news, she didn't want to deal with Colin. Abandoning the idea of finding any peace and quiet at the studio, she drove home frowning.

Tomorrow night Loretta Rose and Max were coming over to the apartment to watch the widely publicized tribute program to Robert Madrid on *The Late Night Chef*. The past two episodes of *Chef* programming had been segments called "Gold Star Viewers's Choices." There had been no official word that Rafael Estrella would actually take his brother's place. Perhaps he would. They'd learn more during the program.

Chapter X

MARGOT MOVED AMORY THE CAT and sat down on the sofa between Sophie and Max. The black cat snarled his displeasure at being displaced and leaped down to the rug, sitting under the coffee table, staring at them with his peculiar yellow eyes. Loretta Rose had the large chair on the right. Ivy was curled up on the floor.

This was not a pajama night. They were together to watch the special *The Late Night Chef* memorial to Robert Madrid.

The remains of the evening's fire glowed in the fireplace. Max got up and loaded two logs onto the embers. It was a chilly night. Margot could feel the cold behind her hovering along the thin old, poorly insulated walls of the apartment.

"Why does it come on so late," Max complained.

"Don't be a baby, Max." Sophie yawned. "It's only nine."

"Do they have any new ideas about what happened to him?" Ivy asked.

"Nothing concrete I've heard about," Max said. "But, hey, do you wanna know whodunit in *my* movie? After all, everyone's in a twit about that stupid life imitating art bit. Hell, don't they understand that everything is fiction?"

"So whodunit?" Ivy said.

Max smiled. "If I told you, you wouldn't go see it, would you? Anyway, my pet theory for Bobby's demise is that one of his beloved family members dumped him in that freezer."

"Max!" Margot said. "That's terrible."

"Come on. It's just a theory, babe. See, maybe we've got some sort of family feud going on. Because, believe me, people simply do not go wandering into kitchen freezers in the middle of the night. What was Bobby looking for—a frozen snack? No way. So since most of the Estrellas are working as extras on *Extreme Cuisine,* the murderer's probably right there on the set, *my* set everyday. I bet I'm looking right at the bad guy through the camera lens."

"Max! You really believe that?" Margot said. "But they're still saying it was an accident, right? And, anyway, all those people are so nice."

"Sure, they're nice. But how do you lock yourself in a freezer unit equipped with an alarm system that's rigged to automatically unlock the door if it slams behind you. And the alarms just happen to be on the fritz that night. What a coincidence. Hell. Unless he was totally blotto, which he was not at our party, old Bobby wouldn't wander into a frickin walk-in freezer and let the door close behind him."

The room was quiet. Margot stared at the flickering screen. In fact, everyone was staring silently into space in the face of Max's storytelling.

"Well," Max shrugged. "My theory's as good a theory as anything else. Hey, here we go," he said.

The distinctive theme music for *The Late Night Chef* came

on. The camera pulled back revealing the kitchen set, but this time there was no grand entrance by Robert Madrid. Instead, a man in a wheelchair wheeled onto the stage into the light. The camera panned slowly toward him.

"Hey." Max leaned forward. "That's old Elliot Ferrigan."

Loretta Rose sat up. "He's the one who's backing me for the wine bar."

Margot stared at Loretta Rose. Elliot Ferrigan? Of course, Elliot must have money. Everyone who worked more or less regularly in the business had *some* money. And so he was Carlos Estrella's backer, too. Cafe Estrellado must make a mint for its backers. She glanced at Max. She'd never mentioned her unsettling run-in with Jonathan and Elliot in her editing room. Max would have been furious and there was no sense in getting him on a Jonathan bashing binge, especially when the film was in production. He might dislike Jonathan, and certainly vice versa, but they needed each other right now.

"Oh, this is so sad."

The lament came from Loretta Rose as Elliot Ferrigan's introduction to the special ended and the tribute film began.

And it was a touching and well-done piece, Margot decided. Nicely edited, too. Robert Madrid had been so vital and handsome. And now… What a terrible waste.

"That was pretty classy. I think I can work with this Ferrigan guy," Loretta Rose said. "He's done a good job for Robert. I'd better record this." She pushed the record button as still black and white photos of Robert Madrid as a child and young man began scrolling across the screen.

Remarkable, Margot thought, to see the man as a child surrounded by the Estrella family, his brothers—tiny tots in the early stills—the mother she'd recently met, here all beautifully youthful, everyone carefree and looking full of fun. Well, all of them gathered here tonight around the television could probably drum up a similar assortment of idyllic-looking photos. Of course, nothing was really idyllic. No one took photos of family squabbles and fights. It was just the good stuff. She'd lost her parents in an accident as a young child, but she'd had happy days with her aunt and uncle…

"So where's the dad?" Max asked. "Those kids didn't happen by themselves."

Margot leaned forward. Max was right. It was a curious omission. Unless she'd missed it, no one had even mentioned "dad." Hmm, a story in there someplace. There always was. Now the voiceover—who was narrating? The voice was so familiar. The unseen actor was bringing them up to date with more contemporary data on Robert Madrid.

They watched Robert as he moved from the studio commissary (he'd worked at the commissary? Margot glanced at Loretta Rose who seemed equally surprised by the news), to his working side-by-side with his younger brother Carlos at Estrellados ("No kidding," murmured Sophie. "He used to be a working chef and at Estrellados?") to a few cuts from the gala first episode of *The Late Night Chef,* three successful seasons ago, with star chefs from all over the country making cameo congratulatory appearances. The show had been an immediate hit and suddenly there was news coverage of Robert Madrid everywhere.

The fire crackled and flared throwing warm light around the room.

Max sat forward. "So who's that beauty?"

"That beauty" was an attractive blonde woman wearing a

slim black dress. She was holding the hands of two youngsters, smiling into the camera and nodding as she escorted the kids through wide doors into a public building.

"Mrs. Robert Madrid with Dierdre and Bobby junior," the narrator said, "shown at the Claremont Museum Charity Dinner in 2000, shortly before the eleven-year marriage broke up."

"*Mrs.* Robert Madrid?" Loretta Rose's voice stood out over the television sounds. "He was married for *eleven* years and forgot to mention *that*? And who are Dierdre and Bobby junior?"

"Must be his kids," Ivy said.

Loretta Rose sat back. "Well, well, well!"

"It's not that surprising," Max said. "Marriage happens all the time."

"He *might* have mentioned something about it," she said.

"Would it have made any difference?"

"No. I'm just surprised."

There was silence. Then, "Great set," Max said. "And the show is really done in a basement?"

"Yeah, it's right under where we're filming," Loretta Rose replied, "under Cafe Estrellado."

"I think I saw it," Margot said, glad they'd shifted from that prickly topic of conversation. "Well, not the basement, but the corridor that leads to it. It's right off the big kitchen. It has an elevator, too, a really old decrepit looking thing."

"What were you doing around there, babe? You gotta be careful in old buildings. I'll have to check it out down there. Maybe I'll need it for something. So, hey, there's old Ferrigan again, live and up close. Looks like someone else we know, doesn't he?"

"We all look like someone," Ivy said, her mouth full of popcorn. "Everyone of us has a perfect twin somewhere in the world."

Max frowned. "Do you think Ferrigan's really his name? He doesn't look Irish. Why does everyone change their name around this burg?"

"Oh, hush, Max. You did it, too."

As the *homage du* Madrid film finished and faded out, Elliot Ferrigan wheeled back across the empty kitchen set. He sat quietly as the camera panned in close.

Ferrigan sat straight in his wheelchair, his feet resting on the foot guard. He was dressed all in black, in a trendy "I am a producer-director, even if it's just television," attire of silk polo shirt and slacks.

"Friends of *The Late Night Chef* and of our dear friend Robert Madrid. As I'm sure you recall, Robert's untimely and unseemly death has shaken us all."

"'Untimely?'" Max said. "Duh, Ferrigan. Yeah, his death was definitely *untimely*… Jeeze."

"We are asking the public, you, our public, to please call us with any information you might have concerning this tragedy. If any of you know why Robert might have been in the Arcturus Studio Commissary on the night of his death, please call the number on your screen. All information will be turned over to the detectives in charge and be held strictly confidential. And now, as a special treat and a hint of the future segments of *The Late Night Chef,* here's our new star chef, Raphael Estrella, the beloved brother of our own Robert Madrid. Raphael will be preparing Robert's famous *Saint Angel quesadilla filled with black figs and Madeira wine*… "

"Wow," said Loretta Rose. "So they did tap Raphael to replace Robert."

Margot watched the television screen as Raphael's attractive face appeared and he began earnestly discussing the origins of the recipe and showed the prepared bowls of ingredients. The recipe was carefully printed out on a chalk board behind him. Raphael seemed a bit nervous. Who could blame him, taking on this huge enterprise.

She stared hard at the list of ingredients, feeling a strange chill of recognition. Finally she stood up and hurried to her bedroom, straight to her closet. Burrowing into her brown suede skirt pocket, she pulled out a folded piece of paper. She peered at it in the half light and went back out to the living room. Everyone was as before, eyes staring at flickering images crossing the screen.

"Maybe I should call that number," Margot said and watched the heads turn her way. "I found this on the floor of the executive dining room the morning we found Robert, Loretta Rose. It's that recipe. Robert's favorite *Saint Angel quesadilla…*"

Max snatched the paper from her fingers.

"Wow," he said, "I think you've got a real live clue, babe." He glanced back at the TV. "No, look, Raphael's left out the Brie."

"Maybe he doesn't like Brie."

"Don't be silly, Sophie, everyone likes Brie."

"Maybe he forgot," Ivy said. "No," she said, narrowing her eyes. "He left it out on purpose. Raphael is a very handsome, ambitious boy. He wants his recipes to be better than his brother's."

"You don't forget the ingredient in a testimonial *recipe,* for heaven's sake," Loretta Rose said. She reached for the recipe in Max's hand.

"Believe me, he did it on purpose. You know," Ivy said, "like your mother-in-law leaving out the best ingredient so yours won't be as good."

"Where did you hear that nonsense?" Sophie asked. "You've never had a mother-in-law."

"I read Dear Abby or whoever it's called after now. I know what's going down," Ivy said. "Anyway, look at him. Rafael knows exactly what he's doing."

Max shrugged. Rafael Estrella had finished the preparations and presented the plate toward the camera. It looked delicious, Brie-free or not.

"Funny," Max said. "I think Ivy's right. Rafael reminds me of certain problematic up-and-coming actors I've had to deal with. I'll bet he could be a tad troublesome if crossed…. So what was the real recipe doing in the executive dining room?"

"Obviously someone dropped it."

"Like Robert?"

"Yeah, I guess. Though why his recipe ends up there is beyond me."

"There was gambling going on in there that night," Loretta Rose said. "And drugs, too. But Robert didn't do coke. So maybe he met someone there after I left him."

Margot stared, visualizing the fancy dining room. She'd noticed the two cups of coffee on the big table.

"Well, you've got something there, babe, something that shows where else Robert was that night, but don't call that number," Max said. "You'd probably be connected right to Ferrigan who seems to be really getting off on this whole thing. I don't get his playing this 'America's Most Wanted' schtick, either. Maybe he knows something we don't. I can't see why he'd make an announcement like that for a stupid accident. So talk to the police, babe. Go direct. Bypass the entertainment bit. Hey, listen, what's he saying now? Oh my God, what's he blabbing on about now?"

His lament echoed through the living room as they watched the camera creeping close to a huge black and white still from the familiar kitchen location set at Café Estrellado. There was Max in animated-looking conversation with the late Robert Madrid. Superimposed over the still was an ad for "*Extreme Cuisine,* the up-coming movie."

"Oh, my God," Max repeated. ""How completely tasteless. Talk about absurd product placement. This isn't the time to plug a stupid *movie,* even one of mine. This is embarrassing. Now let's guess whose fancy work this was..."

"Colin's." Margot stared at the TV screen, the promo for Max's film frozen in time and space.

"Yeah, Colin Peabody, Elliot Ferrigan's old buddy in high places. Both of them with the taste and grace of a...a...well, something totally tasteless and graceless."

Loretta Rose moaned. "Hell, and I've just signed my life away to this Ferrigan guy on this new venture. Maybe he's just so emotionally involved, he made a tasteless slip."

"Maybe," Max said.

Loretta Rose's cell phone bleeped and she flipped it on, stepping behind the sofa. Margot could hear her voice, a low murmur, full of questions. The phone clicked shut and she sat back down. Margot looked at her questioningly.

"That was Colin. I don't think Colin and Elliot Ferrigan are buddies anymore. He told me he knows it's Elliot Ferrigan's money that's behind my wine bar. He's furious. This little PR thingie must have been worked out before he knew."

Max shrugged. "So Ferrigan's financing you, so what? It doesn't matter who does it. Money is money. Television money buys as much as any other. And people in the business are always fighting over this or that. They get together, however, no matter what, if it's in their best interest to do so. Like countries do, know what I mean? Everything's done for their own self interest. So if it was before or after an argument, I'd still like to know which of those jerks thought up this crass advertising. It's lousy. It's bad enough that the news is circulating that my new brilliant film forecasts a death, a *friend's* death. Jeeze. I'm really pis..."

"Coffee?" Ivy interrupted brightly, a tray of steaming mugs in her hands.

ON MONDAY Margot went to the police station address listed on the card the policeman had given her during the initial questioning. It named a Detective Wilson and gave an address for a police station close to Arcturus Studios.

Leaning over a heavily scarred wooden counter, she pushed the card and the crumbled recipe paper along with one of her business cards toward a uniformed clerk.

"Hello," she said. "I found this in the Arcturus Studio executive dining room and it might have to do with the death of Robert Madr..."

The clerk nodded and taking her card and the recipe off the counter, started punching numbers into a console on his desk.

Margot waited for something to happen.

Finally, "He'll be right out," the clerk said.

Margot took a chair and wondered why she'd come. What difference was a recipe card going to make? What difference did it make if Robert had wandered through the executive dining room. They all did that. Why did she always listen to Max?

"Ms. O'Banion?"

She looked up to see a tired looking man in a slightly rumpled suit standing in front of her. He was squinting at her business card held out at arm's length.

"Yes." She felt at a distinct disadvantage having to crane her neck to look up, but he was standing so close that if she stood now, it would be even more awkward.

"I'm Detective Wilson. You had my card. You brought in this paper?"

The recipe, she noted, was now encased in a small plastic bag.

"Yes, it's a recipe. I found it after I saw Mr. Madrid's body in the commissary kitchen freezer."

"Yes, I recall your statement." He peered at her. "You were summoned by your friend, Ms. Loretta Rose Cinefucco, the dining room food manager, right? She needed you for moral support, she said. And where did you say you found this?"

"It was laying on the carpet in the executive dining room. We were watching the testimonial to Robert Madrid Saturday night and I remembered I'd picked it up. It's supposedly his favorite recipe."

"This stuff?" He held out the scrap of paper she'd found.

Margot nodded. "I don't know if it means anything…"

The man suddenly smiled. "I don't know either, but I'll put it along with the other things we have. So, did you know Mr. Madrid well?"

"Not really that well. He was working on this film I'm editing. He was an advisor on restaurant lore and he and my friend, Loretta Rose Cinefucco, were friends, too. Everyone seemed to like him a lot."

The man raised his eyebrows. "We've gotten several calls about a scene from the movie you guys are making."

Margot's heart sank. Then, "It's just a terrible coincidence, I'm sure."

The detective tapped the plastic baggie with an impatient fingertip. "It doesn't really help us, you understand. I'm led to believe that approximately three hundred people knew what was in that scene long before Mr. Madrid's death."

She nodded. "It was an accident, wasn't it?"

The detective stared at something over her head and said, "Well, thank you for coming in."

"Detective?" He turned, looking not so much impatient as simply fatigued.

"Yes?"

"Was his death an accident? I mean are you still thinking that Robert Madrid somehow got trapped in that freezer and couldn't get out and died there of hypothermia?"

The detective paused. "We're waiting on the results from a lot of lab reports. Even in our digital age, some of these tests take time." He paused. "Why? Don't you think it was an accident?"

Margot stared, trying to read the man's enigmatic expression. His face was round and creased with dark pouches under his eyes and a definite double chin developing. The dark hair was thinning and there was the hint of a chronic five o'clock shadow on his face, even at this early hour. He'd be a good character actor, she thought—perfect casting for the old school politician or, yes, the long-suffering detective.

"Do you?" he repeated. The two words floated between them.

Did she? What could she say. Just because all the players in this scenario seemed to be bigger than life… That Robert Madrid was too familiar with restaurant kitchens to make a mistake like that. Did those questions make the circumstances suspicious?

She shook her head. "I work in film," she said. "I guess I have an active imagination."

"You'd make a terrible policeman," he said. "We're not allowed to have imaginations." With that Detective Wilson nodded and turned, disappearing down a long corridor.

Margot stared after him and left the police building.

Chapter XI

AT TWO O'CLOCK SHE LEFT HER WORK AND DROVE to St. Anthony's church. It was the Estrella family's formal memorial for Robert. Max had promised to meet her there. He'd be taking off from the restaurant kitchen location shoot along with the production crew. Everyone on set, relatives or not, had liked Robert Madrid.

Stepping into the church she was caught in the dim coolness that she always associated with practicing her religion. Not that she actually participated these days, but she thought about it occasionally. Some childhood habits were hard to break.

She waited, letting her eyes grow accustomed to the soft light and saw Max sitting in a middle row. She slipped in beside him and sat down on the wooden bench. He smiled and took her hand.

"Hey, babe. Nice crowd," he whispered. "Check out who's here."

She looked around, seeing backs of heads from the shoulders up. She shrugged. "Who?"

"*Everyone,*" he answered. "All the Estrellas, Carlos, too, and the TV group from his show—there's Ferrigan—and, over there, I think that's Robert's ex-."

Margot followed his glance. Yes, she recognized the blonde woman identified as the former Mrs. Madrid, from the tribute program. She was sitting in the front row with two teenagers. The clip had been filmed years ago. The children had grown up.

The religious service was a short one. The priest seemed to have actually known Robert Madrid and spoke kindly of him. Margot saw the back of the ex-Mrs. Madrid's head bow slightly. Perhaps they'd even been married here. She sighed and felt Max take her hand again.

The two younger brothers, the famous chef Carlos and the new TV star Raphael, each told a story about life with Robert. The anecdotes were touching and Margot felt her eyes tear again. There was something about *ritual,* she decided.

"Shit, I missed it all." Loretta Rose whispered. She was sliding into the pew next to Margot as the organ chords swelled and ended. The ceremony was over.

"Where were you?"

"Having a showdown with old Colin about ducking out on him, project-wise. And watch out, he's around here somewhere."

"Best thing to do is ignore him," Max said. "That's what I do at every opportunity."

"Okay, I will. I'm really excited about the wine bar," she said. "That Carlos Estrella is great."

"Is he married?" Margot whispered.

Loretta Rose smiled. "Let's go pay our condolences to the family. Come on, I'll introduce you to Carlos."

They began wending their way through pockets of people toward the Estrella family clustered together on the church porch.

"Uh oh," Loretta Rose muttered. "Jeeze, I thought they decided to hate each other."

And Colin was there, standing next to the wheelchair bound Elliot Ferrigan, talking to Raphael Estrella. Max was right. Whatever differences Colin and Elliot might have over who was backing Loretta Rose in her new venture, their primary interests were similar, making sure their production projects worked. Now Loretta Rose sighed and walked toward the men, her hand under Margot's elbow propelling her forward.

Max mumbled something and peeled off toward another group. She didn't blame him, but still, she was stuck. Goodness, she didn't like either of these men. Elliot had seemed all right until that day she'd found him squirreling through her work. Both men deserved to out-business one another. She nodded toward Colin and Elliot and expressed her sympathies to Raphael.

Loretta Rose managed to maneuver Margot between herself and Colin.

Margot understood. She didn't blame her friend for using her as a shield. "Hey, Colin," she said.

"Margot, darling," Colin said. He was looking rather retro-resplendent, she thought, in his conservative funereal dark suit, his thinning baby fine blond hair blowing in the breeze like soft bird feathers. "Sad, sad day for us all. You know Elliot here, don't you? Elliot is, well, he *was,* dear Bobby's producer and director. Now of course, he's taken Raphael under his *Late Night Chef's* wing. So how are the ratings, Elliot?"

Elliot Ferrigan smiled at Margot, sardonic humor in his expression. If she hadn't been so angry at his showing up in her office that morning, she might have liked him for this.

"There's just been the one show so far, Colin," he answered.

"High ratings. Of course, it was the testimonial. But I'm sure Raphael here will keep us on the same winning track as Robert did. You're already getting fan mail, aren't you?"

Raphael smiled. "I'm going to do my best," he said. "I have some ideas for the format, stuff Robert didn't want to include. Not to put down my brother's show, but I plan to do more with the cooking concept."

"Not like some people." Colin glanced at Loretta Rose who ignored him.

Elliot Ferrigan nodded. "Robert was a wonderful person, but Raphael's got the driving ambition. Right, Raphael?"

Whatever Raphael might have said was lost as the crowd parted and Margot found herself face-to-face with his older brother, the inimitable and unmistakable star chef Carlos Estrella.

Loretta Rose gravitated to his side and Margot suddenly found herself feeling flustered being this close to celebrity. She should be used to famous people, she thought. But, generally, she just saw the familiar faces on film or far off on a sound stage under artificial conditions. This Carlos Estrella was dazzling in true Estrella tradition; the inky black hair and eyes, finely pored skin the color of an expensive coffee drink, smooth skin most women would kill for. As Ivy would say, the man was drop-dead gorgeous.

Formal introductions were made and expressions of sympathy and remorse were shared. Then she watched as Carlos took his younger brother's arm and led him a short distance away. She thought about Max's death theory. Was one of the brothers a murderer? But Max couldn't be right. His family killer theory was crazy. The Estrella family was so close they were like something a Disney screenwriter would invent. Now Carlos was leaning down to Raphael saying something that certainly had impact. She watched as Raphael's complexion took on that faint flush of either embarrassment or anger. Which was it this time?

"Whatcha checking out, babe?" Max had returned. His voice was quiet in her ear.

"Family dynamics."

He followed her glance and nodded as Raphael jerked his arm away and strode off. Carlos was still frowning when he saw Max and started over. The frown didn't disappear.

"I can't have you doing your movie at my restaurant any longer, Max," he said.

She felt Max tense up beside her.

"What are you talking about, Carlos? We've got a deal. I'm almost through shooting the kitchen. I've kept my end of the bargain. We haven't messed up the place and we've been out by one o'clock sharp…"

"It's not that, Max. I didn't know then who you were working with."

"Who?" Max waved his arms. "I work with a million people. I work with Margot here. You're not mad at her are you?"

Carlos Estrella didn't smile. "Of course, I'm not angry at this lovely woman. I'm talking about your producer."

Max relaxed. "Oh, *him*. Hell, Carlos, *everyone* hates Colin. You are talking about Colin Peabody, aren't you?"

"Yes. He's trying to move in on our restaurants. He's like a telemarketer. He calls all the time. He's always hinting at weird things in my financier's background. You know, Elliot Ferrigan. As though I care about talk like that. It's like listening to high school trash talk. Know what I mean? See, there he is, still talking with Ferrigan, probably trying to move in on us still and we've been open for four years with Elliot's backing. We're set."

"What's he doing playing financier, anyway? Hell, he's supposed to be producing my damned movie."

"He wants to back a restaurant, period. I dunno. Maybe he wants free meals or something. Ferrigan doesn't need his money. Elliot likes to be in the background like a good financier should be, anonymous and generous. Loretta Rose is lucky to have him backing her. We just want Colin Peabody to leave us alone. They've held some momentous shouting matches at the restaurant. It's embarrassing to listen to. The man is impossible."

"Tell Colin to go climb a tree," Max suggested. "I don't get it. Doesn't he make enough money outta movies?"

"I think he's worried he might be fired," Margot said. She probably shouldn't relate what Colin had said about the problems with the studio, but she felt no obligation to him. "You know, if Monolith takes over Arcturus. He figures he'll be let go."

"Good move," Carlos Estrella said. "Okay, Max, finish it up, finish your kitchen movie at my place. We can't let the Colins of the world dictate what we do. There is one other thing." He glanced around and lowered his voice. "The family got some pretty serious news this morning and then a couple of my cousins mentioned that you have something in the new movie…"

Max slung his arm around the tall man. "Hey, I'm way ahead of you there, Carlos. That crazy scene, my murder scene…I'm gonna delete it. It's not worth the trouble and I sure don't want to cause any more pain to your family."

Carlos Estrella nodded, looking relieved.

Margot was taken by surprise. This was the first she'd heard that the controversial prescient scene would be removed. She wondered why the news caught her off guard. Max usually did do the right thing. He'd think of something else for that plot line.

The conversation reverted to standard consolation phrases revolving around the real reason for their all being together today. And Margot found herself scanning the crowd, much as she'd scan the scene of a film looking for this or that important detail.

Across the courtyard she noticed Elliot Ferrigan watching her. Still feeling angry, she excused herself and walked over. Leaning down slightly toward him, she said, "That scene from *Extreme Cuisine,* the one you and Jonathan were searching for, has been eliminated from the film. You two can stop going through other people's property now."

Elliot looked surprised. "Really?" he said. "Well, that's fine. That ought to stop the gossip."

She nodded and looked away. Louisa Estrella, handsome in a plain black dress so deceptively simple-looking it must be couturier, was shaking hands with a long line of mourners informally lined up like guests at a wedding reception. She saw numerous somber faced men in dark suits, all looking a bit like Robert and Raphael and Carlos. The Estrella genes at work, she supposed. She was still glancing about when Loretta Rose swooped back over.

"Have you heard? Here," she said. Her eyes were wide. "Alisandro gave me his copy," and held a newspaper in front of them. *Death Ruled Homicide,* the black headline proclaimed. In smaller print, Margot read, as they all bent closer to the fluttering pages, *TV Star's Freezer Death A Murder.*

Margot met Max's stunned expression.

He snatched the paper from Loretta Rose's shaking hand.

She watched as his eyes quickly skimmed the story. Finally his hand dropped, the newspaper rustling in his clenched hand.

"See? Didn't I tell you? But, oh my God," he said, reading.

"Look at that. Someone slipped Robert a mickey."

"Who?"

"Not *who,* Loretta Rose. A mickey's a *what.* Someone drugged Robert. That's how they did it. That's how they got him to stay in that freezer."

Beside her she heard Colin gasp, a wheezing unnatural sound. His normally pink face was gray, his pale eyes round and staring. "Bobby was murdered."

"Are you all right?" Max said.

Colin nodded.

From the corner of her eye, Margot saw a man standing on the edge of the crowd slowly surveying it, not unlike the way she'd been looking about a moment before the startling news. Her stomach gave a lurch. It was Detective Wilson from the L.A.P.D., the tired man she'd spoken with that morning.

Uh oh. She'd grown up watching *Columbo* on television. She knew what it meant when a detective just happened to be in the crowd at a murder—oh, good Lord—victim's funeral service. When Columbo did this on TV, he was searching for suspects, the person who looked or acted suspicious at his victim's ceremony. Suddenly she felt distinctly uncomfortable. *Who* was Detective Wilson watching? She couldn't very well keep staring at him to find out. She toyed with the idea of walking over to talk with him but decided this, too, would look suspect. And what could she say? Protest her innocence? No, she'd stay put, hidden in the group.

And as she watched, the detective approached Louisa Estrella. Heads bowed together, they were talking, talking. Mrs. Estrella must already know the awful news. The police wouldn't allow that terrible headline into print without the next-of-kin knowing…would they? That news must have been what Carlos was hinting at earlier. Suddenly she saw the brothers materialize together across the way. There was a sudden bit of tentative shoving, a punch to a shoulder. Both men's expressions were furious. As Margot watched the two men dancing about, she could almost imagine she could hear the angry exchange. Tempers were definitely flaring and during a funeral, too.

"Oh no," said Loretta Rose. "They're fighting, aren't they?"

"Is it about the newspaper story?"

She heard Max chuckle. "No. I think they're fighting over who's going to ask you out first, Loretta Rose."

"No! Really? Oh God. Not more complications. And see that guy with them? He's the one who quizzed me at the police station. He's a cop."

They stood quietly, the reality of the newspaper story and the change it made to everything, overwhelming the occasion. But the detective wasn't walking toward their group. In fact, he suddenly disappeared. Margot craned her neck searching for the man.

"Where'd he go?" Loretta Rose whispered.

"I don't know."

"Do you suppose he's going to make an arrest?"

"Here, at a memorial service? I don't think the police would do that."

"It must be one of us."

"No." It was Colin, sounding firm. "It was not one of us. It was some stranger, some person who broke into the commissary. Bobby found him stealing and, well, that was that."

Loretta Rose took Margot's arm and walked them away. "Yeah, right. The thief was stealing a case of artichoke hearts.

Really, I'm getting so I can't stand that man. He was saying the most awful things about Elliot Ferrigan and Elliot was standing… well, sitting… right there."

"What was Colin saying?"

"Nothing. I mean nothing substantive. You know Colin. It was all veiled threat-type language. Hell, he does the same thing with me."

"He *threatens* you?"

"Not exactly *threatens*. He *intimates* things. With me he hints about impending failure all the time. I ignore him. He's just being Colin. You know. The man can't believe that everyone has other things to think about or to do besides thinking or doing them with *him*. The man has a massive ego."

"But what was he saying over there?"

"Well, he told Ferrigan to watch his back or something original like that. And then he told me that Ferrigan and I would work well together since we both have 'pasts'."

"What did you say to that?"

She leaned toward Margot. "I told him *everyone* has a past. I mean how did we get where we are now if we didn't have a frickin *past*. Honestly, he's such a jerk."

"So what's your past?"

Loretta Rose turned her dark gaze on Margot, a small smile on her lips. "*My* past? Well, I guess it has to do with knowing a murderer. Remember? As I recall, you were right there. But you know what? We probably all know murderers. We just don't know that we do. My personal fave unsolved crime concerns whatever Colin's up to all the time. He's truly got a criminal mind."

Margot nodded. Now that she thought about it, Loretta Rose was exactly right. Colin had no morals *per se*. He shifted like a stalk of hay in the wind, going this way or that depending on what was best for him.

"Let's get out of here," she said. "I'm tired of these people."

"Do you think I'm doing the right thing, Margot? I mean doing the wine bar right next to Carlos's chi-chi place? Does it look like I'm coming in on his coattails, or worse..." Loretta Rose grimaced. "Like I'm after the guy or something like that, because he's such a success? You know, Loretta Rose Cinefucco takes up with the Estrella brothers, one after the other."

"Of course not. Elliot Ferrigan set up the position for you in the wine bar and, of course, Carlos Estrella had to sign off on who would be in charge. He must think you're good. Don't worry."

MAX FINISHED THE SHOOT AT CAFE ESTRELLADO later in the week without any new problems arising. By the time the production crew was packing up for what, they hoped, was the last time, construction was in the final stage for the café's new wine bar, manned by the almost-movie star, Loretta Rose, whose part on film was also completed.

True to his word, Max had shelved his version of the murder scene and substituted another, one that didn't utilize a restaurant's walk-in freezer. Margot had already viewed it and it was just as eerie and unsettling as the first, but without the coincidence factor.

The night of the grand opening of Cafe Estrellado's wine bar was star bright, dry and cold, especially cold for Los Angeles in

February. Margot shivered inside her seldom worn, heavy coat.

The restaurant looked warm and inviting and very crowded from the outside as they drove up, uniformed valet parking attendants swooping down on Max's car. Margot could see swarms of people inside the dining room, moving from the main room over towards the wine bar. Loretta Rose must be swamped, not that a little thing like that would faze her.

She took Max's arm as they walked to the entrance. "Hey," he said, looking down at her, "your dress matches the ring!"

And it did. The shimmering ruby was exactly the same hue as her swirling silk dress. Any further conversation about her color matching skills was impossible as they stepped into the noisy warmth of Cafe Estrellado. Max led her expertly around the busy dinner tables and into the room where Loretta Rose reigned behind a rosewood bar. She looked exquisite in a simple ivory dress complimenting her dark hair and pale skin. Margot glanced at Max who smiled at the beauty he was seeing. Good old Max. He'd probably find a way to put the exact scene with the exact colors in the new film.

Later, carrying glasses of a magnificent ruby-colored—yes, ruby again—Cabernet Sauvignon, they moved toward a quieter corner and she stood there, sipping and observing the handsomely dressed crowd as they moved like the sea from one area of the restaurant to another. Carlos Estrella came and went, resplendent in his crisp chef's coat smiling and accepting congratulations for adding yet another dimension to his famous restaurant, another showpiece. Max was right. The entire restaurant was like a brilliantly lit stage, the perfect backdrop for the heady drama of the dining table.

"Hey, babe, let's go check out that TV studio they've got

underneath here," Max whispered in her ear. "I may wanna chat with Ferrigan about using it for something."

"I don't know how we get down there," she said. "I didn't see any stairs by that elevator."

"Stick with me, babe, I'll find the place. Come on." He took her hand and led her through the crowd toward the kitchen door.

Ducking into the kitchen, Margot was nearly overwhelmed by the chaos in front of her. Across the room, Carlos Estrella waved a long handled spoon at them. The central counter top was alive with steaming plates. The room was noisy with the sound of sizzling pans, the clanking of china being moved from here to there with lightning speed and above it all, the sound of voices shouting directions, acknowledging instructions, pleading for this or that missing from their orders, all of which seemed to be late. And everything and everybody, she noted, flowed around the chef, like a stream swirling around a massive boulder.

"Isn't this cool?" Max said.

He held her arm close and they wove their way through the kitchen and the sea of dancing chefs, the line cooks, sous chefs, heavily laden waitpersons passing each other with scant inches to spare. Finally they were at the old door leading to the corridor. Max gave a final wave to his crew extras and opening the door, they slid through. He shut it firmly behind them and suddenly the cacophony of semi-organized bedlam and chaos was muffled as though someone had turned down the sound.

"Whew," said Max leaning against the door in relief. "How can they work in conditions like that?"

She shrugged. The chaos in the restaurant kitchen didn't seem any worse than many hectic scenes she'd watched being filmed on soundstages for Max.

"Jeeze," Max said, "what a hole this is. Couldn't they paint it or something?" He looked around the dingy corridor. "So where the hell is the basement? They've gotta have stairs someplace. Come on."

And unfortunately and as she'd feared, he slowed down as they walked past the tiny, dark elevator door. "Hey, look at that. It's something right out of *Alice in Wonderland.* I wonder how you get in," and with that he pulled at the small tarnished brass knob and the door opened. "Cool," he said. "Let's try it."

Margot shook her head. "No, no way. I am not getting into that thing. And don't you, either. The floor could be rotted."

Max looked at the dark wood and stepped back. "Think so? Hmm, you could be right. Well, let's find those stairs."

They walked on, further than she'd gone that other afternoon. A door was propped open at the end, and as Max gave a thumbs up, she saw that it was, indeed, a flight of stairs leading downward.

There was a light switch and the overhead lights illuminated a surprisingly clean stairwell and the plain wooden stairs in a bright and efficient-looking manner. They stepped down into a huge, modern space. The room was so immaculate it could have been a surgical suite. The familiar set of *The Late Night Chef* was set up against the far wall. Overhead were banks of lights and several television cameras were on the floor, neatly covered by protective tarps. A bank of consoles filled one wall for the producer and engineers and everything looked as though it could begin production at a moment's notice, which of course, was the advantage of a permanent set.

"I'm gonna hafta have that chat with old Ferrigan," Max

said. "I wonder if he'd let us use this place for a couple ideas I have in mind."

"What do you suppose is back there?"

Max looked over her shoulder past the bright, white set into what looked like a black void. "Must be the rest of the basement. That's what this is, after all, just an old basement." He took a few steps forward, peering between the white painted plywood walls separating the set from the darkness. "Rat city. I wouldn't go back there." He paused, his eyes widening. "Good God, what's that?"

Margot whirled around, her skin tingling. "That" was a disembodied pale, oval face wafting toward them through the blackness . "Max!" she shrieked.

The face kept coming, closer and closer. Then, "I'm sorry. Did I frighten you?" The voice echoed slightly through the vast space as it floated toward them. "Are you investigating down here, too?"

Margot clutched Max's arm as they stood like statues waiting for the dark-clad figure to emerge into the lights from the unlit portion of the basement.

"Shit! It's Mrs. Madrid, I mean Estrella," whispered Max. "Robert's mother. What the hell is she doing down here?"

Chapter XII

"OH, IT'S YOU MOVIE PEOPLE. I know you two." Louisa Estrella stood in the bright lights of the renovated basement and stared at them, first at Max, then at her.

Margot felt the intensity behind those black eyes. Beside her she felt Max relax and saw him smile his charming smile. "Mrs. Estrella, and how are you this evening? What are you investigating down here?"

There was a short pause and Louisa Estrella said coolly, "Investigating? Did I use that word? Perhaps I meant something else. I wanted to see the place where Robert, and now Rafael, spend so much time on the television show. It's quite impressive." Her arm in the flowing sleeve of her black satin blouse making a sweeping gesture around the space. "Don't you think?"

"Is there anything we could help you with?" Max asked.

The woman turned her imperious gaze on him. "I have learned that my son was murdered. Do you think you could help me with that? Do you know who murdered Robert?"

Max mumbled something that still managed to sound kindly and charming.

"Well, I must return to the wine party upstairs that your pretty friend and my other son are hosting. Life goes on." Her gaze passed from Margot to Max. "It always does."

They watched as she walked gracefully across the room, her black mid-calf skirt swirling about her shapely legs.

"Wow," Max whispered. "*Que formidable.*"

"Is that Spanish or French?"

"Both, I think. So what was that all about? What the heck was she doing back there in rat land? Can she see in the dark?"

Margot peered into the murky section of the basement. The only light came from small dark rectangles that must be street level windows, dirty windows at that. Did that mean the rest of this entire space was below ground? Where they were standing right now. She shuddered. "Let's go back up." She hurried toward the stairs, the sound of Louisa Estrella's delicate heels still audible in the quiet.

"Margot, wait!"

She turned. Max was picking something off the floor. He held it out to her, walking quickly toward the stairwell. The lights picked up the glitter of a fine gold chain dangling from his hand.

"Treasure," he said.

"I don't know about that. Loretta Rose told me all the Estrella brothers wear chains like that. From their grandfather in Mexico I think she said. You'd better see if Rafael or Carlos is missing theirs."

He nodded and slipping the chain into a pocket, took her arm and hustled her up stairs to the landing, carefully turning out the basement light as they headed for the kitchen entrance and the crowds at Loretta Rose's wine bar opening.

THE PARTY CELEBRATING THE OPENING had grown even larger during their absence. Carlos had canceled the last seating in the restaurant and the dining tables had disappeared. Now the two rooms were combined, filled with people talking loudly, trying to carry on conversations above the din of the party. Many of the women were in bright parrot-colored dresses of red, orange, electric blues and yellows. Margot surveyed her ruby silk and knew she'd never reach the cutting edge of trendy fashion. The men, including Max, were in Hollywood "casual," rumpled linen trousers paired with open-neck shirts under expensive designer jackets. She shook her head. Every man seemed to be wearing the same pair of loafers. Everyone held a wine glass, dutifully—even gleefully—sniffing, swirling and sipping. Loretta Rose glowed from behind the crowded bar, deftly filling and refilling glass after glass, a patter of continuous wine lore going back and forth across the gleaming wood.

The few seats available for the weary were a row of cut down wine barrels lined up against a wall. The barrels must have been made especially for the wine bar, she thought. The staves were of burnished copper matching a beaten copper top. They couldn't be real wine barrels. No winery could afford fancy barrels like that.

It was hard to hear herself think. The decibel level seemed to rise higher and higher. Margot was amazed at the size of the crowd. This was it, she thought. Loretta Rose's big break into the food profession. If noise level was any criteria, the wine bar was a massive hit. Across the sea of bobbing heads, she saw face after face she recognized. The one person she didn't see was Colin Peabody. He was undoubtedly here somewhere, probably hoping against hope that Loretta Rose's endeavor without him would be a total failure. Still, she thought, Colin was so short, she'd never see him unless she stood on a chair.

Trays of tapas were being passed. Margot helped herself. They'd promised to wait around till the end and take Loretta Rose for a congratulatory late night supper. Max was deep in conversation with one of his actors. Margot wandered over and took a surreptitious glance at the expensive watch on his famous wrist. 10:45. Almost winding down time.

She listened with half an ear to the conversation. It was business, something about reshooting a scene from the day before. Probably, she thought, looking around the throng, most of the people here were talking business. Carlos Estrella had emerged from the frenetic confines of his kitchen again looking exhilarated at the sight of the obviously successful wine bar opening. A few couples were heading for the door. Margot smothered a yawn.

Twenty minutes later, a dozen diehard party-goers lingered. Loretta Rose abandoned her place behind the wine bar. No more bottles were being opened. This usually accelerated the ending of an evening.

"Ready, babe?" Max said. "I'll just get Carlos and Loretta Rose and we can catch a quick bite at Pete's. It's just a block away. Let's walk."

Loretta Rose materialized beside them, her arm through Carlos Estrella's. "Let's go," she said. "I'm starving. Carlos wants burgers. Anyone up for that?"

"Yup, at Pete's," Max said. "I was thinking burgers too."

There was the sudden sound of breaking crystal. People

halfway out the door turned to see what unfortunate person was responsible for the noise. Margot turned too. A woman was standing by one of the wine barrels looking embarrassed at the remains of her wine glass scattered across the shining floor.

"I'm sorry," she said to no one in particular. "I thought I'd set it down straight." She lurched slightly and bumped the barrel which moved on the polished wood of the floor. Margot stared. The base wasn't flush to the floor. That was the whole problem. Then the barrel swayed and fell on its side, rolling a turn or two before stopping in the center of the floor. The remaining guests hurriedly stepped away from the unpredictable object. There was a loud creaking as the burnished copper lid separated from the wood, then a thump as the lid gave up and rolled off. Margot was left staring into the darkened interior of the barrel. Only it wasn't really dark. She took a step forward. What was that? What had they filled the interior with? Something for ballast? Well, it hadn't worked very well.

There was a silence as people crowded close. The barrel lay where it had come to rest in the midst of the glittering crystal shards from the woman's broken wine glass. The lid had rolled away. Everyone moved slowly toward the gaping barrel. Margot stopped. She was right, the interior wasn't empty. There was a vaguely familiar shape emerging from the open end. It was round and covered with wispy blonde hair. Margot gulped and reached for Max's hand.

"What the hell…" Loretta Rose said and then, "Oh my God, not again," she shrieked. She pointed a shaking finger at the floor. "Who did this?" she shouted. "Somebody murdered Colin Peabody."

THE ROOM ERUPTED from dead silence into a hum with gasps audible at intervals. People were turning away from the sight. Carlos immediately flicked on the room's work lights. Everyone looked pale and shocked under the onslaught of bright overhead lights. No more soft hues to glamorize their faces, not with this turn of events.

"I'll call 9-1-1," Max said. Margot's eyes followed him as he went toward the small desk at the main entrance, the roost of the maitre d'.

Margot caught Loretta Rose's eye. Loretta Rose just shook her head in a disbelieving way. She looked as though she might faint. "How did he get in there?" she whispered. "He was fat."

"He wasn't that fat," Margot said. "And he was pretty short. I guess someone stuffed him in there, that's all."

"Like a pimento in a martini olive."

"Loretta Rose!"

"Oh, face it, Margot. Half the people in this room tonight won't shed a tear over Colin Peabody being dead." Loretta Rose promptly burst into tears. Margot handed her a handkerchief.

Ten long, quiet minutes later the entrance door opened. Margot didn't know whether to groan or rejoice. It was that same detective, the TV star lookalike. He was followed by a team of plainclothes officers, a paramedic, and a man carrying a large case. The coroner? She shivered. What was the detective's name? It should be Columbo. The only prop he needed was the worn raincoat. No, Wilson. That was it.

The detective was immediately in deep conversation with other officials. Then the group walked over, surrounding the fallen wine barrel and its horrific contents.

At length, Margot saw the detective's sharp eyes survey, individually, the people standing about.

"I think you all will be more comfortable in the other room," he said.

This was definitely an order and they all began shuffling silently toward the archway leading into the main dining room. As they passed by, the detective looked again at each of them in turn. Pointing, he gestured to her. Margot suddenly felt the way she had in grade school when chosen for the team—part elation, part fear. She nodded and followed as he led the way into a corner of the restaurant.

"So, Ms. O'Banion," the lieutenant said. "What can you tell me about this latest disaster?"

"Nothing," she said, shaking her head. "I can't figure out how he got in there."

"You mean Mr. Peabody in the barrel?" he said.

"He *is* dead?"

"Of course, he's dead." He paused. "I don't mean to be abrupt, but he wasn't hiding out in there, if that's what you thought."

"I'm sorry." Margot took a breath. "It's rather a shock. I've known Colin Peabody for a long time. We all have."

The detective sighed. "That's the trouble, isn't it? Here you all are again. The second death in your circle in what…a month? Again, you all knew the man. You all worked with the man. Half the city was in and out of this restaurant tonight." He put his chin in his hand.

"You know the kind of murder I prefer?" he asked. "I like

a nice clean family-type homicide. One where the husband did it. Or the wife did it. Out of jealousy or pure hatred. Something straightforward. Something my people can *solve*. Instead, we've had the murder of a famous member from a local family numbering approximately six zillion people and now an equally famous gentleman whom everyone in the movie business knows."

"I can't imagine what I know that might help. You must realize how shocked we were…to find him like that."

He stared at her silently, reminding her suddenly of Kevin Spacey's character in *The Usual Suspects*. The eyes focusing on her were dead, unblinking, reflecting nothing at all. He'd probably developed the look from years of interviewing people like herself, people who couldn't or wouldn't tell him anything.

He pulled out a small, worn notebook. Flipping it open, he pulled a pen from his jacket pocket. "So, tell me who would want to kill Colin Peabody? Whom did he offend?"

"Oh, he offended practically everyone. He was powerful and opinionated and he had an abrasive personality. He was a perfectionist and difficult to work with."

"Sounds like my boss, but no one's murdered him yet. How about your boyfriend over there?"

"Max?" Margot raised a hand to her mouth. "You mean would Max murder Colin? No, of course not. Max and Colin go back more than a decade. Colin has always produced Max's films. They may not agree on everything, but they agree on what makes a good movie." She shook her head. "They argue a lot, but it's just business."

"Yeah, I'm a big Max Skull fan myself. Great films. Great films…" The detective nearly smiled. "You understand we've had a month to check up on all of you. You also understand that this is the sort of background work we do for all murder cases, right? Well, how about your glamourous friend over there?"

"Loretta Rose?" Margot's voice raised. "No, Loretta Rose doesn't murder people."

"She was letting Colin mentor her, right?"

"Kind of. She sort of used him—not in a negative way, but just as a stepping stone to the sort of work she wants to do, like the wine bar here. But she was already out from under his thumb. She had no reason to hurt him."

The detective nodded. "But both victims, Mr. Madrid and Mr. Peabody, were connected with the film most of you are working on now."

"That's right," Margot said. "I can't imagine why these things are happening, but, yes, both were involved in different ways with *Extreme Cuisine*."

"Have there been other problems associated with this movie?"

"Not really. There are always problems with a production, but, no, nothing out of the ordinary this time." She paused. "It's a story about a fancy restaurant, that's all. I'm sure this film is just like any other."

He fixed her with a steady gaze. "Most productions don't generally have two vacancies caused by murder, do they?"

"I'm sure they don't."

"You've described him as a difficult person to work with, but was Mr. Peabody a popular person outside of his job?"

"I don't think so. As I said, he didn't have the greatest personality. I really can't think of any close friend he had."

"Family?"

"He never mentioned any family."

"Wife? Significant other? Was he gay?"

She shook her head. "I really don't know. I've known him professionally for years. But he never talked about anyone besides himself. It was always business. He never gave any personal details. I never heard any rumors about him, either. I think I would have heard…"

"Okay," he said. "Well, I think that's it for now. We'll be getting statements from everyone. I think we can use what you've just said for yours."

She looked up. He couldn't be satisfied with her silly, ambiguous answers, could he? Or perhaps he was just tired, too, and wanted to go home.

He pushed back his chair abruptly, then leaned over the back toward her. "Funny, isn't it?" the detective asked.

"What?"

"How much we don't know about the people we know."

"I only worked for him…"

"Of course." He walked quickly away, back into the wine bar, back to the official crowd clustered about the broken wine barrel.

Chapter XIII

"WHAT DID HE WANT?" MAX ASKED.

"He wanted to know what I thought."

"And…"

"Well, Max, I can't really think right now and I don't *know* anything. He wanted to know if you did it."

"Really?" Max looked charmed by the idea. "Hey, I hated the little bastard, but murder, no."

"That's what I told him. Anyway, we're all suspects."

Max looked around the room. The rest of the party-goers were exiting slowly, white business cards from the police clutched in their hands. "We're all suspects, for sure. Poor old Colin. Shit." For the first time since the grisly discovery, Max looked truly horrified. "Holy hell, there goes *Extreme Cuisine*, my favorite flick of the moment. We've lost our producer. I bet the studio'll dump it." He shrugged. "I'll do another one." Grabbing her arm, he propelled her towards the door.

"Margot!" Loretta Rose wailed. "What am I going to do?"

"Come on," Carlos said. "We'll get something to eat.

Something at someone else's restaurant. I'm sick of this place. Rudolph!" he shouted toward the kitchen. A gray-haired man poked his head out. "Close up for me after everyone's gone. Okay?"

"Sure, boss," he said.

Margot took one last glance over her shoulder. Uh oh. She shouldn't have looked. Somehow they'd extricated Colin from his barrel and the body was lying spread over the polished floor, surrounded by uniforms and men in suits.

"I'm not hungry," she said.

Beside her, Loretta Rose was crying. Max was frowning intently at some inner thoughts and Carlos was looking around at all that had happened to his fabled restaurant during one festive evening.

THEY SAT OVER PLATES OF HAMBURGERS AT PETE'S, the burger joint of choice for those interested in their specialty, people who didn't mind paying fifteen dollars for a regular hamburger. Only Carlos and Max ate, and apparently with great appetite and enjoyment, Margot noticed.

She and Loretta Rose, sitting opposite, had taken a few bites—it seemed somehow disrespectful to the dead to admit how delicious the burgers tasted—and were toying with the thin-cut French fries that accompanied the sandwiches. Loretta Rose was taking tiny sips of her coffee. Nearly midnight and the place still full.

"Say, Carlos," Max said, "we ran into your mother tonight."

"At the opening?"

"No, in the basement where the TV production shoots."

"What was mother doing in the basement?"

Max shrugged, finishing off another huge bite of his burger. "I dunno. What did she say, babe? Something about seeing where her sons worked or something. Was that it?"

Margot nodded. Suddenly she thought of Max's find.

"Show him, Max. Show Carlos what you found down there."

Max retrieved the thin gold chain and placed it in front of Carlos. "From what Margot says, this probably belongs to someone in your family."

Loretta Rose reached over and picked up the chain. It hung from her long fingers in drapes shimmering under the bright lights. "Robert lost his. Did you know that, Carlos?"

Carlos shook his head. "I've still got mine. I'll ask Rafael if he's lost his," he said and reaching into his collar pulled out a portion of identical jewelry. "If it's Robert's, I'm sure mother would like to have it. Where did you find it?"

Margot sighed, remembering. "It was right in the middle of the studio. Funny, you'd have thought it would have been found before now if Robert had dropped it. The production part of that basement is totally clean."

"Now those barrels tonight, Carlos, the ones in the wine bar. Where did you get them?" Max asked.

Carlos rubbed a hand across his face. "Oh God, the barrels. Don't remind me. I guess I'll have to burn them or something. Yeah, well, I had Jimmy Gottfried make them up for us. He does a lot of our fancy work. It was his idea to do the removable copper lids so we could use them for whatever. Hell, they looked good. How did I know they'd be used for hiding a body."

"How long were they in the restaurant?"

"Came in last week. Do you remember what day, Loretta Rose?"

She shook her head.

"So who saw Colin last?" Carlos asked.

Margot thought back. "I ran into him last week. Loretta Rose?"

Again her friend shook her head.

Margot and Max exchanged a glance. "Time to head for home, I think," Max announced cheerily. He picked up the check and pushed back his chair.

"I'll take Loretta Rose home. Okay?" Carlos said.

Loretta Rose nodded and stood, her dark eyes red-rimmed, darkening circles underneath. "I'm sorry to be such a drag," she said. "Do you think it's someone who's after one of us? I knew both people. We all knew both people. What do they want from us?"

Max put his arm around her. "Don't worry. It's just some weird thing going on that we don't know about, that's all. Probably some crazed maniac…" He paused. "Look, Loretta Rose, the motive could be anything. Our business has a lot of agendas, people with hurt feelings that fester, that sort of thing. Both Robert and Colin were really successful people. They probably attracted a lot of wannabes and misfits, the jealous types who gravitate toward the wealthy and successful."

"I'm safe then," Loretta Rose said caustically. "I'm neither of those things and the way things are going, I won't be for a long time. Come on, Carlos. I'll pick up my car from the restaurant tomorrow. Do you plan to serve tomorrow or what?"

"I'll contact the police. See what they say. I'll let you know soon as I hear."

"Oh. And I want to take my hamburger home."

"Sure," he said and with a quick finger pointed at their waiter and the sandwich. Twenty seconds later, the container was in Loretta Rose's hand.

"I like them cold in the morning."

Carlos smiled. "So did Robert. But you knew that, didn't you?" Still fingering the fine gold chain, he slipped it in a pocket. "Thanks for this, Max. I'll ask Raphael and then give it to mom if it turns out to be Robert's. She really misses Bobby. It's been a tough month for her, for all of us."

Margot and Max stepped out into the cold night. It was unusually clear and she could pick out the brightest planets even through the city lights. They waved and turned to the parking area.

"I'll drop you off, too, hon," he said. "Tomorrow's gonna be disaster control."

"Will they shelve *Extreme Cuisine?*"

"Dunno. Maybe they'll just put it on hold. If we're lucky, they'll find someone to take Colin's place. God, I hated the old bastard, but he was good. He was a good producer."

"So whodunit, Max?"

He shook his head, unlocked the car and ducked inside still shaking his head. "I dunno, babe. The deaths have to be related, don't you think? I hope they aren't related to the movie. What's going on here, Margot? Is someone trying to screw up production? Like I started to tell Loretta Rose, is there some crazed killer on the loose? Someone holed up in a corner of the basement of that crazy restaurant, someone deformed, insane, striking at random?"

Margot squeezed his hand. "You have the most vivid imagination."

She got out at the apartment and she saw Max wait till she was inside before driving away.

What a day, Margot thought. The apartment was quiet. Tiptoeing to her room, she noticed the message light blinking on her phone.

Settling down on the edge of the bed, she pushed it. It was Jerry, Jerry Lake, her famous agent ex-husband. Jerry would have heard the latest disaster practically immediately. He was on the cutting edge of gossip.

"Babe!" She grimaced at the word. "Just heard about old Colin. Goddamn, what a way to go. And you were there, right? Heard he was in a frickin barrel? Could that be true? What's going on with your boyfriend's production anyway? So I'm probably almost out of tape here, but give me a call. Okay? I suppose the police are looking into that business Colin was in back in the seventies. They must be looking. Police never forget our mistakes, do they? Now keep in touch, babe, and tell old Alisandro to get his shit together. He's too old to be hysterical and he's blabbing all over town that the Mayan gods have cursed the production. God, I'm glad I'm not *his* agent. There's going to be a memorial service for Colin. Are you coming?"

She shut off the machine, undressed and lay in her bed in the dark, the cat at her feet, thinking, thinking, thinking.

"ANYTHING ELSE YOU NEED, MS. LAKE?" Ken's voice came over the intercom. "I can set it up again if you want."

She jumped slightly, startled, and waved at the man visible behind the glass of the projection booth. "No," she called out. "It's fine. I'm fine. I'm leaving now."

Margot picked up her dailies notebook and clutching it to her side, left the room. Max had already left the projection room and she'd just been sitting there musing. Was the work they were doing today all for nothing? She wouldn't know for certain until Max filled her in on whatever decision the executives made about the film. Until then, it was work as usual, but she couldn't stop thinking about everything else.

The morning paper had been full of the tragedy. Since this was a bona fide murder investigation, it was an even bigger story than that of Robert's death, the initially proclaimed "accidental death." Margot had scanned the columns and learned absolutely nothing new. There was no mention of his family, no mention of a link between the two men, the only link being Max's picture in production.

She hurried down the hall and stepped into the cutting room. Her assistants, Dusty and Barry, stared back at her without expression. Sitting at the old Moviola machine was the familiar, slightly rumpled figure of Detective Wilson.

"Hi." Wilson stood up. "Just learning some of the finer points of your profession from your nice assistants. Could I have a few words with you, Ms. O'Banion?"

Margot's mouth went dry. "Sure," she said.

Barry glanced at Dusty. "Hey, we'll go get some coffee. We'll be right back," he said.

They left the room and the detective smiled. "Nice kids," he said.

"Yes. They're good workers, too." She held out her notebook as though it would explain everything.

He nodded. "I won't keep you long. There's just this one matter I'd like to ask you about. It turns out that your Colin Peabody had a brush with the law back in '71. Do you know anything about it?"

"He did? The law? Colin? Actually, I don't know any details, but a friend—he's my ex-husband…well, that part isn't important, is it? Anyway, he hinted that Colin had done *something* or *something* had happened back then. No details. Colin always seemed so… well, above board, I'd say." And as she said that she thought back to all the un-above board shenanigans she'd witnessed that Colin had done or *tried* to do through the years. It was almost as though the man had been a criminal wannabe, not quite having the felonious talents to pull off his schemes.

"Above board?" the detective repeated.

"Well, he *acted* that way. I've been in the business a long time and no real gossip about Colin has ever reached my ears." She looked at the detective. "But you know what those rumors are about, don't you?"

The detective cocked his head. "It may be of no relevance. It's a twist, that's all. We like to examine closely anything that seems out of the norm." He smiled. "It seems that Mr. Peabody started out in Hollywood producing pornographic movies under another name. Now it's not illegal to make these movies and it isn't illegal to show them or attend them. It's just that most people don't want to be associated with those enterprises. Bad for the reputation once you move up. Know what I mean?"

Margot shook her head. "I never heard the slightest rumor."

"Background checks are a mainstay of my profession. I'm afraid we sometimes forget just how carefully people try to hide portions of their lives. Not," he turned a palm up, "that I don't understand completely. Hell, I've always figured that computers are why I've kept out of politics. I certainly wouldn't want anyone digging into some of the darker corners of my past."

Margot studied the man's concerned face. He looked uncomfortable.

"You mean the paternity of my son? Everyone knows about that. Max and I have been together for years now. No, we're not married. Yes, Luis knows exactly who his father is. Is that what you're talking about? How very Victorian."

"Actually I wasn't concerned with your private life," Wilson said. "I was thinking more about that scrape you and Ms. Cinefucco were in a few years back."

"You mean the murders in the vineyard. Oh, that."

"Exactly. Didn't you think it appropriate to mention them?"

Margot held his gaze. "You're not thinking that Loretta Rose Cinefucco and I are some sort of murder magnets, are you? That murderer was tried and convicted. There was no question that it wasn't the right person."

"I've noticed that Ms. Cinefucco is ambitious and has a bit of a temper, that's all."

She stood. "Well, I have a temper, too, for that matter. Now I've answered enough questions. I've signed my statement. I have nothing to add."

"Thank you for your time. If you think of anything else or have anything to add…"

"I won't. I'm sorry."

"One last thing, that freezer murder scene that Mr. Skull

deleted from the film? Do you suppose I could see it?"

Margot stared at him, then reached into her desk drawer and pulled out the film canister. She inserted the footage of the deleted scene into the Moviola. Gesturing for him to sit down at the machine, she waited until he was peering into the screen, then pressed "on."

Twenty seconds later, the detective sat back. He looked at her intently. "Interesting concurrences," he said. "Interesting script, interesting film. Still the scene isn't conclusive of anything by itself, is it? At least, not yet. Why did you keep it?"

"As a curiosity."

"I'll bet you could get a lot for it, selling it to a TV news station or on Ebay," Wilson said. "Ever thought of that?"

Margot laughed. "I make a good salary. Still, as you point out, it could be good insurance against a rainy day."

"Thank you, Ms. O'Banion. Very interesting notion. Very interesting place you work in."

She nodded and waited until he left before sitting back down.

Dusty stuck her head in the door. "Okay, if we come in. Is the interrogation over?"

"For now. Yes, let's get back to work. I'm not in handcuffs yet."

Dusty nodded and moved over to the cutting bench. Margot sat down and spent another hour bent over the Moviola. About noon, Jonathan Keller opened the door. Without knocking, she noted.

"Max sent me over," he said, making himself comfortable leaning against her desk, feet in worn cowboy boots casually crossed at the ankles. "He was in meetings all morning. He wants you to know that for the moment we're still greenlighted. We're supposed to keep on doing what we're doing."

"We are."

Jonathan nodded. "Well, keep up the good work," he said. "I'll go back playing slave to your boyfriend."

Margot watched him leave then picked up the latest edition of the *Modern Film Encyclopedia.*

She looked up Colin first. Poor old unpopular Colin. What had he been up to in his youth? The mind boggled at the idea of a youthful, bad boy Colin. His vita, as shown, of course, was extraordinary. Good films to great films and the great films were with Max. No mention of family, nothing but film after film, all done for Arcturus Studios. He'd been fifty-five. She thought about Colin. Well, he wouldn't have to worry about being fired for being "too old" now. The idea made her sad. There was no title listed that even hinted of being the least bit pornographic, not that she'd expected there would be. As the detective said, it's not as though it was illegal to make these films. Heavens, they were sold all over the Internet, no questions asked. *Her* email was always full of invitations to view or buy....

Thumbing to the F's, she read on. Elliot Ferrigan's career had followed much the same pattern as Keller's. He'd never made it above assistant for either picture or sound editing. Still he'd certainly "made it" with *The Late Night Chef.* It really just took one big hit to make a career and a fortune and the TV show looked as though it could continue for many years to come. She stopped reading and pushed the bulky volume aside, considering the data.

Next, just for the fun of it, she looked up Jonathan Keller. Nasty old Jonathan. To her surprise, there was quite a lengthy paragraph devoted to his career. But this was definitely quantity, not quality, and at least half of it was as first AD on Max's string of first-rate films.

Her finger traced the list of his earlier film work. He'd worked his way up to first assistant director on one dog of a picture five years ago. Somehow he'd gotten stuck in that position, however, and had remained as an assistant director in a number of less than memorable films until Max had taken him on. Why the two men worked well together was beyond her comprehension. But, they did.

In her opinion, all this waiting for his big chance to direct was certainly taking its toll on his personality, or there was always the possibility that he was just an unpleasant person, period. Of course, he was a longtime friend of Elliot Ferrigan. That was a connection. And where did Jonathan fit in there? The rumor was that Elliot had some sort of "checkered past," which in this town with these ambitious, competitive people, could mean practically anything at all.

She considered the possibilities. Could Ferrigan and Keller possibly have been on that porno film team with Colin all those years ago? Could they have been blackmailing him all along, finally forcing him to hire them for this film or that?

Damn, maybe she was getting fanciful. Fanciful was born of desperation in this instance. Just because people knew each other and worked with each other meant nothing. Networking was the name of the game in Hollywood, the preferred way of doing business. What was the point of hiring some young upstart when you already knew the qualities of these other people you'd worked with before—even if you didn't like them much.

Chapter XIV

"HEY MARGOT!" Loretta Rose said.

Margot shifted the phone to her other ear. She was in the editing room on a gloomy morning a week after Colin's murder. The studio was a grim workspace these days. People were glum and subdued, even people who hadn't liked Colin. Death was shocking. Murder was super-shocking.

"What's up?" Margot asked. "I'm working, trying to keep busy. Where are you?"

"At the restaurant. Carlos is reopening tonight. That means I'm reopening tonight, too. Your Max is doing a last scene in the dining room. Well, he isn't here, but a bunch of production people are in the kitchen and the barrels are gone. Come over for lunch. Carlos said he'd fix us something special."

Margot looked at the clock on her desk. Something special to eat straight from star chef Carlos Estrella?

"I've got to watch some rushes with Max and then I'll come over. I'll be there in an hour."

She walked down the hall to the small screening room. Max

was already seated. He reached out a hand for her and pulled her down in the seat next to him.

"What's this about?" Margot asked.

"This you've gotta see, babe. I don't know whether to laugh or cry over it. Loretta Rose hasn't said anything to you about it, has she?"

"Anything about what?"

Max started to grin. "She didn't tell you? Cool. Well, wait till you see this scene. Okay, are you ready, Ken?" he yelled up at the projectionist. "Let's get going."

The lights dimmed and they sat side by side in the darkness, waiting.

"Just a second, folks," Ken's voice crackled from the intercom. "Having a little trouble getting it going."

"So here's the story. I'm all ready to shoot this tiny little piece, just a teeny little scene between the star chefs, Loretta Rose and Carlos Estrella..."

"I didn't know you were using Carlos in the film."

"Well, obviously I am," Max said. "I mean, the guy gave us access to his incredible restaurant kitchen, didn't he? It seemed the least I could do was put him in a couple shots. Plus he's got a great voice. So anyway, the shoot went fine yesterday until Carlos hit this one line. It's the most straightforward line on earth. It means nothing. It's a throwaway. But what happens? It made some strange connection in Carlos's little brain and the weirdest stuff started coming out of his mouth. It took an hour before we got it right. Loretta Rose must have cued him two dozen times. We were going crazy trying to finish the scene. Wait till you see what happens..."

Margot shook her head. "I had no idea you were doing this."

"Yeah, sorry, babe, but I figured Loretta Rose would mention it and it's no big deal, really. I got kind of sidetracked what with Colin's untidy demise. I just wanna see if you can do anything with this piece. Oh," he added, "and the ending's the best part."

"Well, okay. We've all been kind of sidetracked."

"For sure we have." Max sighed. "And there's the usual downside. Here I am trying to keep on schedule with a bunch of union people and Carlos has to go bonkers on me." Max shook his head. "The crew loved it, of course. The guy was outrageous. It really was funny. He was jumping all over the set. Marc was going crazy trying to keep him in focus."

"What was he saying?"

"You'll see. It's all on film. Hey, Ken, what's going on up there?"

"Just a hitch. Give me a minute."

"Damn."

The dark screen suddenly came to life. There was plenty to work with in the first scene and Max was clearly delighted. Then on the screen appeared a sharp closeup of Loretta Rose, with her fine-boned, expressive face looking more beautiful than ever under the lights. Loretta Rose turned to the camera, her eyes haunted.

"I did the Chilean sea bass last night," she said. "You do it today."

Max slumped in his seat. "Here we go."

The screen filled. It was a closeup of Carlos with his storybook good looks, masculine and sensitive, his dark eyes filled with deep expression. He stared past Loretta Rose into the camera

"A great love," he said, his voice deep and resonant, "is complete in every moment it exists."

The camera moved to Loretta Rose, hovering, waiting for her line.

"It *what?*" Loretta Rose said, her lovely dark curving eyebrows raised in astonishment.

The camera retreated as Carlos burst into a huge smile and fell out of camera range.

"What the hell, Carlos?" Max's voice came loud and clear from off stage.

"Cut!"

The second, third and fourth takes were nearly exact repeats.

"I did the Chilean sea bass last night," Loretta Rose said. "You do it today."

"A great love is *still* complete in every moment it exists," said Carlos Estrella, staring intently into Loretta Rose's bemused face.

Cut!

Margot decided her friend's dark eyes were beginning to look unfocused. Loretta Rose looked nearly hypnotized.

In the fifth take it was Loretta Rose who burst into laughter and fell out of camera range.

"Cut!"

"I gave them a pep talk here," Max whispered. "Watch how much good it did."

"I did the Chilean sea bass last night," Loretta Rose said. "You do it today."

Carlos nodded vigorously, his blue-black hair gleaming under the lights. "Right. Right," he said, pulling her to him, his hands on her waist. "Do you know why?" he whispered into her ear. "Because a great love is complete in every moment it exists."

Loretta Rose shrieked with laughter and they both fell off screen. The camera gave a wild jolt.

"Cut!"

"Hey, you guys," someone shouted. "Watch your marks. You're getting too close to each other. You're wrecking the sound."

"I did the Chilean sea bass last night. You do it today."

Carlos shook his handsome head. "By the time we get the damned sea bass done, it'll be tomorrow."

"Cut!"

"I did the Chilean sea bass last night. You do it today."

Carlos's face was serious. He nodded. "I think it's endangered, anyway," he said.

"Cut!"

"I did the Chilean sea bass last night. You do it today."

Carlos smiled. "Hey cool. Who cares? A great love is complete in every moment it exists."

The back of Carlos's head blocked Loretta Rose's face completely. He took her in his arms, bumping the camera.

"Cut!"

Margot turned to Max. His look was unreadable. "Is Carlos on anything?" she whispered.

"You mean drugs? God, no. I almost wish he were."

"Well what on earth is Carlos supposed to be saying here?"

"He gets the line, finally," he replied. "You'll see."

Another barrage of takes followed. In some Margot could hear Max's voice shouting beyond camera range. Loretta Rose alternated between giving her line and responding directly to Carlos's oddball readings.

Once again the screen was a closeup of Loretta Rose. Once again she frowned. And once again she said, "I did the Chilean sea bass last night. You do it today."

Carlos shrugged. "Okay," he replied.

"Cut! That's it!"

There was a smattering of applause audible from the crew off camera.

"There," Max said with a sigh. "*That's* the line *I* wrote. I wrote 'Okay.' Hell's bells." He shook his head. "That's what I worked so hard to get on film, 'Okay'? Shit."

"But where did that other line come from, the one about great love being complete in every moment it exists?"

Max shrugged. "Jeeze, you got me on that one. But watch this, babe. This is the really good part."

Margot watched. The camera tracked the actors. She sat forward.

"Are they doing what I think they're doing?"

Max laughed, relaxing. "Yup. They went into this big clinch behind the refrigerator. It was wild. Hey, Ken, freeze it!"

"Wow! Is that for real?"

"Well, it sure as hell wasn't in the script, kiddo. Man, there was some heavy chemistry going on there."

"Double wow. Loretta Rose hasn't said a word about any of this. Goodness. Well, Carlos did say an interesting line."

Max groaned. "Interesting? Jeeze. We should use his."

They sat in silence for a time. "What would happen," she said, "if we stuck the whole series of takes in, as is? You know, showing the repetitive side of being a chef, even a star chef, kind of a surreal spin on life in the kitchen."

Max thought for a moment and then grinned at her. "It could be good," he said. "Oh, man, it could be great. Hey," he said glancing at his watch, "I've gotta run."

"Speaking of star chefs, I'm off to Café Estrellado for lunch."

"They don't do lunch."

"Apparently they do for our beautiful friend. Loretta Rose called me to come over to share something Carlos is cooking up for us. Things are definitely moving along, aren't they?"

"Maybe she wants to confide about her new boyfriend! Cool.

Hey, could you take old Jonathan over with you? He's doing some make up work for me in the kitchen there and is whining that his car's kaput or something."

"If I *must*, I will. He's a pain."

"Yeah, he is that, but it's kind of a 'must.' You've been a great help." He paused, taking her arm, squeezing it against his side. "So what did you think of Carlos's line, the great love line?"

She smiled. "I liked it a lot."

Max bent over and kissed her lightly. "Me, too."

They left the room, Max going to the sound stage while she walked toward the editing room to pick up her purse. Speaking of the devil—Jonathan Keller was lounging against the far wall. Had he been waiting all this time?

"Hey, Margot," he said. "Are you going off the grounds for lunch? I'm off to that Estrellado restaurant for the last day's shoot. I'm gonna be handling the scene. Max said maybe you could give me a lift. Truck's on the blink again."

"Okay, Jonathan. Actually," she said, "I was on my way there, too. My car's out front."

They walked down the corridor toward the lobby, Jonathan was curiously quiet. Usually he raised her hackles immediately with his acerbic observations on everything, mostly Max. But today he just trudged along, hands deep in his worn jeans pockets.

"Anything wrong, Jonathan?" she asked.

"Oh, the usual. I feel pretty bad about old Colin. Granted he wasn't someone you wanted to hang with much. I guess it's the surprise, that's all."

"Maybe the fact he was murdered by someone we probably know?" She couldn't help it. The words just came out.

Jonathan fixed her with his pale gray stare. "Yeah, that's it. I bet it's someone we know. That little thought gives me the creeps, too."

They stepped out into the gloomy day. Margot clicked open the car door and Jonathan got inside, folding up his Icadbod-like legs in the passenger side.

"You worked for Colin for a long time, didn't you, Jonathan?"

"Yeah, same as you and Max, I guess. Weird guy, but a good producer. Think they're gonna shitcan the film now?"

"We're still going ahead with it. Max says..."

"Oh, I know what Max says. Something about the execs are weighing all possibilities, some bullshit like that. But I thought he might have told you something different."

"He didn't tell me something different, Jonathan. I guess that's all he knows at this point."

"I just don't wanna be the last to know that we've all been frickin downsized because our beloved producer bit the dust." Jonathan looked out the window. "Hell, most of the execs couldn't stand the man, either."

"They didn't complain about the money his films brought in."

"True, but anyone of them might have done him in." He paused. "Actually, how *did* someone do it?"

"Max said he heard it was the same method as with Robert Madrid—drugged and suffocated."

"And then stuffed in a barrel. That's a weird thing to do."

"Is it any stranger than putting a body in a meat locker?" she asked.

"Maybe it's some sort of message," he said.

"Like what?"

"Oh, I dunno, really. Don't eat meat…"

"And don't drink wine?"

They both laughed.

Margot thought it might be the first time she'd shared a laugh with him. "Someone told me you went way back with Colin, back before he became rich and famous," she said.

Jonathan gave her a look. "Jeeze, not that old rumor again. No, I was not a party to the porn boys' productions, if that's what you're asking. I was already on a legitimate film. I dunno who they got to take my place. Thank God, I was busy during that artistic period of Colin's career."

"Who is 'they'?"

He stared at her. "What are you after, Margot? I'm not going to rat on the group. They went through enough, you know? Besides, it was decades ago. Water under the bridge. Time heals all…"

"Okay, Jonathan. Just asking. So here we are. I'll let you out and find a parking spot."

"Thanks," he said. "Be careful out there, Margot."

Margot turned, surprised. Jonathan Keller was leaning into the car. He smiled at her puzzled stare. "Read the script."

"I've read it," she said.

"Read it again," he ordered. "Don't forget what happens to Max's star chef," he said in a low voice. "He disappears down the rabbit hole."

Margot watched the lanky figure disappear into the restaurant. What did he mean, "rabbit hole"? She knew the script for *Extreme Cuisine* backward and forward. The ending had the star chef tearing off his apron and leaving the restaurant. He wasn't angry or anything, he just had something else to pursue in life. Hmm. Was Jonathan drawing some analogy here for all of them, that they all might be starting over on another project if the studio shut down production? Well, everyone was aware what the ramifications of their *producer* being *murdered* during production were. Heavens, one or more people she knew would probably be carted off to jail before too long. Life was full of uncertainties. They weren't children here. Rabbit hole, indeed.

The downtown street was busy at lunch hour. Today the studio vans were already loading up unnecessary equipment since, according to Jonathan, today's shoot was just a catch-up scene Max had decided to do at the last moment. She finally found a space a block away and walked toward Cafe Estrellado. Loretta Rose must have been watching for her. She had her head poking out the main door, waving wildly for her to hurry.

What now? Margot thought. "What's happening?" she asked as Loretta Rose pulled her into the restaurant foyer.

"Shh," she whispered. "They're setting up a scene. Come with me."

They stepped across the room where Jonathan Keller was already in a huddle with the cameraman and into the wine bar, Loretta Rose carefully closing the door shutting them off from the main dining room. Margot looked around. The barrels were gone, all of them. Otherwise the room looked much the same. She didn't know what she'd been expecting, perhaps a yellow chalk outline on the floor? She shuddered.

"What's the matter with you," Loretta Rose asked. "Too cold in here? Well, whatever. Cool is good for the wine. Anyway, I wanted you here. Louisa Estrella is prowling around again. Honestly, Margot, she's everywhere these days."

"I know. We told Carlos how Max and I ran into her the

night of your opening. She told us she was determined to find out what happened to Robert. It was strange. She was downstairs in the basement, way back in the unused part, doing something."

"What?"

"Well, I don't know, do I? I couldn't very well ask. We pretended it was perfectly normal social behavior to find a guest emerging from a deserted, pitch dark basement area while the party's going on a floor above us."

"No kidding? Well, it really wasn't much of a party if you count the ending. Still, old Colin's bizarre demise gave us a lot of publicity. I'm just hoping, after all the ghouls come in and are satisfied with looking around our crime scene, that people might want to come back again, just for the wine." Saying that, she handed Margot a glass of lightly chilled Sauvignon Blanc.

"Who do you think did it?" Margot asked.

"Offed old Colin? Well, there must be a hundred prime candidates. But I'd place my bet on someone with a really whacked out sense of humor. That barrel bit had got to be seen to be believed. What's your best guess on whodunit?"

"Well, Jonathan Keller and I were talking about that on the way over here. Think about this—Robert was a chef and he got put in a restaurant meat locker and Colin fancied himself a wine buff and ended up in a barrel. It might be a real reach, but we can make a connection there. Say, where are those fancy barrels?"

Loretta Rose shivered. "Oh, Carlos had them taken out and burned. All but the one Colin was in. The police have it."

"Then why did he burn the others?"

"Guilt by association, I guess. Barrel-guilt. It's almost funny. He's panicky it will happen again. You know, a lookalike crime. He didn't want art to imitate life again, especially not with his barrels and not in his restaurant. I was thinking last night...I wonder what Colin would have made of his final resting place?"

They were silent a moment, sipping wine.

"No one is exactly mourning over what happened, are they?" Margot said slowly. "Frankly, Jonathan Keller is my first choice for murderer. He's so grim. Well, actually, he wasn't as grim as usual this morning, but he's usually incredibly grim. I don't know if he'd qualify for your sense of humor theory since he's so dour. Then, if they should connect Robert's death with Colin's, well then I just don't know who I'd accuse. I'm not sure Jonathan even knew Robert. Heck, I guess he isn't a very good suspect, after all."

"Okay, he's off the list for now."

A young woman walked in carrying a tray. She smiled and put the two plates and appropriate cutlery on the bar.

"Thanks, Janet. Wow, look what Carlos's made for us."

Margot looked. Lunch was beautiful.

"It's *Crab Cakes with Cabbage Slaw and Blood Orange Mayonnaise,*" Loretta Rose said, a mouthful already halfway to her lips. "Let's eat and then we'll go down to the basement."

"Whatever for? Oh, this is delicious."

"Because I'm gonna be a genuine, live guest on *The Late Night Chef* show. Can you believe that?

"That's terrific, Loretta Rose. I know you'll be a smash. So what'll we do in the basement? I've already seen it and it's just your basic TV studio. What do you want to check out?"

"I wanna see how I'll look behind that cool workspace."

Margot gave her friend a sharp look. "Has Carlos said anything about all this stuff going on?"

"Carlos? Not really." Loretta Rose chewed thoughtfully. "We've just been working to get things going here again. Elliot's been great, so far. He set me up for this job. Got us through the unexpected barrel burning phase and seems to me to have logical expectations of what we'll get out of the wine bar once the publicity wears off and people who are truly interested in wine come in."

"And he backs both the restaurant and the wine bar?"

"Sure. It's easy. Same kind of clientele. Same premises. Heck, even his show is taped right here. "

"How did he react to Colin's murder?"

"I dunno. I've just spoken with him on the phone. He sounded the way we all feel…shook up and bewildered. There wasn't any love lost between those two, but they were cordial enough together in public. Their's wasn't a hate thing."

"We're all nice enough in public. It's called being civilized. Well, let's go exploring, if you want. I've got a ton of work waiting."

They paused at the sound of yelling bouncing off the walls of the elegant dining room behind them.

"Uh oh," Loretta Rose said. "It's Carlos. Sounds like Max forgot to tell him about this catch-up scene they're doing."

"My brother was *murdered* because of something about this frickin film," they heard Carlos Estrella shout.

There was a chorus of answering low murmurs.

"Yeah, right. That's easy for you to say. And then this pig of a producer was dumped in my wine bar on *opening night,* for God's sake. What's with it with you guys, anyway? Does one of you have some sort of vendetta against my family? Can't you leave me alone in peace in my own restaurant? Wait, I'm going to call your boss. Does Skull even know you're here?"

"Come on, Margot," Loretta Rose whispered

She watched as Loretta Rose cautiously opened the door

leading to the main kitchen. The room was blessedly deserted. Carlos was in the dining room taking on Jonathan Keller and the crew. Margot couldn't help but smile. Jonathan's big chance to direct a scene and he was being confronted by a *very* angry chef, a *star* chef, no less. There was a certain ironic justice about all this. Poor old Jonathan, who never seemed to catch a break.

They ducked through the old door and stood in the quiet of the dusty corridor. "Do you fancy the handsome chef?" Margot asked.

Loretta Rose smiled her foxy smile. "Which one?"

Margot stared at her friend. "You mean Carlos *and* Raphael?"

"Yup. I've gotten phone calls from each of them, separately, every night this week. I really don't know how to handle this."

"Maybe Carlos got the wrong idea when you kissed him on the set."

"How did you know about that? Anyway, Margot, what's wrong with *kissing?* Heck, if you'd been interacting with that hot guy in that crazy scene, you'd have kissed him, too. Chemistry is chemistry and you can quote me on that one. And I hope I get to kiss him again. But this brother rivalry...I just don't know about that."

"Uh oh."

"Yes. Just what I need, a *romantic* feud in a family that's already as volatile as my own. And," she said, lowering her voice, "I'm afraid neither of the guys is looking for a plain old friendship, either. Carlos asked if I'd like to see a space he's thinking about in Palm Springs this weekend. And Raphael said he's considering opening a restaurant on Catalina and have I ever been to the island. Jeeze. With my track record for boyfriends and just *men* in general, I sort of wish I fancied ladies. I'm serious. I feel like a witch or something. Even Colin, and heaven knows I didn't fancy *him*...but look where he turned up. I sure don't want anything to start tearing those brothers apart, especially me."

Margot couldn't think of anything logical or comforting to say.

They walked quickly down the cheerless hallway to the stairwell. Flicking on the light, Loretta Rose led the way down the stairs to the TV production set. The room was lit by the overhead lights. The space as pristine and professional looking as it had been the night of the opening. Loretta Rose went and stood behind the counter.

"So you're really going to appear on the show with Rafael *and* Carlos?" Margot asked.

"Yes, the plan is to have Carlos introduced and then he'll introduce me as the queen of the wine bar at his esteemed restaurant. Good PR all around. Still, I don't know if I should bring a little gun to keep those guys apart and I don't know what to wear. Come on, let's get out of this place. You can take an hour off. I'm going to call up Sophie and see if she can meet us on Rodeo Drive. She's got great taste in clothes. Let's go shopping."

Chapter XV

MARGOT AVOIDED SHOPPING ON RODEO DRIVE, but Loretta Rose and Sophie seemed to thrive on the high-powered atmosphere. While she hung back in the nether regions of each store fingering this or that luxury item, the other two women—strong contrasts with the curly black hair of Loretta Rose and the tawny mane of Sophie bent over each item—asked, interrogated, and manipulated the prickly salespeople with ease.

An hour later, after the purchase of a killer peach-colored silk shirt—after all, as Loretta Rose pointed out, she was only going to be seen from the waist up, and she'd be wearing an apron to protect it—they headed for a sidewalk café where the rich and powerful liked to sit and be admired by the people in the cars passing slowly by on the wide avenue.

Sitting in the mild sunshine, over iced tea, salad and rich, buttery cookies, Margot listened as Loretta Rose explained her snowballing romantic situation to Sophie. Sophie listened with deep concentration.

She sat forward. "You're kidding," she finally said.

"It's all true. The Estrella brothers hate each other as much as my own do, but both of these guys are coming on to me, separately, of course. What is it with these men?"

"No idea," Margot said

"So you're working in the restaurant of one foxy brother..."

"Well, a spin-off of the restaurant..."

"It's in the same building, isn't it, practically the same room?" Loretta Rose asked. "And then you're gonna be on this hot TV show starring the *other* brother. But wait, then the *other, other* brother will be looking over your silken shoulder, watching every move on you his very own brother might make, right?"

Loretta Rose nodded.

"Well," drawled Sophie, sitting back in her seat, "I'd make 'em go through a weapons search before you get behind the counter with them."

Margot smiled, but her mind was racing. The star chef and the TV star, the two handsome brothers, face-to-face, in combat over the ever-glamourous Loretta Rose. What a scene that would make!

"But I really, really like him. I like him a lot," Loretta Rose said.

"What? What did you say? Well, who is it?" Sophie asked.

"Carlos," she said. "I think I love him."

There was a pause. "But Loretta Rose, I thought you were the original I'll never fall in love with anyone ever gal. Isn't that right?" Sophie asked

"I know. I know I act like that. And I know Raphael will kill us both if he finds out...what...ah... happened. He's taken rather a liking to me, too. And then it's his TV show that's gonna give me my big break."

"Surely hooking up with a star chef, especially one that looks like Carlos Estrella, can't hurt, either."

"Well, I'm not falling in love with him for *that*."

Margot thought tough-acting Loretta Rose looked suddenly close to tears.

"Really, I'm not," she said. "It just happened. It all happened during that scene Max had us do. Carlos kept saying this crazy line that wasn't in the screenplay. It was kind of magical…"

"What was it?"

"I saw the takes," Margot said.

"Tell her." Loretta Rose dipped her mouth to the tea glass, classic roses blooming on her cheeks. "Tell her what Carlos kept saying, Margot."

"He said to Loretta Rose, over and over again, 'A great love is complete in every moment it exists.'"

"Wow. Then what happened?"

"He kissed me. I mean he *really* kissed me."

"He really kissed you. On camera?"

"Oh, no. We were off camera."

"No, you weren't," said Margot. "The camera was still rolling. And Max plans to use all the takes, the whole thing."

"The whole thing. Really?"

"Including the kiss."

"Wow!" Loretta Rose looked pleased and picked up a cookie.

Sophie chuckled. "So did you guys hear about Colin Peabody?"

Loretta Rose's cheeks were still flushed. "That he's dead?" she said. "That he died at my wine bar opening, right in the middle of the room?"

"Not that. Although I did hear rumors of his disgraceful behavior that evening. No, I heard from Jack Spivey on the set that Colin had no relatives, nobody. Nobody's come forward to claim the body."

"I thought he must have been lonely," Margot said. "Maybe that's why he threw himself into his work and was into so many different things all the time."

"If he'd only been a *nicer* person," Loretta Rose said.

"Once he even asked me to steal a famous bottle of port from Cinefucco Cellars when we were up visiting you."

"Really, Margot? He asked you to *take* a bottle of our illustrious porto? You mean rip one off? Well, did you?"

"I said 'steal,' and of course I didn't."

"Of course you didn't. I used the last bottle in existence to kabosh that jerk of a guy, remember?"

They sat back in their chairs remembering and enjoying the sun. Suddenly Sophie sat up. "Look," Sophie suddenly whispered. "Look who's here!"

Margot turned slightly, following Sophie's surprised gaze. There, sitting comfortably at a table beneath one of the restaurant's expansive, dark green umbrellas, was Detective Wilson and the leader of the Estrella clan, Louisa. The two were sitting companionably close, sipping glasses of white wine.

"He didn't bring *me* here for interrogation," Loretta Rose said.

Sophie's nails clicked on the table. "Doesn't look like an interrogation to me."

"Or me," whispered Margot. "Do you think they've seen us?"

"Margot, this is a public place. We won't be under suspicion

for anything but having tea when we're supposed to be at work."
Loretta Rose adjusted her dark glasses. "Do you think we should
go over and say 'hi'?"

"Gawd," Sophie said, "a chummy murder investigation.
What's next in this crazy town. What do you think?"

Margot shrugged. "Louisa Estrella is pretty famous in the
city. Maybe they've known each other a long time or something."

"Or something," Sophie. "Get a load of that."

"That was not your basic air kiss or kiss on the cheek kiss,"
Loretta Rose said. "What do you guys think?"

Before anyone had a chance to answer they saw Mrs. Estrella's
dark gaze zero in on them. They watched as she patted Detective
Wilson on the cheek, adjusted her sunglasses and began walking
over to their table.

Margot felt an inclination to stand up, as though royalty
was paying a call. She compromised and made an awkward
little bobbing motion from her chair. Louisa nodded briskly and
immediately made herself at home, sitting down in a fourth chair,
drawing it up close to their table.

"Good afternoon," she said, her gaze rested on Sophie. "Do
I know you?" she asked.

"I'm her housemate." She pointed at Margot.

"Then you know everything, too, I imagine, everything evil
that is going on," Louisa said. "I was speaking with Detective
Wilson. He convinced me that the deaths of my son and that
movie man are related. What do you think of that?"

Margot wanted to say that she thought this café was a unique
spot to be speaking with a Los Angeles police detective, but
decided that might sound snippy. Anyway, what business was it of
hers? Theirs was obviously something deeper than a policeman's

and a member of a victim's family relationship.

"Well, ah…about the two deaths," Loretta Rose said, "I'm not surprised they're linked. Did Detective Wilson say *how* they are linked?"

Louisa's eyes were invisible behind her designer shades. "Linked by method is, I believe, the correct police terminology. They are also linked because they knew each other. The minds of the police I do not always understand, but that is what he said."

"We all knew both men," Margot said. "Did you know Colin Peabody, Mrs. Estrella?"

Louisa Estrella lips pinched into a thin line. "I knew *of* Mr. Peabody," she said. "Robert did mention him once and, of course, Rafael and Carlos couldn't bear the man. Still that's no excuse for murder, is it? But Mr. Peabody had many enemies and I cannot find one person who hated my Robert. My son didn't make enemies."

"I wondered, Mrs. Estrella, if Carlos showed you the chain?" Margot asked.

The woman put a slim white hand to her neck and brought out the gold necklace. "Carlos told me where you found this. It was Robert's. His was the only one missing. I will wear it for him. You see, you do find things for me."

"Margot found a recipe from Robert, too," Sophie said. Margot cleared her throat.

"A recipe?"

"Yes, I found it at the studio. I gave it to the police. I don't know what it means…"

"Ah, they will place Robert where it was found, but, of course, that doesn't make a difference. We know where Robert was put. All these clues, as the detective tells me, add up, he says. I hope so." She covered her face with her hand. "I'm sorry, the scars are not yet healed." She stood up as though to leave. "Please," she said, "if there is anything you might know about Robert's death, please call me."

She made a quick, elegant exit from the patio and onto the sidewalk where a black car pulled up to the curb, the door opening automatically as she ducked into the dark interior.

Margot watched the car pull away. Glancing across the tables she saw that Detective Wilson still sat beneath the umbrella across the patio, staring into his half finished glass of wine. She watched as he pushed the glass away, stuck a bill under the check, and stood up. He caught her eye and nodded.

She nudged Loretta Rose and Sophie as the man made his way toward them. Coming close, his shadow lay across their table as the three of them looked up, squinting in the bright sunlight. It was difficult to see his expression.

"Ladies," he said. "Lovely day for an outdoor lunch, isn't it? May I sit down?"

"Please do," Margot said.

"I saw Louisa stop by your table."

Louisa, Margot thought. She doubted that he referred to any of them by *their* first names.

"Ladies, I ask you as an old family friend to please not join her in this terrible, dark vendetta she is planning."

"But she didn't ask us to join anything," Loretta Rose said.

The detective raised an eyebrow. "If she does ask, consider the consequences."

Sophie looked cross. "I can't blame her for anything she might do or want to do. But she certainly didn't give us any details or ask for our assistance. Surely, detective, you understand her feelings as a mother. If it makes her feel better to plot, what...

revenge…so be it."

"So long as the revenge is applied to the correct person." He stood up.

Margot caught the chronic weariness in his eyes.

"If she requests things of you, think about what she's asking." He handed a card to each of them. "Call me if you become aware of anything."

"Detective Wilson?" Sophie said. "So you knew Robert Madrid, too? I mean before he was killed."

Wilson stood. "I know all the Estrellas. I told you I am a family friend. I am first of all a friend for Louisa. We knew each other long, long ago. We have remained close."

They watched him disappear through the maze of umbrellas, tables and chairs.

"Wow," Sophie said. "What do you think? A long ago romance?"

"Close means close. Definitely a romance."

"I've never seen him smile," Loretta Rose said. "Shit, look at the time. I've got to get back to work. Tomorrow night's my TV debut!"

THAT NIGHT MARGOT'S PHONE RANG. She glanced at the caller I.D., but could only tell it was a local number.

"Hello?"

"Ms. O'Banion?" The voice was throaty and with that distinctive soft accent. "This is Louisa Estrella."

"Yes, Mrs. Estrella?"

"Ms. O'Banion, to me you seem a most discerning person. I would like you to visit this evening. I have someone here I'd like you to meet. *Es importante.*"

Margot glanced at her bedside clock. It was nearly seven. She and Ivy had already had a quick dinner. Ivy was off to a rehearsal. Max was at a late meeting. She'd been drafting some ideas on the latest scenes. Still, she couldn't think of any reason not to go. The detective's warnings echoed in her head, but, at this point, she didn't know anything anyway. She didn't know whether to be suspicious or nervous of the invitation. And then there was the very real fact that she was feeling just plain curious about the woman.

"I'll be happy to come over. Just give me your address."

She drove west on Sunset, the bright neon lights of the boutiques and movie theaters receding as she reached the impossibly verdant, plush green of the Brentwood area. Turning onto a wide street, she searched for the right address. There. She parked at the curb and locking the car—although in this neighborhood with each house sporting a sign warning of armed guards, it seemed a bit superfluous—she walked up the curving brick walk toward what looked like a medium-size Spanish castle.

The door opened before she found the doorbell and, once again this day, she was looking at Louisa Estrella, still in black, but wearing trousers and a shirt this time.

"Please." The woman gestured for Margot to enter.

The ornately tiled floor of the foyer opened onto a stretch of polished pine flooring with a few thick, colorful hand-woven rugs breaking up the spacious room. The furniture was burnished leather in a dark shade of brown. Just right, she thought, against the apricot colored walls, the exact color she wanted for Max's bedroom.

"Ms. O'Banion? I'd like you to meet my daughter-in-law. This is Mirella Estrella-Madrid. I shall return with some drinks."

Margot blinked as a pretty woman, her pale gold hair piled on top of her head, stood up, reaching out to shake her hand. Of course, Mirella was the wife on Robert Madrid's tribute film. The ex-*wife*...

She smiled. "How do you do? And please, my name is Margot."

They took seats on the smooth leather chairs and silence fell. Louisa Estrella returned to the room. She carried a tray holding three small crystal glasses of a smoky brown liquid. She handed a glass to each of them and placed the other one on a small table, sitting down behind it on a chair of wood so dark it was nearly black.

"Now," she said, "let's get started, shall we? Mirella, my beautiful daughter-in-law, who will always be family no matter what the circumstance, is also concerned that the official investigation is going nowhere. Our get-together tonight will help us to put the facts together."

"But Mrs. Estrella," Margot began, "I really don't know how I can help you."

"You don't know, because you haven't heard." Louisa Estrella's fingers drummed on her knee. "You must listen, Ms. O'Banion... Margot. Just listen and then tell me if you cannot bear to help."

Margot leaned forward.

"You see, Mirella and I do not trust the police in their investigation."

"But I saw you today with Detective Wilson. Isn't he an excellent policeman?"

"We were not discussing Robert this afternoon," said Louisa Estrella. "But I know Wayne ("Wayne," Margot thought? Detective Wilson didn't look like a "Wayne") has no idea what happened. He keeps telling me not to worry, not to be concerned, but what does he know. They say that to every victim's family. It's police talk. It means nothing, *nada*. Robert is worth more than that."

"But what can you possibly do?"

Louisa stared at Margot, one curved eyebrow raising at her question. "What can I do? I can find out what happened. I can find out why someone would do that terrible thing to Robert. Oh, I know they are looking into the fact he was gay and that he was a celebrity and so on and so on. But I know Robert led a blameless life. Isn't that right, Mirella?"

Mirella nodded.

Margot realized she hadn't heard the woman's voice yet. Perhaps she was used to being a silent muse for the dynamic woman who was once her mother-in-law.

"So when someone like Robert has done *nothing* he shouldn't have done, one looks to other motives for this sort of tragedy."

"But perhaps it was…" Margot shrugged, "…one of those aberrant things that happen."

"You mean an *accidental* death or murder done by one of those deranged humans who do terrible things spontaneously?" Mrs. Estrella shook her head. "No, no. If it had just been Robert, but it was also that movie man. This other person fancied himself a knowledgeable wine lover, *si?*"

"*Si,*" Margot repeated and then froze. She was so intent on listening, she was taking on the flavor of the conversation. But, surely the woman wouldn't take her parroting of her language as an insult, would she?

Instead Mrs. Estrella looked pleased. Turning to Mirella, Louisa said, "See, Mirella, this Margot agrees with me. I told the police that Robert would never get into a frozen food locker of his own volition. I'm sure Mr. Peabody wouldn't climb into a wine barrel on his own. No, someone is playing grotesque jokes on the dead, like word games, but using the bodies of his victims. The murderer is making a statement. An ugly, perverted statement. He is showing off. He is laughing at us."

"So you're certain the…murderer must have known both of his…victims?"

"Come now, Margot. We must use the words. They are just words. Yes, the *murderer* knew his *victims*."

"But both your son and Colin Peabody knew so many people. Both men were famous. Probably lots of people *thought* they knew them, too."

"You mean those groupie people." Louisa frowned. "Mirella, did Robert ever talk to you about those people? Was anyone, what is the word, stalking him?"

The ex-wife shook her head. "Robert didn't discuss unpleasant things," she said, her voice soft and light. "If something was bothering him, I never heard about it. That was his way of dealing with difficulty."

"Was he…ah…involved with someone?" Margot asked.

"No, Bobby really didn't have time for romance. I know he was seeing a lot of your friend, that beautiful woman with the dark hair. Bobby did love beauty, but he never mentioned anyone close to him, not after that imbecile Paul Bennett."

Margot caught Louisa Estrella's glance. It seemed to say don't ask anything about whoever Paul Bennett was or had been.

"I think I should be going now," Margot said. "You've given

me some interesting things to think about."

"I did not," Louisa said, "invite you over here as a joke, Ms. O'Banion. I want to elicit your special expertise. You are an editor of films, isn't that right?"

She nodded.

"Yes, I thought so. Mirella has explained to me what you do, how you take pieces of film and fit them together to create stories." Louisa folded her hands. "So I will give you the pieces and you will create the picture. The picture will be of the assailant who murdered my child."

Margot glanced at Mirella who nodded. "I told her about you. I'm a set decorator over at Moonstruck."

Okay, Margot thought, so Mirella was in the business and had explained what a film editor's job was to her eccentric ex-in-law. Okay, fine. But how did *she* get out of this? Surely Mrs. Estrella didn't think she was going to create something out of thin air, a portrait of the suspect the way police artists did?

Margot reached for her purse. "I don't know what I can do to help."

"I'm not asking you to pull fluffy rabbits out of hats," Louisa said. "I will give you pieces of the puzzle and you will put them together. *Si?*"

Margot sighed. "Si," she repeated. Damn.

Louisa sat back. The woman suddenly reminded Margot of Amory her cat, smiling contentedly after finishing the last bite of mouse.

Margot rose and reaching in her purse for her car keys felt the sharp edge of the business card the detective had given them at lunch. What had he said? Something about just saying no, in case they were asked to join in a vendetta. That was it. Quite melodramatic. She pushed the card into an inside pocket and pulled out her keys.

She shook Mrs. Estrella's hand, offered palm down as though to be perhaps kissed, and followed Mirella Madrid to the door.

"Louisa is not crazy. She is just driven to find the truth," the ex-wife whispered.

"Oh," said Margot, "I understand." Which, of course, she didn't, but realized she had never been put in the position that Louisa Estrella found herself in, either.

She'd had those sleepless nights before she and Max met each other again after so many years. She'd tossed and turned when their son Luis was late getting in and again when he'd announced he wanted to become an actor—an *actor*! Didn't he realize what he was letting himself in for? But in comparison to having a grown son murdered in his prime, these temporary stresses were nothing. *Nada*.

Chapter XVI

MAX WAS WAITING IN THE APARTMENT. He had let himself in with his key and was comfortably settled on the sofa in front of the fireplace, a full wine glass in his hand. He smiled as she came in and patted the sofa next to him. Sitting down, Margot was all ready to tell of her adventure with Louise Estrella when he handed her a sheet of paper. Squinting, she turned it toward the firelight and read.

"Max!" she said.

He nodded mournfully. "The little prick left us all his money. All his money, his condo, his frickin huge Mercedes…lemme see, what else…oh, and everything else, absolutely everything, even that furniture Loretta Rose told me he lifted from Property." He put his head in his hands. When he looked up, Margot couldn't decide if he were crying or laughing. "And we hated him. Oh, God, Margot babe, we're doomed! What're we gonna do with it all?"

She shook her head. "I'm just amazed, Max. Didn't Colin have some obscure relative somewhere? Didn't he know anybody else who liked him a little bit, someone who would appreciate his generosity?"

"Well, obviously not. Now we'll have to be nice about him to everyone or they'll think we're as bad as he was."

They sat staring into the fire in silence. She twisted the smooth surface of her ruby ring round and round her finger. Finally she reached for the wine glass from Max and took a big sip. All that money and it was an incredible amount of money. And Max was right. They didn't need more, especially from someone whom they would remember, when they thought of him at all, for all the trouble he'd been. Of course, the reason they were so comfortably off now was from the money Colin had made for them as Max's erstwhile, but brilliant producer. For all the strains and pressures of their work, the money always flowed straight to them. Colin may have been a problematic personality but, somehow, he'd made it work for Max and, thus, for her. She was still reticent, even to Luis, about the exorbitant amount of money she made.

"We could start a foundation or something," she said. "Something in Colin's name."

"Well, why the hell didn't he do that?"

"Don't be mad at him now, Max. Colin didn't know he was going to be stuffed in a wine barrel. And maybe he just did it because he liked us. That's all I can figure."

Max looked incredulous. "How could he like us? I was rotten to him. Of course, he deserved it, but I was mostly rotten."

She stared at him. "Are you feeling guilty? What did you do?"

Max gave her a look. "What did I do? Whatever I did, you were with me when I did it. I mean, think about it. We never even invited him over."

"You never invite anyone over."

"Whadaya mean? I had that party and everything. You're over all the time. I mean over for dinner, like with Luis, like a family or something."

"But, Max, Colin was just your producer, an excellent producer, but he was not the sort of person we wanted to socialize with outside of work. I don't think you should turn yourself inside out feeling guilty that he left us all his worldly possessions. It really was a nice thing to do. We just have to figure out what to do with it."

"Yeah, I guess so. The police are all over his place now. I guess we don't have to worry about dividing up the booty anytime soon. Still it's frickin weird. I'll feel funny if anyone finds out."

"Then don't tell anyone. Our secret is safe with me."

He smiled and pulled her close.

THE NEXT EVENING they enjoyed their second dinner in two months at fabled Café Estrellado. Carlos had apparently forgiven Max's production crew for banging around his sacred kitchen again and had invited them to have dinner at the café before the taping of Loretta Rose's appearance on *The Late Night Chef*. She and Max were to be the "celebrity audience" on the show, a job consisting of making yummy noises as the dish was cooked and then sampling the finished product with appropriate looks of pleasure.

Carlos was cooking in the café tonight and he would also be appearing on the episode, but the man was a genuine multi-tasker and seemed perfectly capable of doing a dozen things at once.

Plus, as Max pointed out, he only had to go downstairs to be on the show. No big deal, he said.

She leaned forward to sniff the small bouquet of yellow roses in the middle of the table. "We're the only table with flowers," she whispered. "Wasn't that nice of Carlos!"

"I had the staff put them there," Max said. "They're for you. I'm turning over a new leaf. I'm going for romantic."

Margot's eyes widened. "Why? You've never done anything like this before."

"That's why I'm doing it now. It's never too late. Anyway, you've been putting up with all this murder crappola and everything. It isn't fair."

"Wow. They're beautiful." She leaned into their fragrance, warm and spicy and felt herself blushing. Max, the man she would never completely know. It was quite wonderful.

"And don't worry, babe. We're not involved in all this. I know we're not. We're your basic innocent bystanders. Don't worry. No one's after us."

Suddenly he turned and pointed. "Wonder where he's off to in such a hurry," he said. "He" was Carlos Estrellado. He was without his tall chef's cap, but still wearing the bright white chef's jacket, and he was heading out the door, fast.

"The show is going to be taped in an hour," Margot said.

"Oh, he'll be there in time. He won't want to miss quality time with our Loretta Rose. I can't wait to watch those brothers go at it over her."

"It won't be like that. They're adults."

"Right." Max grinned.

They were finishing their espressos when Loretta Rose hurried over. Margot thought she looked improbably fabulous in her new peach colored shirt.

"Have you seen Carlos?" Loretta Rose asked. Her usually smooth brow was furrowed.

"We saw him leave earlier," Max said. "He's probably come back by now, probably back in the kitchen."

Loretta Rose shook her head. "No, no one's seen him for ages. Well, hell. And there's kind of an emergency downstairs."

"What kind of emergency?" Margot asked.

"The frickin stove gave out. They were bringing over a replacement...well, you'd better come see what's happened."

Margot exchanged a look with Max. Thanks to Carlos, there was no check to settle and they followed Loretta Rose into the routine chaos of the main kitchen. As Loretta Rose had said, Margot didn't see Carlos anywhere but, still, the kitchen appeared to be on autopilot, fragrant laden plates moving about the room at a rapid rate.

They threaded their way through the kitchen as the staff moved out of their way, heading to the door leading out to the corridor.

"What's up, Loretta Rose? Nervous about the show?" Max asked.

They stepped into the relative quiet of the gloomy corridor, leaving the noisy kitchen action behind them.

Loretta Rose gave him a withering look. "Just follow me," she said.

As they walked toward the stairwell, the usually silent corridor became filled with voices—loud voices, frustrated voices, angry voices.

She looked at Max who raised an eyebrow. At the head of the stairs, Loretta Rose halted and pointed. "There," she said.

"There" was midway down the stairs where two sweating men in overalls were wrestling with a huge black box, the new gourmet stove. Out of sight, from the basement level, other voices were heard offering suggestions and recriminations and two more sweating men could be partially seen at the other end of the stove grunting and groaning as they tried to push the unwieldy object upward.

"What is that?" Margot asked.

"I told you. It's the frickin new stove. It's stuck against the walls. They can't move it. Now no one can get up or down the stairwell and we don't have a proper working stove for the frickin *Saddle of Rabbit with Black and Rose Peppercorns* for tonight's show."

"You're going to cook a rabbit?"

"Oh, heavens, Margot, grow up. The rabbit is dead. We didn't kill it. We're just going to cook it. However, as you can see, no one's ever going to see the damned dish since we can't get down there to do the show."

"Use the elevator." Max seemed unperturbed.

"That awful little contraption? We'll all be killed."

"Well, Loretta Rose, unless you plan to climb over that monster in the stairwell and slide down over the top of it into the basement, I'd say you'd better use the elevator."

Max's voice was calm, but Margot could hear the laughter behind his words. Max loved catastrophe as long as it wasn't *his* catastrophe.

"Anyway, there's gotta be a service entrance or something, some other way to get into that basement," he said.

"Well, there isn't," Loretta Rose said. "Elliot said they got all the equipment down there by taking out one of the basement windows. The city engineers got after them because the whole building is supported by the damned basement. So they had to restore everything they'd done. That's the reason they still use the space. It's too much trouble to move everything out now. Think of a tomb."

"Great." Max clapped his hands together. "Well, even if we all get down there, what are you going to cook your bunny rabbit on?"

"We're going to fake it. That's why I need Carlos. He was going to cook the rabbit—oh, stop looking at me like that, Margot—and then bring it down and we'd fake the preparation. No big deal. But now everyone is down there except Carlos. Where the hell did he go? Everyone is waiting for us." She looked at Margot. "Sorry for shouting at you about the rabbit bit. This is just so frustrating. My big break on a hit show and look at us, up here, stranded."

"Could you climb in from one of those little windows in the back?" Margot asked.

"I'm not going to try that. The windows aren't wide enough for a thin cat. Wouldn't that be fun, me stuck halfway through a window giving an interview about my new wine bar. Jeeze, I'd rather risk the frickin elevator."

Max had already opened the fancy little elevator and was examining the innards of the narrow box. "How does old Elliot get down there? I don't think a wheelchair could fit inside."

"He said it does and it's an okay machine. I just don't like the looks of it."

Neither did Margot. Still, with shouts entreating Loretta Rose to get down there, the show was nearly ready to tape and there didn't seem much of an alternative. Except, "Well, you don't really need me. There's no real need for me to go down there."

"You're the frickin *audience*, Margot. Loretta Rose clutched her forearm. "For heaven's sake. You're supposed to be supporting me in this. You're my friend."

"She didn't know you'd be serving her rabbit," Max said. "Margot refuses to eat bunny rabbit."

"Well, *fake it then*, Margot!"

Margot was about to defend herself when the door at the end of the hallway burst open and a disheveled Carlos Estrella entered the corridor in a rush. He stopped, surprised at seeing them clustered about.

"What's up, Carlos?" Max asked.

"You tell me," he gasped. "Someone called about an emergency down at Chi-Chi-Chi, but when I got there, no one knew anything about it. I thought mother had chopped off a hand or something."

"Fat chance," muttered Loretta Rose. "Well, we're stuck up here, Carlos, unless you've got some great idea how to get down to the basement without getting in this frickin death trap of an elevator."

"Oh, that," he said, "I use it all the time. Come on," he said, and grabbing Loretta Rose by the waist, he pulled her into the little dark cell. "Just press "S" when you and Margot come down," he called out to Max as the door was shut in their faces.

Margot listened to a gentle whirring noise as the elevator docilely returned. Max shrugged and opened the door for her. As she stepped gingerly into the tiny rectangle, she grabbed his hand. She closed her eyes as he pressed the "S" button.

"What does 'S' stand for?" she whispered as the bare floor under her feet gave a few tentative jerks and the elevator began a slow descent. "Maybe there are more floors under the basement and we'll never get there. 'S' could stand for anything."

'You got me on that. Anyway, we're already there!" Max said.

The door opened into the basement, the production part of the space right ahead of them. People were milling about the noisy room. She caught a quick glimpse of Loretta Rose, now wearing a tiny, crisp white apron over her two hundred dollar shirt, and Carlos getting made up by a young girl. Elliot Ferrigan was in his chair, hunched over a stack of papers. Rafael, in his smart-looking chef's coat with *The Late Night Chef* 's logo on the breast pocket waved at them from behind the cooking counter, various bright lights were being trained on this or that, as he consulted his notes.

Margot looked at the recipe blackboard behind him. Someone, in a fine calligraphic hand, had written out the ingredients for, as Loretta Rose had said, *Saddle of Rabbit with Rose and Black Peppercorns*. She shook her head. Why did they have to serve *that* on the only night she'd ever get to be present. A rabbit. She just prayed it wouldn't *look* like a rabbit.

Then, "*Sous-sol*," she whispered to Max.

"What?"

"That's what the 'S' meant. I just remembered. *Sous-sol* means basement in French."

He looked down at her. "You are the most amazing woman..."

The lights where they stood suddenly went out and they were ushered to two stools drawn up to the counter, the lights bright and hot overhead. Margot smiled as her nose was powdered and then watched as Max was subjected to the same treatment.

"We want you two to look natural," the makeup artist said.

"Yeah," said Raphael Estrella, "just act natural too. This'll be no sweat."

"Ready?" It was Elliot Ferrigan's voice. "Max and Margot, we're a little behind taping schedule. All that bullshit with the stove…I guess Raphael told you. Anyway, we'll get this in the can, get it to the studio and sit back and watch ourselves, in, hell, two hours. Come on, folks, we've got to step on it."

FORTY-FIVE MINUTES LATER, Max whispered in her ear, "You didn't eat your rabbit."

Margot smiled. "But it *looked* as though I ate it, didn't it?"

The brilliant lights over the counter went out and they stood up, stretching. Behind the counter, Raphael was thanking Loretta Rose and his brother for their help.

When, "What the hell!"

The voice cannoned off the walls and the production partitions practically trembled in place at the sound. It was Elliot Ferrigan. "Who the hell was in charge of the tape?" There was silence and then a mumbled reply. A phone rang as Elliot turned angrily toward the mumble. "Bruce, Bruce, Bruce. There's no tape. Where the hell's the tape?"

Suddenly there was a flurry of activity as everyone in the room reached for their cell phone. Margot looked at Max who was scrutinizing the chaos with obvious interest. "What happened?" she asked.

"We didn't get taped. Someone screwed up. We're all up shit creek."

Elliot, meanwhile, was barking into his cell phone. People were keeping a respectful distance from the furious director. Finally he clicked the phone shut. Silence fell, an uncomfortable silence feeling like the heaviness in the air right before a tornado hits. Elliot smiled—a disarming smile, Margot thought.

"Say, all you movie buffs," he said as though having a conversation at a party. "Does anyone remember the scene in *Tootsie* where they do the soap live?"

There was silence.

"OHMIGOD. We can't go live," said Loretta Rose. "You can't be serious. But it all went perfectly. We can't do it again. We can't go live. We're out of rabbit. We already cut it up!"

Elliot Ferrigan glanced at his watch. "Then put the rabbit back together, please, because we're doing a live feed in approximately twenty-three minutes."

"Really live?" a voice said.

"Live."

A deadly silence pervaded the basement like an unwanted guest.

"Let's get going, people," Elliot Ferrigan said.

Each person began working feverishly at whatever they had to do to get ready. Margot watched as Carlos Estrella somehow put the rabbit they'd been eating, or pretending to eat, back in a semblance of a rabbit shape. Loretta Rose and Raphael were busy grabbing dirty dishes and piling them on platters to be taken away as the crew brought in clean dishes, utensils, and began moping down the entire set.

"What does this mean for us, Max?" She lifted her face as her nose was being repowdered.

"Nothing. I'm assuming none of the three principles are

going to surprise us by divulging that they are, indeed, actually a he or a she, the way Dustin Hoffman did to everyone's amazement and horror. Great flick. So we just do the same stuff we did before. You know, look cool and pretend we're hungry. Good thing you didn't eat any bunny. I'm stuffed. Now I'll have to fake it, too."

Margot noted that Loretta Rose and the Estrella brothers seemed to be taking the chaos and uncertainty in stride. Of course, they had no choice. The person who had forgotten the tape was in heated conversation with Elliot Ferrigan, bending over his chair making some point or other that Elliot flat out rejected.

"I hope the poor bastard has another job lined up," Max muttered.

Margot felt queasy. You could say a lot of things about film production, but you could never say it was ever done *live*. Live was for stand-up comedians and for actors in legitimate theater. It was for people who had incredible composure and nerves of steel. She, of the quiet editing room and abhorrence of the spotlight, was not one of those audacious souls.

She looked at Max who seemed oblivious to the upcoming trauma as he consulted with Elliot. Max was in his element, as always. In fact there seemed to be few venues that *didn't* appeal to the man, where he wasn't at ease, friendly and confident. She settled herself back on her kitchen stool and prepared to observe.

"Ten, nine, eight, seven..." the voice intoned solemnly.

The countdown was on. The lights blazed down as Margot turned her ruby ring over and over. She couldn't see what the crew and Elliot Ferrigan were doing. She was stuck with her back to them. Suddenly Raphael walked out from behind the set into the bright light and took his position in front of her and Max, the celebrity guest audience. They were on. Raphael introduced Max and Max introduced her. Margot smiled as brightly as she could trying to ignore the TV camera dodging about and turned her attention to what Raphael was saying and doing, *again.*

And, once again, Loretta Rose was introduced. Again, she appeared glorious in her peach colored silk shirt barely covered by the minuscule apron, her dark curls gleaming under the overheads. Raphael's face lighted up as she leaned forward to give him the ubiquitous "glad to be here" kiss on the cheek, again. Then Carlos Estrella, star chef extraordinaire, strode out. He was wearing *his* chef's coat with the Café Estrellado logo over his breast pocket. He looked happy and carefree. Who would ever have realized that they'd just done exactly the same gig an hour ago.

Margot watched the two brothers intently. There was certainly that pronounced Estrella resemblance. Carlos was the taller of the two. Rafael was perhaps more picture-perfect handsome. But it really was a toss-up in the attractiveness department. Their voices were similar, even their mannerisms. She wondered at the age difference. It was difficult to say. And the personalities? Well, she didn't know either of them well enough to evaluate that.

Margot winced slightly as a spoonful of something…what was Loretta Rose handing her?…was thrust in her face. "The most delicious sauce," Loretta Rose was saying, "…just right for roast rabbit."

This hadn't been in the first script, Margot noted. Still it was like her friend to put her just a tiny bit on the spot. Well, she could play the game, too. She took the spoon and swallowed the sauce, smiling widely. She managed to conceal the drop of sauce that slid from the spoon onto her skirt.

And on through the scripted episode the trio of chefs proceeded, moving deftly between the complex explanation of the rabbit recipe, *again,* and moving the prep dishes back and forth between the already cooked and precariously shoved together creature. All this was performed in the confined space between the counter and the cold, unusable, broken monster stove.

Margot did notice that during this live take there seemed to be more than a little bit of jockeying for position between the brothers. Were they trying to upstage each other? See who got the best camera angle? No, actually it appeared as though each man was attempting to be the one closest to Loretta Rose at all times. Heavens, they were both practically hyperventilating over the woman. Loretta Rose seemed oblivious to the ardent attentions she was gathering, but she must be aware of what was happening. My goodness, Margot thought, everyone must be noticing. She certainly didn't recall this kind of impassioned behavior in the first almost-taping.

There was a sudden close call as Raphael's arm nearly upset a prep bowl full of olive oil as he attempted to angle Carlos out of the way. Margot reached out and righted the teetering dish just before it slipped to the floor, still a large portion of the oil slid onto the tiles.

Carlos's expression darkened just a bit and he moved in front of Rafael, ostensibly to get the rabbit platter. Too quickly, Carlos moved left. He must have hit the olive oiled floor and the platter and Carlos rebounded slightly off the defunct stove. Miraculously the platter didn't drop. Raphael quickly glided—or was he slipping, too?—across the slick tiles coming to an abrupt stop at Loretta Rose's elbow. Margot looked on, awestruck at the two chefs's bizarre culinary dance.

Beside her, Margot was sure she heard Max start to chuckle. Loretta Rose, meanwhile, appeared ignorant of the men dodging about right and left. She was deftly doing the same tasks she'd done an hour before. Still, she appeared to be trying not to get too close to either of the brothers, a difficult feat in the tiny space. Margot knew she was also trying to avoid the slippery part of the floor. She could see her friend quickly scrutinizing the tiles before making any move.

At last, the reconstructed rabbit—looking, Margot noted, definitely rabbit-shaped—was presented to the "celebrity" guests. Margot and Max made indiscriminate yummy sounds as Loretta Rose and Carlos prepared to carve.

Finally Loretta Rose and Carlos stood shoulder-to-shoulder facing the camera. Of course, their close proximity was simply the only way to present a platter held by two people, but Raphael suddenly appeared between them, shoving Carlos, none too gently, to the side. This abrupt movement made the counter in front of Margot shift several inches toward the stove, as Carlos clung to the platter, the rabbit sliding toward the floor.

Loretta Rose, in an apparent effort to keep from being pinned against the huge black stove, held onto the counter as the dishes clattered and shook. Raphael, sensing imminent disaster, held one edge of the off-balance counter, as Carlos desperately held onto the rabbit platter, obviously unsure what surface was now stable enough to put it on.

Through all the physical activity, Rafael was semi-keeping his composure, uttering little host-like throwaway lines; "Oops," he said brightly, and "Here we are," and "Uh oh." The two guest chefs were silent, looking more and more grim as they attempted to complete the presentation and finally get to the climax of the show.

Loretta Rose shifted her position slightly and still off-balance, careened into Carlos, stopping with a gentle bump, at which point Raphael reached for her as she slid back, in graceful slow motion, toward the counter. From each side, Raphael and Carlos grabbed a silken-clad arm to stop her oily progress.

Still Loretta Rose smiled charmingly as she attempted to stabilize herself and shake the men off. But now the men, dashing in their crisp white jackets, seemed to be doing a mini tug-of-war over her. As Margot watched in horror, Loretta Rose was caught off balance again and her left breast grazed the top of the olive oil in the little dish. A large round dark stain quickly blossomed, the thin silk rapidly turning to a delicate transparency.

The two men stopped their yanking and pulling, staring instead at Loretta Rose's voluptuous, oil-stained breast, each still firmly clasping one of her arms.

"You blasted idiots!" Loretta Rose abruptly roared, righting herself and shaking off the hovering men, the extra olive oil dripping across the front of her costly shirt and down the fabric of the insufficient apron. "Both of you, leave me alone!"

Behind them, Margot could hear increasingly anxious mumbles from the crew. Their voices grew more and more agitated as the cameraman was directed, loudly and emphatically, to do the impossible—to *not* show to the loyal audience of *The Late Night Chef* what had just occurred, live, up-close and personal.

It was too late. The damage was done. Still, Rafael managed, at last, to see Elliot Ferrigan whipping his hand desperately back and forth across his neck in the time-honored "Cut it!" signal. Fixing a smile on his handsome sweating face, he stood in front of the shambles that was the set and thanked the audience and thanked the guest celebrities for coming and the production lights went out.

Dead silence reigned.

"By God," Max murmured in Margot's ear, his voice choking with laughter, "I hope your roomies got all that on TiVo."

Chapter XVII

MARGOT SLID OFF THE COUNTER STOOL feeling like a school child who has not only witnessed, but participated in, inappropriate behavior.

"Let's make tracks, babe," Max said. "We're better off away from this firing range."

Elliot acknowledged their hurried departure with a tired wave as his cell phone began an incessant ringing. Behind the counter, Loretta Rose and the brothers were still in a heated conversation amidst the ruins of the set.

Max and Margot, plus members of the production crew anxious to make a quick getaway before the inevitable critique was delivered, milled about looking for the best way to exit the premises, fast. But the huge new stove was still wedged in the stairwell. Whoever had been working on getting it down to the basement had given up and gone home sometime during the filming fiasco. So they joined a line of fidgeting crew members in single-file at the elevator.

Margot watched as the little elevator obediently rose and

returned, rose and returned. Finally it was their turn. Only Elliot, a beleaguered cameraman, and the mad trio behind the counter remained in the room. Margot could hear Loretta Rose's voice hissing first at Raphael and then turning on Carlos.

Max stepped inside the little box first and after Margot had inched her way inside, he stared at the buttons on the tiny control panel. There was a "S" button. Well, that was where they already were. The other buttons were designated as "2," "3," and "4."

"Where's number 1?" she asked.

"There is no number 1."

"There has to be a number 1, Max. Number one is always the first floor. Those others are for the other floors. How many floors are there in this building, four, right? So where's number 1?"

"It isn't here, is it, babe? Just run on over to Elliot and ask him which button to push. He'll know."

She glanced over. The beleaguered director/producer was hunched over his cell phone taking yet another call. Obviously the powers-that-be at the main studio were not thrilled with this, the first and hopefully the last, live segment of their hit TV show.

"I don't think I should bother him now."

"Bother him," Max said. "He'll be glad of the break."

Margot walked over and stood there, hands behind her back, waiting for the phone conversation to finish. Finally Elliot looked up. "Yes, Margot?"

"We just need to know about the elevator buttons," she said. "Which one do we push?"

He looked at her as though she were invisible. Margot followed his stare. Raphael had disappeared. All she could see were the backs of Carlos and Loretta Rose, their heads close together, his arm around her. The furious conversations were over. They were having a heart-to-heart.

Margot waited patiently. At last Elliot turned his attention to her. He still looked distracted, not that she blamed him one bit. What a night.

"Oh, the buttons. Just push any one of them," he said briskly. "They all stop at the first floor. The other floors aren't serviced by the elevator anymore."

"Thank you," she said. "I'm sorry about what happened tonight."

He looked at her, his eyes somber. "Heavens, Margot. None of this was your fault. We'll survive. Hey, Max," he called past her. "Does crap like this happen to you?"

"Everyday in every way," Max shouted back from the elevator.

What must Carlos and Loretta Rose be thinking of these put-downs? Margot wondered. She glanced over, but the couple didn't seem to have even heard the comments. They were still in the same positions, heads together, still talking, oblivious to the rest of the room.

Walking back to the elevator, she eased her way in next to Max and pushed a button at random.

"What are you doing?" Max said.

"Elliot said all the buttons are the same. The elevator only goes to the first floor." She ignored the irritation on Max's face.

"Don't do another thing. Don't touch anything. I'll ask him what's what," Max announced.

She shrugged and leaned against the side of the elevator as he left, slamming the narrow door shut as he did.

The elevator trembled a bit at the impact and Margot frowned, watching him walk in his usual graceful stride over to

Elliot's chair. Suddenly, the elevator gave a lurch. Had it moved?

Margot stared wide-eyed at the floor of the basement beyond the door. Yes, she was perceptively higher. The elevator had lifted a few inches. "Max!" she called. But whatever failings the contraption had, it was well soundproofed. Max did not turn and come back to rescue her.

Grasping the small tarnished brass door handle, she was preparing to open it and leap out, when the machine gave a groan like a wounded animal and lurched upward. She pressed herself against the back facing the door with its fancy little window showing nothing but bare wall as the elevator slowed, but continued to rise.

Okay, she thought, she'd get out at the first floor landing. The machine could return by itself to the basement for cross old Max. Meanwhile, she'd go through the kitchen—maybe they'd even sell her a cup of coffee—and wait for Max in Loretta Rose's wine bar. In fact, a glass of good wine would be even better, certainly called for after the disaster of her first and last TV appearance.

But the elevator didn't seem to be slowing down or stopping. Surely she should be at the first floor by now. She peered out the grimy window but only saw more wall, moving wall. Then there was a brief glimpse of a dimly lit corridor—*there* was *the first floor!* That's where she was supposed to get out, but then she was plunged into more gloom and up, up, up the elevator kept going. And she was going with it.

Oh God, what was going to happen now? Darkness flooded the small space as the machine persisted in carrying her upward. And then it abruptly stopped with an unnerving jolt, the cables beyond the contrivance creaking and groaning.

Margot stood motionless for a few seconds and then leaning

her forehead to the window, looked out the door. There was a landing that looked like any other landing. She was somewhere. She just didn't know where. She stepped back. At least there was some sort of light out there. She could see shadows and strange wavering forms. From windows? Reflections from outside as the light bounced up from the street? It was impossible to tell from her un-vantage point huddled in the back of the machine.

Finally, suppressing an urge to scream in terror at her predicament, she grasped the door handle and pushed. The door opened and she stepped outside into the gloom, but, at least, she was on the more solid ground of a hallway. Behind her, the elevator made various grinding noises and then it began to descend without her and God only knew where it would end up this time.

Margot blinked in the sudden deafening silence. Where the hell was she? Of course, she had to still be in the building. Elevators didn't go sideways. The windows she'd thought might be here, were here, but they were aligned with the ceiling. Too high for her to peer out and get some sort of bearing. How many stories was this old building? Four stories? There had been a number four button in the elevator. But those buttons were crazy. The whole elevator was crazy. There could be fifteen stories for all she knew. She tried to visualize seeing the building the times they'd driven up to the restaurant. It didn't work. All she recalled were the brilliant, beckoning lights of Café Estrellado and a huge looming dark bulk overhead—where she was now, stranded in the gloom.

She peered down the dark corridor. She was near one end of the building, an outer wall behind her. It looked as though there was a series of doors opening off the hall. All the doors were closed against her.

Would there be electricity up here? The elevator had made it up, but it wasn't *supposed* to and why electrify a vacant area of a big old, firetrap building? Still, she peered about the corridor looking for any sort of light switch. But the light fixtures overhead had no light bulbs in them. Uh oh, her first efficient-thinking inclination was right. Why light up a place no one used.

She took a deep breath. Max would be looking for her. He might track her down eventually up here, but she had to find her way down before then, before she started panicking. Just the thought of panicking made her feel queasy. All she needed to do was find the stairwell. There *had* to be a stairwell. The first floor stairs were at the end of their corridor. These must be in the same general area. So, all that meant was creeping down through the dark, past all the closed doors, and then just inching her way down an indeterminate number of flights of stairs in the dark. Hey, just a walk in the park, as Luis would say.

Taking a deep breath, she began walking slowly down the hall. Did she have to open every door hoping to find the stairwell? But it must be down where the other one was on the first floor. Architects didn't design buildings with staircases meandering through them, did they?

She reached out and tentatively grasped a dirty glass doorknob. It felt sticky to her hand and she automatically recoiled, before finally turning it and pushing the door open. She peered inside. It was an empty room, period. No furniture, no curtains, no carpeting, nothing. Had the place been a hotel? She could just make out two more doors inside. Bathroom? Closet? Whichever. She wasn't going inside to check them out for anything.

But, still, she realized that if she opened the silly doors, the faint light reflected from the solitary windows inside, from the street below, would help illuminate the damned dark hallway. As she walked along she reached for first this doorknob and then that doorknob across the hall and pushed them open. Her mind registered empty room after empty room. Someone had cleared them out thoroughly some time in the distant past.

Was Max worrying about her? Didn't he wonder where she was? Where on earth did they think she'd disappeared to? She paused, but heard no anxious voices calling out her name, searching for her.

Finally she reached the end of the hallway, the outer wall looming in front of her. She pushed open the last door on the right, ready to reach for the next one—it had to be the stairwell—across the hall, and stopped. There was no light coming in from the mean little window in this room. Each room she'd opened and glimpsed had been the same. But this room was much darker. She focused through the gloom. The solitary window was covered over with some sort of heavy fabric. It was like blackout material and it was stapled across the glass with dozens of the things fastened in the window frame. Margot had seen this same technique used on location when a light source was hindering filming.

The rest of the room was as bare as all the others.

Turning her back on it she reached for the last doorknob. Opening it, she was hit by a gusting draft of dusty warm air. The stairs! But, oh my God, this stairwell was in total blackness. She recoiled from the sight. No light from any dirty windows would reach here.

Staring down into the abyss, she hesitated and then took the first step down. She curbed the urge to sit down and make her way to the next landing like a two-year old child afraid of falling. Of course, she *was* afraid of falling. The deep darkness gave her a strange feeling of instant, terminal vertigo. Putting out her hand, she felt the wall and tentatively took another step down, feeling each inch of the stair with the toes of her shoes.

Step after step she took until at last there were no more. The landing wasn't more than a few steps across to another door. She opened this door to more awful darkness and then she was back to picking her way down through the dark again. Down. Down. Down. Her feet were beginning to feel heavy. Finally, she sat down on a step, the darkness hovering around her, just to breathe deeply for a moment and mentally compose herself.

At last, another of the short level landings and then…she paused. She really didn't think she could do another flight of steps right now. Breathing hard, certainly not from any real exertion, she leaned against the wall trying not to think what might be lurking on the grimy surface.

And then, from far off below her, she heard a sound. Margot froze. It was the sound of soft footfalls on the next floor, coming slowly upward. Finally, "Max?" she breathed out. "Max?"

She listened as the footsteps stopped, a slight crunching sound as though the sole of the shoe was turning in grit. Were the steps retreating? But why didn't someone answer her?

Suddenly terrified, Margot continued her descent, faster this time, ignoring the darkness and her claustrophobic panic of a few moments ago. Step after step she took until she was again at the level landing. Was a person hugging the walls here, anxious that she might run into him, hiding? She didn't care. At this point she was ready to take on anyone.

She reached out tentatively toward where the door should be and her arm brushed fabric. Someone silent and invisible was standing there. Margot screamed and recoiled, the primal sound echoing back up the stairwell. Plastered with gooseflesh, she grabbed for the doorknob and pulled. Stepping out, she slammed the door behind her, enclosing whatever or whoever she'd bumped into in the claustrophobic stairwell.

She blinked in amazement. Lights! The first floor. She ran as though the devil himself were pursuing her to the kitchen door, looking once over her shoulder to make sure no one was following.

Throwing the door open, she saw two people piling the remaining stacks of dinner dishes into the gigantic dishwashers. They didn't seem upset or surprised at her sudden terrorized appearance. Margot tried to smile, but felt as though her hair must be standing on end. The dishwashers nodded politely as she ran across the floor, out the opposite door and into the quiet luxury of the deserted restaurant. And across the room, silhouetted against the soft lights of Loretta Rose's wine bar was Max. He was talking in low tones to Carlos.

"Max!" she cried. "There was someone in there with me!"

He turned, looking startled to see her standing there.

"Someone in where? Hey, babe! Where the hell have you been? I thought you were mad at me. I thought you'd gone home."

"The elevator went berserk. I was up there somewhere," she said pointing to the ceiling. "It took me all the way to the top!"

"But it came back down for me." Max looked confused. He took a glass of red wine that Carlos hurriedly handed him and brought it over to her.

Margot sank onto one of the cane café chairs at the small tables that were casually arranged in the wine bar, taking the place of the ill-fated designer wine barrels. Max sat opposite her while

Carlos made a point of being busy doing something behind the bar.

"Margot, babe, you had me worried sick."

"Me, too," she said. "And then I had to creep down in the total dark and Max, I mean it was *completely* dark. There was *no light*. And at the bottom I heard this *person* and it didn't say anything to me and when I got to the landing I bumped into its clothes and it *still* didn't say anything."

Max said, rubbing her hands between his warm palms. "It was probably just someone from the kitchen grabbing an illegal smoke."

Margot narrowed her eyes, remembering. "I sure didn't smell any smoke and who would want to grab anything in a pitch dark stairwell?" Feeling safe and better for the venting, she finally sat back in the chair, looking around the wine bar room. "Where's Loretta Rose?"

"Went to change her clothes." And, as if on cue, Loretta Rose appeared, now in a red shirt and black jeans, scowling at them from the doorway.

"So where the hell were you, Margot? Couldn't stand the heat in the kitchen, right?" She laughed merrily and brushed by Carlos who was grinning at her as though only they knew the punch line of a great joke.

Loretta Rose pulled up a chair and sat down. "God," she groaned, "what a night. Well, Carlos," she called over her shoulder, "there goes our television careers." Both of them seemed to think that was another uproarious thing to say.

"How is Raphael taking it?" Margot asked.

"Uh, yeah, Raphael…" Carlos walked over and sat down next to Loretta Rose, or as Margot noticed, both of them seemed happily scrunched together on the same chair. Interesting. "Yeah, my little brother is kind of upset, to put it mildly. He thinks the Rose and I were in cahoots or some damned thing. Out to destroy him. I told him he was as much to blame for the pandemonium as anyone. Plus, I told him he'll get the biggest viewer turnout known to TV for his next show, but he's still kind of …ah…"

"Pissed off," Loretta Rose said. "So where the heck did you disappear to, Margot?"

"The elevator took me up to the top of this building, I think."

Carlos looked concerned. "It did? How the heck did that happen?"

She shook her head, remembering.

"Well, I'd better get the building people on that machine, first thing."

"So what was up there?" Loretta Rose reached for Margot's wine.

"Nothing. I mean there were dozens of rooms opening off the corridor, but they were all empty."

"Yeah," Carlos said. "This used to be a hotel. In fact, it was still a hotel when the guy who owns it now took over. Caused kind of a flap, I think, when they dumped the remaining tenants out on the street."

"Not little old ladies on paltry pensions?" Margot asked, horrified.

Carlos chuckled. "Nothing so refined, Margot. No, most of the rooms had been turned into…ah…businesses. Uh, you know what I mean."

"He means the place was a whore house, Margot," Loretta Rose said. "Margot is not as shy and delicate as she looks, Carlos.

Yeah, it was an evil house of prostitution. Quite successful too, I heard."

"Who did you hear that from?" Max was clearly curious. A good story always drew his attention.

"From old Colin Peabody. He knew everything about everything, as you know. This was when he was attempting to dissuade me from making my new enterprise here. I think he was trying to warn me that the bad reputation of the old hotel would rub off on me." She and Carlos exchanged a long look, the corners of Loretta Rose's expressive mouth curving up in one of her fetching smiles.

Across the table, Max rolled his eyes at her. Margot smiled in return. This un-fixup looked as though it might actually work for their fiery, eccentric friend.

"Hey, Max," Carlos said, "come over and check out this new Pinot Noir that this beautiful, incredible woman found."

The men walked over to the wine bar and Loretta Rose remained smiling. "I'm that beautiful, incredible woman he's talking about. And he calls me The Rose. I've never had a nickname. Can you believe that? Ohmigod, Margot!" she said suddenly. "Look at your ring."

Margot looked down. The ring was there. Oh no, the stone was gone. The glowing, smooth crimson ruby was missing.

She looked in horror at her friend. Loretta Rose quickly covered Margot's hand with her own. "Don't tell Max. He'll freak out. When do you remember seeing it there last?"

"During your show, before we had to do it live. I was nervous and kept turning my ring round my finger. I remember feeling the ruby then."

"Okay, we've gotta get downstairs. First we'll look in the

basement. But, hell, by now they've cleaned everything up. Still it might be in a corner somewhere or stuck in that frickin olive oil that they'll never get off the floor."

Margot shook her head slowly. "I can't do that tonight. I really can't. You will not get me in that elevator again tonight. Maybe the stairs will be cleared by tomorrow. But, oh, Lord, someone has probably picked the stone up already. Or it might be upstairs, up on one of those terrible, deserted floors. But I can't go up there again, not tonight. Nothing is worth doing that again."

Loretta Rose looked surprised. "Wow, you must really have been scared."

Margot was offended. "It *was* pitch dark, you know. If we go up there, we'll need huge flashlights or something. There's no electricity."

"Except in the elevator shaft," Loretta Rose pointed out.

"Obviously in the elevator shaft."

"Okay. Well, first I'll call Elliot and see if anyone turned the ruby into him. You know, some people still have good instincts and consciences," she added, turning on her phone and murmuring into it.

"No luck there. Elliot said no one was even speaking to him by the end of that artistic debacle, much less handing him huge rubies."

"It's not huge."

"Yes, it is, Margot. It's huge. Okay, tomorrow come by whenever you can and I'll help you search. Bring a flashlight, if you have one. We'll need them even in daylight. And don't tell Max. He'll think you did it on purpose or something."

"Why on earth would he think that?"

"Oh, Carlos said Max said he didn't think you would ever marry him."

"What? We've never even discussed marriage. Goodness."

"I guess they were just having a boy type heart-to-heart. It doesn't mean anything, probably just a comment on something else. I wonder what else they *were* talking about…"

"Well, us," Margot said. "Obviously."

Loretta Rose had two pink circles high on her cheeks. "Yeah, wow," she said. "So how long have you and himself been together now?"

"Just five years," Margot answered. "Of course, there was…"

"Yeah, no kidding. There is Luis."

"That's what the ring was for," Margot whispered, turning the gold band around so the empty setting didn't show. "Luis will be twenty in January. It was to commemorate him, oh, and us, I guess."

"Wow! And people say guys can't be romantic." Loretta Rose looked over to where Max and Carlos sipped a ruby red wine. "Shit, he opened the '92. Oh well, nothing's too good, et cetera, et cetera. So, call me tomorrow or I'll call you at work. We'll coordinate our search plan." Loretta Rose started to get up. "Oh, one other thing. Carlos mentioned to Max that you're in cahoots over Robert's murder with his saintly mother."

"'Cahoots'? How silly. All I did was go over to Mrs. Estrella's, at her invitation, and talk about this and that." Margot thought it best not to mention seeing Robert Madrid's ex- there, too.

"And what do you two have in common to talk about but murder?"

"Shh," Margot said. "Okay, so we chatted a bit about that, too."

"I'll bet." Loretta Rose's dark eyes were sparkling. "Well, keep me informed. I wouldn't put anything past that woman."

Chapter XVIII

I T WAS LATE IN THE AFTERNOON before Margot could leave the studio and drive over to the wine bar. Loretta Rose was just setting up for the evening rush, but was ready to do the stone search, as she called it.

They left the wine bar, carefully examining every step they took, even through the kitchen where the employees suspended whatever prep work they were doing to watch them searching the floor. Walking into the corridor, they scrutinized the hall on both sides, all the way to the stairwell. It was dusty beyond belief, but utterly bare of any precious stones.

The stairwell down to the basement was finally clear. Somehow the gigantic stove had been extricated from the passageway and the two women, flashlights borrowed from the kitchen staff in hand, walked down into the darkened basement. The stairwell was a mess. Plaster from the stove removal project was scattered over the steps, hunks of it all over the place. The dirty white walls were punched and scraped. But the new stove was finally in place, looking ready for the next episode of *The Late Night Chef.*

At the bottom of the stairs, Margot waited while Loretta Rose found the right light switches and the production area of the space lit up theatrically.

"Oh God," Loretta Rose moaned. "Here it is, the scene of my budding dramatic career's chaotic demise. I just hope Raphael isn't around today. I sure don't feel like reliving the horror of the moment with him again. Well, okay," she said. "Let's get busy. You start looking around any place at all you were last night and I'll check out the kitchen area. That ruby might have accidentally gotten swept under something in there during our...ah...little fracas. I remember you attempting to restore order at one point by clutching at the counter. It could have fallen out then and scooted over to our side."

Margot twisted the stone-less ring around her finger and walked toward the elevator. She had been touching the cavity in her ring all day. It was like having a sore tooth. She simply couldn't leave the gaping space alone. Of course, Max would have insured it. But telling him she'd actually lost it was last choice on her list of things to do today.

She turned on the flashlight and gingerly opening the elevator door, shone it all around the interior of the tiny dark floor. Nothing. The floor was simply a floor. There were no cracks or crevices the stone could be hiding in. With a sense of relief that she'd examined the worst first, she shut the door and began investigating the rest of the room.

Loretta Rose was right. The room had been swept but it certainly wasn't clean, even to her less than exacting standards. Dust bunnies cluttered every corner. The stands holding some of the lights were filthy. Dust covered everything, everything but the cameras and the computer and engineering banks. These were pristine.

She poked through the corners, under the debris hiding under every available spot, but no gleaming ruby stone caught her eye. She even emptied the waste baskets onto the floor waiting to here the clink of the heavy stone. Nothing. *Nada*, as Louisa Estrella would say.

Up in the front of the room she could hear Loretta Rose cursing under her breath as she checked under the counter and the various appliances.

"It couldn't have rolled under the stove, could it?" Margot asked.

"Nah," was the muffled reply. "That old thing had a skirt on it to the floor. Nothing could get under it."

At last, Margot stood looking helplessly around the space and Loretta Rose stood up, frowning, wiping her hands on her jeans. "Not here," she said. "You didn't drop it here unless someone already stole the thing. We've gotta retrace your foot steps up there," she said, pointing upward.

"I don't know. It..."

"Come on, you baby," Loretta Rose said. "It's gotta be somewhere and that's the other place you were last night, right? Look, now it's daylight and I'm with you. What other protection do you need?" She looked toward the elevator, sitting in its corner. "So, what floor do you think you were on?"

"I have no idea. I wasn't counting the flights of stairs and I could have been anywhere. I think I was at the top, but I had no way of knowing for sure. And we are not going investigating in *that* damned elevator. Anyway we should walk up. I used the stairs to come down. If the stone is up there, it's either on the stairs or someplace in that top corridor. I couldn't see a thing in the stairwell. It could have dropped off anywhere."

Loretta Rose shrugged. "Okay. Let's go."

"You lead," Margot said. "We'll both search the same places and that way two sets of eyes will be scouring the place."

They trailed up the stairs, over the bits of broken plaster, some of it sticking to the bottom of Margot's sneakers. She stopped to remove it from the thick rubber soles with a finger nail, the beam from the flashlight snaking over the scarred walls.

"What are you doing, Margot?" Loretta Rose asked. "Oh, okay. Well, come on. It's not going to be on these stairs anyway since not a bloody one of us could use the damned staircase yesterday. Oh Lordy, Margot, was last night as terrible a disaster as I think I remember it was?"

"You mean, the show?"

"Of course I mean the show. Were there other disasters around here that could equal what we did? None that I saw. So tell me honestly. Was it the absolute worst? Did I say what I think I said at the end? And could you really see through my shirt? I mean all the way through?"

"Yes. Pretty much"

"Yes? Pretty much you could see through it? Totally?"

Margot nodded.

"Well, at least I was wearing my good lace bra."

"I know. It was nice lace. It just kind of…ah…revealed you. That's all."

"Oh, God, I revealed my breast to the world, to the entire TV audience."

"And to the production crew," Margot added.

"Everyone saw it…Max and those silly brothers, too." Loretta Rose took a deep breath. "Well, I was afraid that might have happened. I noticed how everyone was staring at me. I thought it was because of what I'd said on camera to the brothers."

"It wasn't because of anything you said."

"Yeah, I saw how my shirt looked when I got home." She paused. "Well, that's that. Come on, Margot." She stopped. "Hey, how big was that rock you lost? I know it was huge, but how would it look all by itself?"

"It isn't *that* big. It was in a ring for heaven's sake. It was a smooth stone. That's the trouble, too. It won't catch the light very well."

"Nothing can catch the light in this dirt trap. Okay, we'll just look for a bump in the dust. Don't worry. If it's there, we'll find it."

They'd reached the first floor landing. "No point in searching here. We've already given it a good look. So where's the door to the upstairs? Here?" Loretta Rose reached out a hand and turned the knob.

The dirty tarnished knob turned and turned in her hand. "Shit," she said. "It isn't locked, is it? Did you lock it behind you, Margot?"

'Why would I do that?" And as she said "that" the entire apparatus came off in Loretta Rose's hand.

Her friend stared down at the hardware, a few errant bolts dropping noisily to the floor.

"This building is falling apart. I wonder if Carlos knows about the condition of the place outside his beautiful kitchen. Heck, he wouldn't care anyway. The whole place could fall down as long as the restaurant remains intact."

"Sounds like Max."

Loretta Rose chuckled. "Yeah, they are two rather similar types, aren't they. So here we go."

Putting the broken doorknob on the floor, she opened the door by sticking her fingers through the hole left by the hardware revealing the dingy narrow flight of steps leading upward. "Yuck," she said. "No wonder you got the willies in here."

"You should have been in it last night in the dark..."

They took the steps slowly, one at a time, Margot trailing behind, the beams from their flashlights canvassing every corner, every inch of every available surface. Step by step they climbed until they reached a second door. Loretta Rose carefully turned the doorknob and they stepped into the next landing.

"What floor is this?"

Margot shrugged. "It's got to be the second, right? We were on the first and now we're on the second."

"Cool. And you just walked from that door to this door, right?"

"Right."

Again the flashlights bobbed and weaved across the grime and they were face-to-face with the next flight of stairs.

"Jeeze," Loretta Rose said. "How many flights are there?"

"I told you, I don't know for sure. I forgot to count. Well, why would I have counted? I never thought I'd be retracing my footsteps. Oh, what's that?"

"That" was a tiny dead creature of some sort, so old it was desiccated, dry as a furry leaf. Loretta Rose kicked it aside.

They trudged upward, moving the lights over the bare stairs.

"You know, Loretta Rose," Margot said, "I was sure I heard someone coming up the stairs last night as I was feeling my way down. I know someone was there."

"You were probably hallucinating from fear."

"I know what I heard."

"But why would anyone be coming up here?"

"I can't think of any reason. All the rooms are empty."

"Did you check them on each floor?"

"Of course not. Why would I do that? I was just trying to get downstairs to where there was some damned light."

"Okay, okay. Just checking. But wait…" Loretta Rose stopped so abruptly that Margot ran into her back. "How will we know which floor you started on?"

"Well, I'm pretty sure I had to be at the top. I didn't see another stairwell leading up anywhere."

"Good. Well, let's snap it up then. I think we're both supposed to be working elsewhere, aren't we?"

Up they went to yet another floor. The spaces were so identical, every step was like déjà vu all over again. Finally, after a fruitless search of the last stairwell, they reached the top floor.

"Yuck," Loretta Rose said, "this air is awful. Talk about pollution. We're probably inhaling heaven knows what toxic substances."

"I think it's just dirty."

"Okay. So what did you do up here?"

"I got off the elevator down there and then walked down the hall to here. But I opened every room door for the light. See, they're still open. I didn't go inside any of them, though."

The doors yawned open up and down the hallway, the dark interiors of the closet-sized rooms unwelcoming and foreboding.

"Jeeze, what a dump. Come on. We'll start at the elevator and come back down this way. Drop something. See what way it rolls. I doubt if this floor is level."

"Drop what?"

"I dunno. Something roundish. Let's see." Loretta Rose stopped and yanking a pearl button off her shirt, dropped it onto the bare floor.

They stood fascinated as the button bounced and rolled off to finally stop against the hallway wall.

Margot looked at Loretta Rose. "Okay, now we've learned that the floor isn't level and your bra is showing. Again."

Loretta Rose looked down at her shirt gaping open where the button was missing. "Well, it's less than I showed the world last night, isn't it?" She sighed and picking up the button, tried her trick in physics again. Again it rolled against the wall.

"Off we go. Check the edges of the wall carefully."

Again they made their way down the hall toward the stairwell, Loretta Rose on one side, Margot on the other, heads bowed over the flashlight beams. They each looked into the deserted rooms that seemed even more dusty, deserted and identical in today's late afternoon light.

"Look in here, Loretta Rose," Margot said and pointed into the interior of the last room, prematurely dark thanks to the black curtains stapled haphazardly over the windows, the tarnished staples still visible.

"Weird. Those are blackout curtains, aren't they?"

"That's what I thought, too. Well, let's go. I'm supposed to be at a meeting at four."

"It's already five. You missed it."

Margot shrugged. Her assistants would have gone. They would tell her what she needed to know. She was not irreplaceable.

The same draft of dusty dry air met her nostrils as they began the downward climb. She was feeling depressed. All this trudging up and down and still no beautiful ruby. It had been so sweet of

Max to give it to her and look what had happened.

She twisted the ring round her finger as they went down stair after stair. Finally, Loretta Rose, still in the lead, stopped. Margot's heart began to race. Was it the stone at last?

"Look," Loretta Rose said, "look there."

Margot followed the beam and saw no ruby, but there was a strange pattern of marks in the corner of the landing. She bent closer. There were footprints in the thick dust that had collected at the bottom of the stairwell. Footprints close to the wall. She looked at her friend who had one dark eyebrow raised.

"Well, *we* didn't make those. We went right up the middle, didn't we?"

Margot nodded. "It was from those sounds I heard last night. I told you I heard *someone* down here."

"Yeah, well, let's get outta this place. It's giving me the creeps. And I'm sorry we didn't find the stone. It was really pretty."

Margot sighed and skirted the funny footprints. Loretta Rose flung open the hardware-less door to the main floor and stopped. Margot looked over Loretta Rose's shoulder. Elliot Ferrigan sat there in his wheelchair grinning at them and holding a beautiful, gleaming deep red stone between his thumb and forefinger.

"Yours?" He smiled at Margot. "One of the crew told everyone to be on the lookout for a fabulous lost gem."

Margot put out her hand and he dropped the ruby into her palm. She sighed with relief. Cool and heavy, the stone lay on her outstretched hand before she closed her fingers firmly around it. "Thank you so much, Elliot. Where did you find it?"

"Right over there," he said gesturing at some space against the wall. "So what were you two doing upstairs?"

"Oh, just looking for the stone. You know the elevator went

crazy last night and deposited me on the top floor. I had to walk all the way down in the dark. I thought I'd lost the ruby then."

He smiled again. "No, it was right down here all that time. Well, see you ladies later. Have to do some repair PR work about last night's…ah…show."

Loretta Rose couldn't seem to meet his gaze, bright circles of embarrassment back on her cheeks. "Nice of you to refer to it as an actual show, Elliot. I'm really sorry things got so out of hand."

"Don't apologize, Loretta Rose. I don't know what Raphael and Carlos thought they were doing, but it's done and we'll survive. People probably thought it was all a carefully scripted episode. Kind of a Jerry Springer show on speed."

He nodded and wheeled away down the hall.

"What a relief." Margot took a breath. "And he was nice about last night. He seems a very calm person."

"Yeah, not like some I could name. But Margot, you know it is a little bit strange that he found your ruby. I know I looked up and down this hall. You did, too. Why didn't we see the thing?"

Margot shrugged. "Could we have overlooked it?"

"Hell, no. I even found that piece of mouse. Nothing escaped us. Maybe old Elliot found it elsewhere and was struggling with a bad conscience over whether or not to give it up."

"Elliot Ferrigan doesn't need money."

"I know. There's the restaurant and it brings in a bundle. I think my wine bar is really going to take off, too. We're getting busy. Speaking of, I better get to work."

"Thanks for helping."

"Funny, isn't it?" Loretta Rose cocked her head. "We didn't discover a thing and you still got your ruby back."

Chapter XIX

MARGOT WALKED INTO HER EDITING OFFICE to find Max behind her desk. He stood up and enveloped her in his arms. "Guess what?"

She put her arms around him, very aware of her ringless finger. On the way to the studio she'd stopped at the jewelers and the stone was already being reset. Still she'd be without it for a day.

"What, Max? What's happened now?"

He burrowed his face against her neck. "It's not that bad. The cops called and told me Colin's place is available for us, the beneficiaries of record, to check out. We own it and everything in it. The police knew about the will. How the hell did they know? I guess they know everything, except, of course, whodunit. Hey, I wonder if that makes me a suspect in their eyes?"

Margot disentangled herself from his warmth and perched on the desk top. "Oh, Max. I'm sure we're all suspects of one sort or another. But we're just two of the hundreds that detective told me could have a motive. Colin was not well-beloved. Detective

Wilson was lamenting that neither murder was straightforward enough."

Max grunted. "Straightforward? Shit, murder's a crime of passion. Passion isn't straightforward."

"Maybe he meant something different. I don't know. But about Colin's things…are you going to go through them?"

"You mean *our* things? Yes, and I want company. You'll come, won't you?"

She bit her lip. "I can think of very few things I'd rather *not* do. We've never been to his place. What is it, a condo, a mansion off Beverly?"

"Neither. Believe it or not, he has a big old apartment not far from here, certainly not the trendiest part of town, for sure. Of course, he owns the whole frickin building, but still, that's where he chose to live. I don't think he stayed there all that much. And it's ours now, of course."

"He had to sleep somewhere."

"Yeah. Well, do you wanna do it? We'll check out our 'inheritance' and figure out what to do with it. Someone's gotta want it, preferably someone who didn't know Colin—maybe a nice nonprofit or a school or something."

She nodded and sighed. "I suppose so. Okay, I'll go with you."

"Yeah, babe. Gotta check out your half." Max wrapped an arm around her waist. "Dinner after?"

She smiled. "Lovely."

MAX DROVE SLOWLY UP TO THE OLD APARTMENT BUILDING that had been Colin Peabody's home and hideaway for so many years. The structure looked typical of the 1920s, certainly it had that distinctive California Mission architecture that was so popular then. The massive building, with the characteristic red tile roof parapets, looking like a mock defense for a mock castle, was set back from the street. The lawn was well-cared for, with two gigantic old fig trees drooping over the arcaded entry porch.

"It sure could use a paint job," Max said. "Colin was probably a horrible landlord. Can you imagine owing him rent? It would be a scene out of one of Dickens's more depressing stories. At least I'll finally get to see that wine cellar he was always bragging about. I'll keep the wine."

The sun had set and a queer, slate blue twilight was permeating the environs. But there was a friendly six-sided gold glass lantern shining from the ceiling inside the foyer as Max unlocked and opened the door for her.

"Top floor," Max said.

And what on earth could they do with all the property, all the possessions, she wondered. It was important not to waste everything. She just wished that Colin had included his wishes, or instructions, when he was making them his sole beneficiaries. She'd searched her memory to remember any charities or interests beyond himself that the man had revealed over the years. She couldn't recall one besides his obsessive interest in expensive wine and food.

The elevator—a normal-sized one, she was relieved to see—deposited them at the top, on the third floor, and she trailed after Max down the quiet, carpeted hall. He stood in front of a door at the end and sighing, inserted the key and opened the door.

The living room, long and spacious with arched windows and a gleaming parquet floor, looked dark and opulent in the fading light. Max took her hand and pulled her inside. They stood there, looking around the space, Colin's home away from the studio.

"Creepy," she whispered. "But he had beautiful things." She drew her fingers over the thickly woven, burgundy-colored fabric of an overstuffed chair.

"Yeah." Max stared at an artfully simple credenza, its fine woods glowing against the wall. "Some of it sure looks familiar. Hell, I'll bet half this stuff belongs to the Arcturus Property Department. How did the studio let him get away with stealing their good stuff?"

"That's what Loretta Rose wondered. She said she saw property department tags on some of the pieces when she stopped by for some papers. The studio must not know. They wouldn't allow this. Oh, Max, look at that incredible chandelier!"

"I've seen that piece before…in some goddamned flick," Max said. "Jeeze, it was in one of *our* flicks. We used that in the main house set on *Last Boundary*. Damn, I thought I recognized it. Wow, this is just great, isn't it? Good old Colin. Now we've inherited hot furniture."

They skirted the rest of the room and she followed him down a hallway, peering into the rooms. It was a large apartment, two bedrooms, a study, a huge bright, modern kitchen—Colin had prided himself on his culinary arts—and three bathrooms. Done in the style of the times, the closets were small but there were many of them. She kept her distance as Max opened one, searching for the elusive wine cellar.

"I don't want to see anything else, Max, " she said. "Let's just donate everything to some foundation and let them oversee getting rid of his things. This is creepy."

"Come on. There aren't any bogey men here. Colin was just Colin. We'll probably find some old moldy Playboy magazines he hid under the bed. That'll be the worst. I just wanna check out his study. And I wanna find the damned wine. If anything interesting is anywhere, it'll be where he worked."

"We've already found stolen furniture. Isn't that enough?" Still she followed him back down the hall and stood in the doorway of the study.

It was a pleasant room with only a simple Mission-style desk—also probably borrowed from the studio and never returned—occupying one corner and a comfortable looking chair with a tall reading light bending over it. A trio of narrow windows ranged behind the desk bathing the room in the cool twilight outside. There were no personal photos, aside from some publicity stills of him at this or that professional studio function. Four six-foot bookcases filled with books lined the walls. One also held the two golden Oscars he'd won, thanks to two of Max's films, the dwindling light gleaming softly off the faceless statues.

Max opened a closet door finding glistening, carefully labeled rows of bottles. "Hey, look at all that nice wine," he said. "Hmm, he did have some good stuff. Well, this is gonna be Colin's present to me. Thanks, old buddy. I'll just have to figure a way to get it over to my place.

Max closed the door. "I'm gonna check out the desk," he told her. "The police have already been through everything, but if there were any instructions for us or anyone, they'd be there." He shook himself like a puppy. "You're right though. It is kind of creepy. Can you imagine Colin lounging around in here? It's too nice, too gentlemanly. Colin was no gentleman. Why don't you check out the bookshelves. See if there's anything we'll want. I'll do the desk and then we're outta here."

Margot stepped over to the first shelf and began examining the titles, running her finger along the spines. Lots of books on filmmaking, movie history, specifically Hollywood's history, an entire shelf of scripts that he'd kept for some reason or other, shelves and shelves of wine books, and then the rest of the volumes were the usual books one picked up through life and couldn't bear to part with. The lure of the classics was apparent, even for Colin.

"Hey, what the hell?" Max stood over the desk, the drawers pulled open. "Some bozo's already gone through here."

"You said the police had been here."

"I don't think police people go through someone's stuff and leave it scattered around like this. There are papers all over the floor under here."

"You mean an unauthorized person went through the desk, too?"

"Yeah, unauthorized. You know, like a frickin burglar or something. I'll talk to that detective and see if they did this. If they didn't, I'd sure like to know who else has access to the apartment."

Feeling nervous, she turned back to the bookcase. Interesting, she thought, how little they had known about the man. All she'd seen of Colin were the shenanigans, the studio politicking, the love of intrigue, and the deft way he had of switching sides on practically everything at a moment's notice, no matter who it hurt or whose career he'd just ruined. She saw Max staring at a sheaf of papers. She watched him slid one item in his pocket.

"What was that?"

"Nothing you want to see, babe."

"Max, by the terms of his will, it's half mine."

"I don't think you want any part of this." He made a face. "Our Colin kept a youthful picture of himself *au naturel*, as the French say, with a funny looking feather mask as his only prop."

"How 'youthful'?"

"Not youthful enough. We're not talking about a family photo of the baby on the bearskin rug here."

"You mean he was into self porn? Oh, gross. Tell me no more." She paused, her imagination in overdrive. "Well, what are you going to do with *that*?"

"The picture? Destroy it. We don't want our benefactor to be considered any more peculiar than he already is. But there's more, too, babe." He held out a file. "More bad news. It seems we're the new owners of that building Carlos's restaurant is housed in. Our boy Colin bought the place in the early seventies."

"Oh no. Are you're sure it's that same awful building? The one with that horrible elevator?"

"Absolutely the same. Well, it does have a fine restaurant *and* a wine bar of some renown, not to mention a full TV studio. Just what we needed…"

Taking the papers, he grasped her hand and waited as she turned out lights and reached the front door. "Can't imagine we'll be coming back here," he said. He opened the door and following her out into the corridor, locked it behind them.

THE FOLLOWING AFTERNOON Margot stood in hazy sunshine looking at the crowd that had gathered outside on the lawn after Colin Peabody's memorial service. There were many of the same people attending who had been at Robert Madrid's memorial just a month earlier. The only people she didn't see were the Estrella family. Of course, there wasn't any reason they'd have come. The coincidence of the violent deaths was the only connection between the two murders, well, that and the method, the suffocation. But didn't lots of murderers suffocate their victims? Was all this linkage just conjecture? Louisa Estrella seemed to have hinted at that. Something about the police and their logic…

"I talked to Detective Wilson this morning," Max said. "He assured me his men do not leave papers all over anyone's floor. They're going back over today to check out whether there was a break-in."

"Great. That's just great, isn't it? Now I wonder what we missed seeing, what whoever it was took from the place?"

"We'll never know. Wilson said the police have a box of Colin's things they confiscated hoping they were relevant to the crime, but they turned out to be nothing. And the box belongs to us, too, of course. And I'm supposed to go pick it up. Jeeze, will it ever end? Hey, who are you watching?" He was following her gaze to one of the groups standing about, chatting and looking somber, as befitted the occasion.

"Your new producer. He looks mean."

"Yeah? Old Charlie? Nah, he always looks that way. He's just one of the few who doesn't use Botox to tone down the wrinkles. He's a good enough guy. At least the studio assigned *someone* for us. Sure better than shutting down the whole frickin production. I don't expect him to have any problems—Colin may have been a you-know-what," he said, lowering his voice, "but he didn't leave loose ends once production started. See, there won't be anything for Charlie to do anyway. Hey, Charles!" he called, waving to the thin, gray-haired man who waved back toward them with a certain lack of enthusiasm.

"Look how he's looking at me," Max said with a laugh. "Colin told everyone I was the devil to work with. I love a reputation like that. Keeps 'em all on their tippy-toes. So who else is here today?"

At that moment Jonathan Keller, Max's first assistant director, walked up. His normally vulpine features were sporting a furtive, feral look like a rabbit that's being chased. Margot looked behind him, but didn't see anyone following the man.

"What's up, Jonathan?" Max said.

At least they were talking, she thought. She could think of several instances where they hadn't been and she'd had to serve as intermediary for some crucial production discussion. It had been awful.

"What's up yourself, Max?" Keller said. "Jesus, look around you. Two murders. That's what's up. And we knew both the guys."

"You knew Madrid?"

"Well, sure I did. I used to hang around sometimes when they were first taping the show, before it became Ferrigan's big hit. At least Madrid was a cool guy. Elliot liked him a lot. I mean he was Ferrigan's big star and then Elliot and I go back a long way, as you know."

Margot remembered that peculiar twosome lurking about her editing room looking for that murder scene of Max's and heaven's knew what else was on their agenda that day. Well, Elliot hadn't exactly lumbered, but he'd been just as invasive wheeling about in his electric chair.

"Old Colin probably deserved exactly what happened," Jonathan said. "But I don't get the wine barrel bit."

"Nobody gets it, Keller."

"I meant it might have meaning, at least to the killer, doncha think?" The man looked back over his shoulder.

Margot's gaze followed his.

"Elliot and I are the last ones now," he muttered.

"The last ones *what?*" Max was obviously bored with the conversation.

"Just the last ones. You know. We all started out together here in the seventies. Kept in touch through all the years.That sort of thing."

"So you think you might be *next?*" Max said. "You're thinking that some weird serial killer is offing people who lived in Hollywood in the seventies? Is that what's bothering you?"

And for the first time Margot could ever recall, Jonathan Keller blushed.

"Not really, Max," he said, head bowed. "It's just all so strange, kinda scary, you know."

"You look scared, Keller," he replied. "If someone were after you, this would be a good time for them to make their move."

"Max!" Margot couldn't help it, the conversation shocked her. What if that police detective happened to be listening? Max's nasty comments practically constituted a threat.

At Max's comment, however, the natural Jonathan Keller negative personality gene revived and he gave Max the most hate-filled look. Actually Margot didn't blame him, at least not today. Well, they were all on edge. Two memorials for two murder victims in a month. No wonder Jonathan was acting even more peculiar than usual.

"Lay off, Max," Jonathan snarled. "You hated Colin, too. And then he goes and leaves you guys all his money."

"How did you hear about that?" Max asked, anger in his tone.

"Everyone knows. I dunno who told me, but everyone knows. It's true, isn't it?"

"Yeah, so it's true. So what?"

"So how much are you getting?"

"None of your goddamned business, Jonathan. Lay off."

"Well, you must have had time to go through his papers. Can't you tell how much is there?"

"We haven't determined the amount and, believe me, you'll be the last person to know."

"But you hated Colin," he repeated.

Margot looked around the parking lot, but there was no place to hide from this frightful "B" movie conversation. The car was locked. She was doomed to listen.

"We *all* hated Colin, Jonathan," Max said coldly. "He was a real shit. You know that. Still there's a difference between hating someone and stuffing them in a wine barrel. Did you do that, Jonathan? Did you stuff our old pal Colin in a wine barrel?"

Keller looked at Max and shook his head. "You could be on the list, too, you know, Skull. The kill list. Colin may have been a total shit, but he protected you. Look at them over there. All the studio execs. All those people you've pissed off for so long with your frickin artsy films that don't make as much money as they want them to. Maybe you're the one who better watch out."

He turned and left them without so much as a goodbye or a nod.

Margot watched him walk away. "What was that all about?" she asked.

Max shrugged. "I dunno. Did you listen to him though? Jeeze, what a weird conversation. He made it sound like he's the last surviving member of a goddamn tontine or some other stupid thing. He is so incredibly medieval." He shook his head. "Where the hell did I dig Keller up from? How have I managed to do five films with him as my first AD and not ended up stuffing his skinny body somewhere?"

Margot felt tired. "That's not really a question, is it, Max? It's reverse chemistry or something. You two work well together. You know that."

"Well, I admit one thing. He sure keeps me alert on the set. I have to watch my back with ole Jonathan every moment of every production, just making sure he doesn't have a chance to slip the old knife in."

She shivered. "When do you think everyone else will hear about the contents of Colin's will and us?"

"You heard him, kiddo. People know already. Let's get outta here. That bunch over there is beginning to give me the creeps."

Margot glanced back over. A circle of studio execs, dressed nearly identically in designer suits and light blue ties, heads bent toward each other, were discussing something they obviously thought important. She prayed the conversation wasn't about Max.

There was a great burst of laughter from someone in the circle that floated on the still air. It was quickly quelled with audible shushes. Decorum, real or imagined, reigned again. She took Max's hand and they walked in silence to the car. Somehow, here they were, as much outsiders as insiders, carrying the fast-dying secret of Colin's embarrassing beneficence home with them.

They were nearly to the car when Margot turned at a whirring sound behind them. Elliot Ferrigan was there, smiling brightly at them.

"Quite a show, wasn't it?" he asked. "I never know how to behave at these memorial things. Do we celebrate the life or mourn the death?"

Margot smiled. "I think it's supposed to be both, but one or the other usually gets short shrift, doesn't it?"

"It did today, don't you think? I really thought the studio would have more to say about Colin's career, and yours, too, for that matter, Max. But the accolades were minimal, weren't they? And I don't really see how they can ever separate yours and Colin's work."

Max scowled. "Jeeze, Elliot. What a shitty thing to say. So now I've got to be bound to the bastard through life *and* death?"

She thought Elliot looked unperturbed by Max's outburst. Of course, this man directed authentic star chefs on his TV show. He must be used to seeing adults throw tantrums.

"So what's your best guess on our killer," Elliot asked.

Max shrugged. "Could've been me. I don't mean Robert's, but that Colin… He still makes me mad and now there's no way I can shout at him anymore."

Elliot nodded, eyebrows raised. "I know what you mean. I've known Colin since we both came to town, both of us determined to have it laying at our feet by age twenty-five. So," he smiled again, "it didn't quite happen, but we've all done okay."

"By any standards," Max said. "Yeah, we all do the best we can and hope the idiots at the top don't screw us up too badly. But," he said more slowly, "to answer your question about whodunit…

well, I'm pretty sure it's one of us. Maybe one of those power suits standing over there, looking like a bunch of starving vultures ready for a really fattening meal. Who knows."

"Right." Elliot wheeled closer to the car. "And then you two have a pretty traditional motive now, don't you? I mean the will and all that…" he said.

Margot's heart sank. Jonathan hadn't made it up. The news was really out.

"Where'd you hear that?" Max asked.

"Oh," Elliot made a sweeping gesture. "That's all anyone is talking about today. Quite a windfall, too, isn't it? A zillion dollars or so, right?"

Max frowned. "Yeah, quite a surprise from the old codger. We're trying to figure out what to do with it all," he added.

Elliot made a face. "Plenty of good places for charity," he said. "I have a couple of favorites if you need a list. So, hey, have you checked out the booty yet?"

Max scowled. "Yeah," he said. "We were over at his place yesterday. Funny. Someone else seems to have gone through his desk even before we got there. Had to call in the cops about that."

Elliot looked shocked. "Burglarized? Colin's apartment? That's terrible. Must have been the killer culprit, don't you think? Did you find out what was taken?"

"Have no idea, Elliot. Having never been on the premises myself before, it was hard to figure out what was missing. Well," Max glanced at his watch. "Time for us to mosey on. See you, Elliot. Oh, and sorry about the other night. That was some rip-roaring episode of *The Late Night Chef.*"

"You're telling me," he said. "You ought to see the stacks of emails. And most of the audience absolutely loved it! Loretta Rose is approaching goddess status with the viewers. She was a hit with all the demographics, the feminists, the college crowd, grandmas, little boys under ten, everyone. Even some group calling themselves Dykes with Knives that, my assistant tells me, is a very influential group of female star chefs, was enthusiastic. I may have the daring duo back on someday. Well, then, of course, Raphael *would* kill me. Carlos and Loretta Rose had some chemistry going, didn't they?"

They waved goodbye and climbed into the sun-soaked car.

"What a funny dorp he is," Max muttered. "He's nice enough, I guess. Weird that he and old Jonathan asked the same questions about the murders."

"Oh, that's all anyone is thinking about these days. Anyway, those two are a real team, I think," she said. "As he said, they've known each other forever. And they work together, too, though toward which ends I have no idea."

"I don't care what they've done in the business. They're still a couple of striving wannabes, that's what they are. Ambition sticks out all over the two of them. Not a pretty sight." He shifted gears and they rolled out of the mortuary parking lot.

They were nearly to her apartment when her cell phone rang.

"Margot? It's Ivy. Someone's been in the apartment. Where are you? Come home!"

"You mean burglars? What did they take?"

"I can't tell. Sophie just got here. She called the cops."

"We'll be there in ten minutes." Margot hung up and looked at Max. "You heard," she said. "A break-in, Max, but this time at *my* place. Hurry."

Chapter XX

B Y THE TIME MAX PULLED UP outside the apartment house with a squeal of brakes, a police car was already double parked, blue lights flashing. Curious neighbors stood on the sidewalk.

Margot leaped out of the car, explained who she was to the policeman at the door, and ran inside, Max following right behind her. Sophie and Ivy stood in the living room answering questions from a young uniformed cop busy taking notes.

Sophie excused herself and came over shaking her head. "We don't know what's missing, Margot. I've checked all the obvious things people steal, but just look over there, we've still got the DVD, the TV, all that stuff burglars are supposed to love to fence. But it looks as though they did go through our bedrooms, the drawers and stuff. I can't imagine what they expected to find in our bedrooms. Better check your room."

Margot and Max hurried through the room and down the hall to her bed-sitting room, Sophie following. And Sophie was right. The drawers in Margot's bureau were ransacked, her bedside table drawer left open.

"But I don't have anything of interest or value here, Max. I just have a few work papers and some personal correspondence. What do you think they were looking for?"

"Well, babe, there's only one thing that's different in our lives now. Old Colin's frickin will. You've never had a burglary here before, have you? I bet someone was after some kind of information that Colin had and this idiot heard about the will and figured that we might have it now." He paused. "My God, I hope I'm not next on this character's to-do list."

"But what would a burglar be looking for?"

"Oh, hell, I dunno. With someone like Colin you'd never know for sure, but he was probably into something illegal, or pretty illegal. Colin was forever after easy money. I always thought he would have made a great, greedy blackmailer." Max massaged his chin. "So maybe incriminating information was still in his desk and I just didn't see it when we went through his stuff. I mean why should he hide it? The guy didn't know he was going to be offed, did he? Then, whoever it is doing these break-ins is trying to recover the evidence, save themselves from paying the dough. Hey, it's just like some dumb movie plot."

"But Colin's *dead*, Max," Sophie said. "Why would the burglar be so hot to lay his hands on any incriminating evidence now that the guy he has to pay the dough to is *dead*?"

Max shrugged. "Maybe the information is *so* incriminating that they just figured Margot and I would take over. I mean easy money is easy money."

"Us as blackmailers? When we've got all that money? That's ridiculous, Max," Margot said.

"Okay, but, I don't like this kind of action going on. How did the burglar get in here, Sophie?"

"A window seems to be the cop's best theory. There was one that was open a crack. The cops can't find any other way that looks forced or anything. We've got to be more careful locking up, Margot. And what are you guys talking about, anyway? What will? What money? Did Colin leave you something?"

Margot exchanged a look with Max.

"We were waiting to tell you and Ivy," Max began as they walked slowly back out to the living room where Ivy was entertaining the policemen with an anecdote from her life as a daytime soap opera star. He seemed eager to ask for an autograph. The officers snapped to attention as the three of them reentered the room.

"We've dusted for prints on the sill," the younger officer said. "That's about all we can do until you determine what exactly is missing."

Well, that's the strange part," Max said. "There doesn't appear to be anything missing."

"Must have been scared off by something. Well, that's your good luck." The other policeman handed Max a card. "Please call us if you find something gone that we can trace. You know, all the electronics have serial numbers on them, things like that."

They shook hands all around, the younger officer lingering over Ivy's handshake, and left.

"So?" Sophie said crossly. "What's going on?"

"What's going on where?" Loretta Rose poked her head around the open front door. "Hey, did you know cops have been in this apartment house? Wonder what's going on with that. Is that what you guys are talking about?"

"Come in," Margot said. "We've got some news we've been waiting to tell you all."

"No!" Loretta Rose said. "You didn't?'

Max looked bemused. "Didn't what?"

"You know. Get married!"

"Jeeze, you guys. Don't you think we'd mention something like that? No, this is pretty nasty stuff we want to tell you about." There was silence as the three women focused on him. "Colin Peabody left Margot and me everything."

More silence followed this pronouncement. Finally, "Everything?" This was from Ivy, eyes wide. "You mean *everything*? But the man was fabulously wealthy. Why did he do that?"

Max shook his head. "We don't know. But he did. I've got his stock in the studio. We have that apartment building he lived in. And the restaurant building, the whole building. And other things, too…" Margot heard his voice pause and stop. "It's all too much. We don't know what we'll do with it all."

Loretta Rose sank down onto the sofa. "Give it to me. I'm deserving, especially after all the crappola I put up with old Colin."

Max wagged a finger at her. "No, I get that honor, Loretta Rose. Can you imagine what it was like to have him hanging around *five* feature film productions? Producers are supposed to disappear after they raise the money and get us all hired. Not Colin. He used to just pace around offering everyone suggestions—even the electricians, believe it or not—day after frickin day." He sighed. "It was ludicrous. So, maybe he just thought I'd paid my dues and he gave me the honor of disposing of his, probably ill-gotten, gains."

"What about me?" Margot said. "He left me half, too."

Ivy and Sophie looked at her, shocked.

"I know he did, babe. And, you know what?" Max said, "I

don't really get that part of it. Why should he give you half? Were you nice to the old bastard when I wasn't looking?"

"Of course not."

"He thought of you two as a team," Ivy said. "Face it, guys, you are a team, a Hollywood team, a romantic Hollywood team. Just because you don't live together or anything doesn't change that."

"Whadaya mean 'or anything'?" Max said. "I'm a real romantic guy. And Margot knows that. Margot knows I love her, don't you, Margot?"

Margot looked at him. She guessed that she knew. It really didn't matter. Ivy was right. She and Max were a team and they just seemed to go on and on together, enjoying each other's company, without a pause. Maybe that's what love was all about. And Luis, of course. Luis shared their love. But the subject wasn't something she felt like discussing in depth with her housemates and her flaky friend.

"No sense in making Margot blush," Loretta Rose said. "So, big deal. Now our best friends are filthy rich. We'll just have to live with it. This won't make us love you guys less."

They all laughed and the slight tension eased. Margot walked with Max to the front door.

"I'll be in touch later." He caressed the back of her neck. "Let me know if you figure out if anything's missing." He looked over her shoulder. "You know your housemates are nuts, don't you? Loretta Rose is nuts, too. I don't know how you all live together."

Margot laughed and watched him go. Love? Did she really love Max? She wasn't sure but whatever it was she felt, she knew she didn't want to live without him.

She was on her way back to her bedroom to check out the

damage when her cell phone rang. It was Max.

"Hey, babe," he said. "Forgot. One of us has to pick up the stuff the police confiscated from Colin's. They said they have a whole box. I've got a meeting in half an hour. I'd skip it but it's with the studio execs and our new producer. Can you do it? The cops said to just tell the desk that they have something for us. It'll be waiting."

"Max…"

"Come on, babe. Do this for us. The sooner we get all the loose ends squared away on this Colin thing, the sooner we'll be out from under his infamous executive thumb. Take Sophie or someone. Sophie or Loretta Rose would probably enjoy going to the police station. Hey, and lock everything up. I can't believe you guys left a window open for some bozo."

"Okay. I'll call you later. Maybe there's a great new script in the box or something fun."

"That's the spirit, babe. I knew I could count on you."

He hung up and she made a face at the little phone before putting it down.

"Who wants to come to the police station with me?" she called out.

"Boring," called back Sophie. "Who's under arrest?"

"No one. I just have to pick up something they took from Colin's apartment."

"Still boring, Margot. You do it and we'll see you back here. Loretta Rose and Ivy and I are going to make dinner. Himself, the star chef is joining us."

"Really? Carlos is coming?"

Loretta Rose smiled broadly. "The very same. I told him I'm introducing him to the family tonight."

Margot picked up her car keys, the damned cell phone that Max insisted she carry at all times, and left the apartment.

FIFTEEN MINUTES LATER she was inside the police station, back at the desk she'd come to with the recipe she'd found after Robert's death. It could have been the same clerk who listened to her rambling explanation of why she was here and then pointed down the hallway. "Door 12," he said. "They'll be able to help you in there."

She thanked him and walked into the corridor, checking the doors for number 12. She knocked on the door. When no one answered, she peered inside. The room had a counter and two uncomfortable plastic chairs sitting vacant. The room was deserted. There was another door, half ajar, behind the counter. From inside, she could hear voices. Walking to the counter, she rapped on it with her ring.

A uniformed policeman stuck his head out. Seeing her, he closed the inner door behind him and took up his position behind the counter, looking suddenly official.

"I've come for the box the police took from Colin Peabody's house," she said. "I'm Margot O'Banion and they said I could pick it up in here."

The officer scanned a list on the counter top. "I have here that a Mr. Max Skull will be picking it up."

"Well, he couldn't come because he's in a meeting. We're both beneficiaries of Mr. Peabody's will and what you've taken rightfully belongs to us."

The man looked at her. "I.D.?"

She pulled out her driver's license and waited while he read it through.

"Okay," he said. "I'll just call Mr. Skull and make sure it's all right with him. We have a number for him right here. Shouldn't take a minute."

She nodded and looked at the wanted posters crookedly fastened to a wall with stick pins while the phone call was made. It was probably interrupting Max at his meeting. She didn't care. She just wanted this loose end, as he'd described it, taken care of so she could go home. Maybe Sophie or Ivy would have some good ideas about what to do with their unsolicited windfall.

"Mrs. O'Banion?" the officer called to her, putting down the phone. "Mr. Skull says it's okay. He said to check your I.D. I told him we always do that."

Margot nearly laughed. Wait till she saw Max. Check her I.D., indeed.

"Okay, now," the officer was saying, his head bent over a cardboard carton. "Let me make sure that what's here goes along with the manifest."

She waited as he appeared to be ticking off this and that item.

"Just one thing missing. I'll be right back and you can take this off our hands."

Margot watched as he covered the top of the carton with the cardboard flaps and opening the door behind him, stuck his head inside.

"She's out here," she heard him say. "Come on, give it over."

Curious, she quickly walked behind the counter and peering

over his shoulder, looked into a small room. The lights were off but she could see a couple of figures sitting inside, back lit by the light of a small projection screen. Dancing across the screen were the grainy figures of three people in a small room.

Margot stepped back quickly. For heaven's sake, they were watching a porn flick. How embarrassing. The policeman turned as she hurried back to her place on the visitor's side of the counter. She could feel her face flushing, but it could be no redder than that of the cop's, now with a video cassette in hand. Oh no, he was putting it with the other things in the carton.

"Sorry about that," he said. "It all belongs to you now. Just sign here."

She picked up the box. "Thanks for your help."

The box wasn't heavy. Probably just papers, oh, and, of course, that damned video. What on earth was Colin thinking, leaving something like that laying around for just anyone to find? Of course, as she'd pointed out to Max more than once, Colin didn't know he was going to be killed. He didn't know the police would be searching through his things. And heavens, what did he care now? Any ancient indiscretions of the dead were always left for the domain of the living to attend to.

On the drive home, Margot's mind whirled. So much had happened in the past couple of months. But Max's film was still on schedule. It was nearly finished. That was good news, but she didn't trust any of the suits she'd seen at the memorial to really care, one way or the other, about *Extreme Cuisine*.

So Carlos Estrella was coming for dinner. No wonder Loretta Rose had looked so cheerful. They must be pretty serious for her to have him over with all of them there. She must know they'd each be carefully evaluating the new relationship with the usual critique offered, if asked for, or even if not asked for. There had certainly been plenty of discussion over the breakfast table after the famous live *The Late Night Chef* episode had aired. Sophie maintained she'd never seen a more lustful TV show. Margot smiled at the thought. Well, maybe Sophie was right. So after dinner, she and Ivy and Sophie could watch a video in Sophie's room and leave the happy couple to the romance of the fireplace…a video….

Margot thought of the nasty piece she was carrying back to the apartment in the carton on the back seat. She saw again the black and white frames going across the screen. Three very underdressed people, the depressing-looking, tiny room, really just big enough for the unmade bed that was the only set decoration.

The room! She nearly pulled over to the curb, feeling herself flush as a realization hit her. She *knew* that room. She'd seen it twice. There was no way two rooms would have the same awful pair of blackout curtains stapled to the window frame. The porn flick had been filmed in those little hotel rooms above Café Estrellado. Oh God, in the old building that she and Max now owned. So why in heaven's name did Colin have a copy of a video like that? Maybe Max was correct. Blackmail.

She dug her cell phone out of her purse and at the first red light, speed dialed Max's private number. He answered on the first ring.

"What's up, babe?" he whispered. "I'm in this meeting, remember? Already this yahoo from the police department called me up to verify you."

"I know. He was just doing his job. But Max, this is important. Come to the apartment as soon as you can."

"Are you okay? Is anything wrong?"

"I'm fine. I just want to show you something. I'll have it at the apartment."

"Soon as I can, babe."

He hung up and she tossed the phone onto the passenger seat as she negotiated the heavy commute traffic.

Fifteen minutes later she pulled up to the apartment. A slick, low slung, black car had her usual parking space. It must be Carlos's. It certainly looked like a car a star chef would drive.

The apartment was alive with people and chatter and wonderful smells drifting out from the kitchen. Margot lugged in the box of Colin's things. She smiled at the group and made her way to her bedroom. After dumping the contents on her bed, she began sifting through the accumulated things from Colin's desk. The video in question was on top and she put it aside. Finally she upended the box and spread the papers across the surface of the bed. She picked a few up at random. They appeared to be legal documents, mostly for stocks and property Colin had acquired and sold through the years. Egad. More properties? Max would have a fit. Well, he could go through all this.

She picked up the video and walked out to the kitchen. She greeted Carlos Estrella more formally and blushed as he kissed her hand.

"Sophie?" she said. "Okay if I check out something on your VCR?"

"Sure. Dinner's going to be ready in…what, Ivy?…about half an hour. Is Max coming?"

"I called him. Don't wait dinner for him though. He's in a meeting."

She walked into Sophie's room and slipped the video in the slot. Taking the remote, she sat down in one of the two easy chairs the room provided. She took a deep breath and switched on the machine.

The film was more of exactly what she'd seen, albeit briefly, at the police station. It was a rather carefully done hardcore porn epic, about grade D, she estimated, instead of the usual F. After two minutes, she put the machine on pause. It was awful to watch. But there, behind the contorted figures of two of the actors, was the same pair of blackout curtains in the room above Café Estrellado. She could see the staples. Or maybe she couldn't, but just knew they were there. The mind was a curious thing. What significance this had, she couldn't decide, but now the building was partly theirs and, boy, this better not have been a recent production. She could imagine the reaction of the diners spending God-knew-what for dinner if they thought something like this was going on several stories above the famous chi-chi restaurant.

She heard the living room door slam and Max's voice greeting everyone. She shut off the VCR, leaving the video inside. "Max?" she called. "Could you come down to Sophie's room? There's something I want to show you."

She heard some laughter at something someone said and then Max's distinctive, brisk stride was coming down the hall. She poked her head out the door.

"Max! I have the papers from Colin, but wait till you see what they were watching down at the police station. The guy had to go and get it away from the others so I could bring it home."

He came in and sat down in a chair. "Go for it, babe. What hath Colin wrought this time?"

"Well, " she said, picking up the remote, "it's not that surprising, really, considering that photo you found of him…"

"The nature study?"

She relaxed, glad as always to be able to discuss the undiscussible with Max. "Exactly," she said. "It's definitely a porn film. But what caught my eye was *where* this atrocity was filmed. Right in that building we own now. Right over Café Estrellado and the TV studio. What I want you to determine is *when* this thing was filmed. What if it's going on right now, right now in our very own building?"

"Well, babe, filming porn ain't illegal. You know that."

"I don't care about that. I just don't want it being done where I know it's going on and especially if we're the owners of the place. Wouldn't we have some liability or something?"

"Hmm, maybe so. Well, switch the beauty on. Lemme take a look at the thing."

Ten minutes later, he sat back with a loud groan. "Jeeze," he said. "What incredible dreck. What's the name of this thing?"

"*Hot to Trot.*"

"Shit. We're not going to see horses join the fray, are we?"

"I don't think that would be feasible, thank heavens. If I'm right, they're filming on the fourth floor in an old building with a broken elevator. Well, it's *supposed* to be broken."

"Okay. Start her up again and I'll try to figure out when this literary wonder was filmed. Holy smokes, what are they doing now?"

Margot didn't answer.

Sophie came into her bedroom. "Hi guys. Good Lord, what are you watching on my VCR?"

Margot quickly put the remote on "pause" but it was too late. And Sophie's VCR was famous for its freeze-frame quality. The scene she paused at was clear as a bell. Plus this particular frame was even worse, if that were possible, than several preceding it.

"It was in Colin's things," she said. "The police were watching it. I think it was made in that building we own now."

"Oh great," Sophie said. "Another star in old Colin's crown. So what are you watching it for, or should I ask?"

"We're trying to figure out when it was made, smarty," Max said. "Any ideas? How about clothes. Do the clothes tell you what era we're in here?"

"What clothes?" she said.

"Aren't they supposed to be wearing condoms?" This was from Sophie who was staring intently at one of the figures.

"Are they?"

"Sure. AIDS and all that."

"Well," Max said, staring intently at one figure. "If that's the case, then we're talking what…mid-seventies here. I'd bet anything the porn industry wasn't exactly on the cutting edge of social awareness then. Anyway, remember when the second guy came in, Margot? I swear he was wearing trousers with a flare at the bottom. Not quite bell-bottoms, but close. Seventies."

"I didn't notice."

"Yeah." He chuckled. "I saw you with your eyes closed."

"Maybe they got the trousers at a used clothing store. That doesn't tell us anything."

"Okay." Max snapped his fingers. "But it was done on celluloid. You can tell it was transferred from celluloid. As Loretta Rose is so eager to point out, no one does celluloid anymore. This isn't digital. That makes it not current. Is that enough for you? It is for me. And I've seen more than enough." He stood up, stretching. "So big deal. It's an old tape. No one's running a blue production company on our time now. What's for dinner?"

Chapter XXI

MARGOT AWAKENED TO THE SOUND OF RAIN pelting her window. The air from her open window smelled thick with scents from the garden, the wet asphalt of the street, the accumulated dust and debris of the past six dry months being swept away.

Rainstorms in L.A. were rare. They were also highly inconvenient for a population that viewed them as a novelty that generally happened elsewhere. The streets would be hazardous. No one owned an umbrella. She looked at the clock. She'd need extra time to get to the studio this morning.

Last night had been fun. Carlos was a riot. Margot and the roommates agreed that he and Loretta Rose made a great couple. There had been ample teasing about Colin's taste in movie fare, but mostly they talked about inconsequential things. It was nice to have an evening filled with laughter, for a change.

Before leaving the apartment, she retrieved the nasty video from Sophie's VCR and tucked it into her purse. The police had confiscated it, but had Detective Wilson viewed it? She knew some police had been watching it, but it didn't seem to her that they'd been actually investigating anything. And this was not a fun and games video. Laughter aside, it was a part of something else. Why else would Colin have kept it and stashed it in his desk? Plus Detective Wilson must know it had been produced in the very same building they'd discovered Colin's body. Was that a link? If not, it was a heck of a coincidence. She'd drop the cassette off when she could.

Margot spent the day in her editing room putting several scenes together with Max's notes from the dailies guiding her. She knew he felt the strain of wanting to finish the film quickly and his subtle exhortations to get things done quickly now were not lost on his crew, including her.

The rain continued throughout the day and the darkened sky made the time feel later than it was. She began to clean up the clutter at five-thirty when the telephone rang.

"Margot. It's me," said Loretta Rose. "Carlos says you are to get over here, immediately."

Margot blinked. "To the restaurant? What's wrong? What is Carlos talking about?"

"His mother is here. She told him to get in touch with you. She needs you."

"Louisa? What on earth is she doing there now? What's going on?"

"They're all down in the basement studio." Loretta Rose's voice was barely a whisper. "Carlos caught one of the scenes from that video you and Max were watching last night. He's really upset. Hurry, Margot."

Margot put down the phone. Carlos upset about the porn video? It was a joke when Loretta Rose and Sophie showed him briefly what she'd been given at the police station. Surely he didn't think she and Max were watching that garbage for *fun?* What had Loretta Rose told the man? Carlos must be thinking the entire apartment was filled with crazy women with kinky tastes, not to mention their significant others.

Well, whatever it was, it sounded like a huge misunderstanding. She'd drop by the restaurant. Maybe Loretta Rose would give her a glass of wine.

Rain fell as she parked behind the building in the restaurant lot. She hurried to the front entrance and stepped inside. There were already a few patrons at this early, by L.A. standards, dinner hour. The room smelled great and she suddenly realized she'd skipped lunch. She nodded to the maitre d' and walked into the wine bar. The wine bar was definitely busy. People stood two deep at the counter and the little tables were occupied. She stepped to the side and waited until Loretta Rose put down a wine bottle and came over.

Her friend was looking her usual calm-under-stress self. Margot didn't know how she did it.

"Margot," she said, "what took you so long?"

Margot gave her a look.

"Better get down to the basement. Louisa Estrella's waiting for you."

"I'm not going down anywhere until you tell me what's going on."

"Okay. Hey, Esteban," she called to a young man carrying in a wine carton. "Take over for me for five minutes, will you? And, remember, we're just serving the Cabs and the Zins tonight, no Merlots."

The man nodded and stepped to the center of the wine bar, thirsty customers at the ready, their glasses held out like the mouths of famished baby birds.

Loretta Rose grabbed Margot's arm and led her to a relatively quiet corner, near the door to the kitchen. "Look in there." She opened the door a crack.

Inside the kitchen, noisy pandemonium reigned. This wasn't the usual chaos. This felt like panic. She felt her eyes widen. "What's going on?"

"All the sauces curdled. Carlos is having to make them all over again. He'd talk with you about mama, but he can't leave those pans right now. Really. This is a culinary crisis of the first order, Margot."

Margot nodded. What did she know about sauces? "So you fill me in, okay, Loretta Rose? I've worked hard all day and I'm hungry."

"Okay, okay." Loretta Rose cast a look at the wine bar, then pushed Margot through the door into the kitchen. Carlos didn't look up. He had four copper pans on top of a stove. Somehow he seemed to be stirring the contents of all four at once. The rest of the kitchen crew was keeping a safe, diplomatic distance from him, eyeing him nervously, ready for whatever command he might issue. Loretta Rose was right. This seemed a major kitchen crisis.

Loretta Rose propelled her through the room and out the mean little door leading to the corridor. As soon as they stepped through, Margot could tell this wasn't an ordinary day in the usually quiet part of the building, either. Far off, muffled by the stairwell, came the sound of angry voices. People were arguing in the studio basement.

She looked at Loretta Rose, eyebrows raised.

"It's Ferrigan and that dreadful Jonathan Keller. Come on. That's where Mama Estrella is, too."

They hurried down the hallway, coming to a stop at the head of the stairs. Staring down the flight of stairs, Margot could just get a glimpse of a corner of Elliot Ferrigan's wheelchair. Someone else—was it Jonathan?—stood next to him.

"Go down there," Loretta Rose said. "She's waiting for you."

"Waiting for me to do what?" Margot stopped moving. "You'd better come with me."

"Okay, but I've got to get right back to the wine bar. Come on."

They walked down the stairs, their heels making tapping noises on the bare boards. Not that any noise made any difference. The closer they got to the basement landing, the louder the voices became.

"You both be quiet," a voice ordered.

Margot glanced at Loretta Rose who nodded. "Mama Estrella," she said.

Margot took the last step and stopped so suddenly she felt Loretta Rose's weight on her back. She blinked. The men, their backs to her, were frozen, staring fixedly ahead of them at the black clad figure of Louisa Estrella who was pointing a pretty little pearl-handled gun at them.

"Is that real?" Margot whispered to Loretta Rose.

"Looks real to me. I don't think Mama Estrella would mess around with a toy."

"There you are, Ms. O'Banion," Louisa called out. The gun never wavered. "Come over here, if you please. I need your opinion."

Margot turned to Loretta Rose. "Go call the police. Get that Detective Wilson. Tell him what's going on."

"What's going on?"

"Are you blind. She's got a gun pointed at two men. Get Carlos. That's *his* mother who's run amuck."

"She won't do anything. Anyway, I told you. Carlos can't leave the sauces. Tonight's menu will be ruined if they curdle again. You've got to understand the significance of good sauces…"

Margot shook her head. "Well, call *someone*. Call Max. Find Raphael. Call *somebody* and do it right away. She's got a damned gun!"

"I'm sure she won't hurt them. But, okay," Loretta Rose said. "I'll hurry."

Margot heard her friend's light footsteps as she sped up the stairs.

The bright lights of the TV studio seemed unnaturally harsh after the gloom of the rainy day. She skirted the two men, still as statues, and walked to Louisa Estrella's side. She looked down at the gun in the woman's white hand, the knuckles even whiter as she firmly clutched the weapon. Mrs. Estrella had a very steady hand, she noticed.

Margot looked at the two men, their eyes never straying from Mrs. Estrella. Jonathan Keller, his normally pallid face even more so this evening. Amazing, she thought. His complexion had truly turned gray. He steadied himself with one hand, pinched fingers showing the strain, on the back of Elliot Ferrigan's wheelchair. Elliot didn't look any happier than Jonathan, his gaunt face haggard and white.

Now Margot looked at Mrs. Estrella, the woman's smooth hair slicked into a thickly braided roll at the back of her neck, shining an improbable blue-black under the overheads. The woman's expression was unreadable.

"One of them is the guilty one, Ms. O'Banion. You will tell me which one."

"But guilty of what? You mean Robert's murder? Is that what this is about?"

"Yes, one of these wretched men put my boy in that freezer. But there is more. Much more. Will one of you please explain to this lady the things you have done? Tell her why I am holding you here now."

"But I didn't do anything." Jonathan held up his free hand.

"The hell you didn't, Jonathan," Elliot snarled. "You're not going to get out of anything this time."

"You see my problem, Ms. O'Banion. There is no honor amongst thieves. All they say is to accuse the other of the crimes."

"How many crimes?" Margot asked.

"*All* the crimes. My Robert, your fat movie friend, and my darling daughter. One of these pieces of excrement killed my son *and* my daughter, as sure as day turns to night."

"Your daughter?"

At the accusations, the men's voices began roiling through the room again, each shouting down the denials of the other. This was beyond finger pointing. At one point, Jonathan began vigorously shaking the arm of the wheelchair, Elliot Ferrigan holding on to the arm rests for dear life.

Oh Lord, thought Margot. What was Loretta Rose doing up there? Had she called for help yet?

"Your daughter?" she repeated. "I don't under-stand."

Mrs. Estrella turned her gaze on Margot, never once lowering the gun. Would it be loaded, Margot thought. It probably would be. This was Mama Estrella.

"Carlos called me this morning," she said. "He told me he saw a scene from a dirty movie when he was at your apartment last night. He said it was his sister. The poor little girl in the movie. It was my little girl, my Paloma, my little dove."

"Mrs. Estrella," Margot said. "I got that video from the police. It belonged to Colin Peabody. I don't know why he had a copy."

"Well, no one killed your daughter, anyway," Jonathan Keller said. "It was in all the newspapers. Your daughter killed herself."

"You destroyed my baby. You forced her to do those things. She was desperate." Silvery tears were coursing down the woman's cheeks. Margot's blood froze. The situation was way, way beyond her ability to control. She listened in vain for footsteps hurrying toward the basement stairs. Surely Loretta Rose had called *someone* by now.

Jonathan Keller finally moved. "I swear to you, Mrs. Estrella. I had nothing to do with any of this."

"Oh shut up, Keller." Elliot rolled forward a few inches. "You were the goddamn *director*. Don't lie about it."

"But I didn't hurt Robert or even Colin Peabody. You did that."

"Yeah, right. I just hopped right up and did 'em in. Are you serious, Keller? How about it, Mrs. Estrella? You can't believe that, can you?"

For the first time, Louisa Estrella's gaze wavered. "You could have used your wheelchair to move those men. You could have used it to put my Bobby in the freezer."

"Even if that were possible, which it isn't, I couldn't have done those things. I had no reason to hurt anyone."

Louisa looked at Margot. Her eyes which had looked so hard, were still filled with tears. "You see," she said. "You see what

I must decide? You are the one who puts the pieces together in those movies. You must decide which of these men is the guilty one."

Margot cleared her throat. "Perhaps they both did the crimes, Mrs. Estrella. Perhaps they worked as a team. Have you thought of that?"

"No," she said flatly. "They hate each other. Look at them. Those two couldn't team up to eat dinner together. No. They kept the secret of making their filthy movies all these years. Movies of my *fourteen-year old* little girl. I can't believe anyone would sink to doing that."

Abruptly, Louisa Estrella dropped the gun to the floor as though it had become too heavy for her hand. She put a white hand to her face and wiped at the tears. She looked close to collapse.

Margot made a lunge for the gun, the contents of her purse spilling across the floor as she reached for the weapon. She picked it off the dusty floor. It felt cold in her hand. She'd never held a real weapon before. Mrs. Estrella's eyes widened. She pointed at the video cassette lying there, along with Margot's wallet and lipstick.

"Is that the movie?" she asked. "Are those the pictures of my little girl?"

"I don't know," Margot said, feeling breathless. "I just know the film was shot in this building. That's all I know for certain. I was going to take it to this detective I know…"

"Which would prove exactly what?" Keller's face twisted. "Okay. We did some porn stuff when we first started out. Big deal. We needed the money. And old fat ass Colin Peabody was in on it, too. He acted as our esteemed producer. He thought it was all a grand idea. How the hell did we know the kid was so young? She had an I.D., didn't she, Ferrigan?"

Elliot nodded. He, too, looked close to collapse. "She did, Mrs. Estrella. What we were doing wasn't illegal, not till we found out afterward how old she was. I'm sorry. What can I say? We paid the price, believe me. We've been living two lives all these years. And I don't care how liberal people say they are, no one would have let us continue in the business if the story got out again. Not at this stage of our lives. Not with that phony frickin family values political climate the execs preach. Peabody, too. We'd have been toast. His career would have been ashes."

"Was Colin blackmailing you?" Margot asked.

"Oh, hell, sure he was," Jonathan said, brushing a hand over his sweaty face. "But I didn't kill that pig. He was as much to blame for the cover-up as we were. He knew it, too. Playing so holier than thou and innocent. Bullshit. He made plenty off our little movie ventures back then. Blackmail was second nature to somebody like Peabody."

Margot looked at the man. He was furious, hands clenched to his sides. How had they all gotten to this point?

"Oh, go away. Go away, you terrible men," Louisa said. "You disgust me."

Jonathan Keller paused, amazed, and looking like a terrified rabbit, scurried toward the stairs. Margot took the older woman's arm and gently led her to the stairwell. Still clutching the gun, she walked her slowly up the stairs and down the hall to the restaurant door. Keller was nowhere to be seen.

As they stepped into the kitchen, Carlos Estrella looked up, snapped out an order in Spanish and two of the kitchen helpers ran over to them. Margot found Mrs. Estrella released from her grasp and escorted toward the restaurant as Carlos flung down his wooden spoon, and wiping his hands on an apron, hurried to his mother's side. Margot shook her head and handed him his mother's little gun. She hoped the sauces were okay.

What would happen now was anyone's guess. She didn't think she'd learned anything new. Well, the fact was that the men had done blue movies. But, as Jonathan had said, even that wasn't illegal, just the tragedy of having an underage girl who'd then been unable to face the shame, the tragedy of losing face inside her family's ambitious, upwardly mobile circle.

She sighed. Where was Elliot Ferrigan? He must have taken the elevator up. She wondered how on earth Raphael would ever manage to work for him again when this news broke. Perhaps the police would be able to put the pieces together about any other criminal activities. It was certainly beyond her talents.

Margot felt infinitely weary. Hell, and she'd left her purse and belongings scattered downstairs in her desire to get upstairs and get rid of the Mrs. Estrella and the damned gun. Time to get out of here. The Estrellas could work at resolving the family ghosts all by themselves. The police would handle the rest. She was going home. Margot hurried back down the gloomy corridor to the studio basement.

At the bottom, she froze. Flickering lights and shadows were bouncing off the flat white partitions of the kitchen set. And there, on one of the TV monitors, the video she'd been carrying around all day was playing. There was no sound, just the jerky stilted movements of the two men and a young girl making a travesty of sensual love. She looked around, her eyes wide. The studio, deserted. The overhead lights were out, the room as dark as night except for the light from the monitor. She reached out for the light switch and stopped, her hand hovering in space.

Something moved. She peered into the blackness beyond

the white walls of the studio. Out from the shadows emerged a wheelchair, its shiny wheels glinting in the half light. It was empty. Pushing it was a tall man, slowly walking toward her. She blinked. Stopping the chair, he set the brake and moved around its side, easing himself awkwardly down into the seat.

Elliot Ferrigan looked up at her from his chair. "It's called Palindromic," he said. "My arthritis. Quite debilitating, but sometimes it allows me to walk. Why are you back here, Margot?" he asked, concern in his voice. "What is it now?"

"My purse. I just need my car keys," she said. She stared at the man across the ten feet of dimly lit space.

"Of course. They're right there," he said pointing to some dark objects on the floor.

She hesitated. There was something in the sound of his voice that was sending needles of apprehension up her spine. Good Lord, the man had been down here in the dark, watching his terrible old film, watching her come down the stairs. And he could walk. *"Why are you back here?"* he'd asked? Margot suppressed a gasp. *Why are you still here, you bastard,* she said to herself. *You just had to watch your filthy handiwork again and I've caught you at it.*

"I want to take the video with me, Elliot. It should go to the police."

"Yes," he said. "Of course." He wheeled over and stopping the machine, extracted the tape. He held it out to her.

Margot stood frozen. Should she go over and take it? What would he do if she got that close? Ferrigan sat looking at her, waiting for her to move. Suddenly the heavy silence between them was abruptly broken as the elevator cables sprang to life.

"It's coming down!" she said. "Someone's coming!" She dodged around the wheelchair and ran toward the elevator. She was halfway across the floor when the narrow elevator door swung open with a bang and the lanky form of Jonathan Keller stepped into the gloom. Margot had never been so glad to see anyone in her life.

Keller blinked hard in the gray light, first at Margot and then at Elliot. "What the hell are you two still doing down here?" he demanded.

"I had to get my purse," Margot began. She stopped and fought to get her breath. She couldn't seem to get enough air into her lungs. "And he was watching the video," she said. "But why are you back here?"

Keller stared at Margot as though he were listening to a foreign language. "I thought I'd gather up the evidence," he said, pointing at the cassette. "Guess you beat me to it. And so what?"

"But you were right," Margot whispered urgently. "He could have done the murders. He can walk."

Margot looked at Jonathan's face. He seemed preoccupied, indifferent to her explanation. Margot dove for her purse, picking up the keys, her wallet. "Let's get out. Let's just get out of here."

"Margot! Stop!" Elliot Ferrigan's voice bellowed. She turned and stared at him. He lurched forward in his chair, the muscles in his neck corded with effort.

"For God's sake, Margot," he pleaded. "Can't you see? He came back for me. I'm the last one left. The only one left to tell on him. He killed the others. Did Madrid find out you were involved, Keller? Is that what happened? Did he challenge you?"

There was a moment of absolute silence and then Keller grinned, an improbable grin revealing his teeth. "My God, you're still sticking with that story? Well, yeah, that's part of it, isn't it, Elliot. But you're right. I came back for you, you damned cripple."

"Don't you see, Margot?" Ferrigan said. "Don't go with him, Margot! *He's* the goddamned murderer! Can't you tell which of us is telling the truth?"

"Don't listen to him, Margot," Keller said. "I was his frickin production designer for Madrid and Colin's 'accidents,' but he was the goddamned director. You're a witness, too, now. You shoulda kept going when you left here."

Margot looked from man to man and suddenly felt herself caught in Jonathan Keller's grip. The power in the his body pulled her off balance, yanking her backwards toward the elevator.

Screaming, she twisted in his grasp as he fumbled behind her for the handle of the elevator. She yanked sideways as it swung open and she planted her feet firmly. Keller fought to drag her inside. but there was no way she would get in that elevator again, not with *anyone*.

"Elliot!" Margot yelled. The man was frozen in his chair. Finally he reached down and set the chair's brake. He grasped the arms of the wheelchair, lifted himself and stepped stiffly out, the cassette falling to the floor with a clatter.

Picking up one of the heavy microphones from the table, Elliot walked toward them, the steel rod held high in his hand. As he approached, Margot thrust her free elbow hard into Keller's chest. A muffled cry and she was free.

She leaped out of the way as Elliot Ferrigan raised the microphone and brought it down—in slow motion, it seemed—with tremendous force onto Keller's gray-cropped head. Margot distinctly heard the dull thud as it crashed onto his skull.

Margot screamed. The shrill sound of her voice hung in the air and she watched as Jonathan's knees crumbled. The man dropped in a heap to the cement floor. The weight of his body raised a cloud of fine dust.

Margot looked up at Ferrigan in horror. "Is he dead?"

He stared. "I don't know. I think so. Oh Margot, I did a terrible thing." She looked at him in horror. He cleared his throat. "I told Robert Madrid that Jonathan Keller was director on his sister's film."

"You told Robert that? But why? You were there, too." She shook her head. "Why did you turn on Jonathan after all these years?"

"I'm afraid Robert had his suspicions. It was those damned rumors following us around. We couldn't seem to shake them. And then there I was directing *him* week after week. We were together a great deal. So that night we were doing some gambling late in the exec's dining room, just Madrid and me. We started talking about what happened and Madrid got angry. I didn't plan to kill him. I really didn't. I mean Robert Madrid was my *star*, for God's sake. But those Estrella boys really have terrible tempers. I had to defend myself. Then I called Jonathan and he helped set up the scene."

"The scene? You mean the scene in the freezer?" Margot swallowed. "Was Robert already dead or did you put him in there to freeze?"

Ferrigan smiled thinly. "We are not sadists, Margot. The man was unconscious. The freezer was Jonathan's idea. He'd told me about the murder scene in your boyfriend's film. We just did it for real this time. Anyway, I was sick of the lies. I thought I could just live on with paying Colin the money."

"Colin Peabody was blackmailing you, too?"

"Of course, he was. All these years. And then old Colin had to figure out what I'd done. I don't know what tipped him off.

Maybe old Jonathan over there. So Colin started dropping all those hints he likes to drop to everyone. He'd figured out that Robert knew who we all were, and that Keller and I had killed him. Hell, it was in self-defense, but who would care about that after our freezer trick. And now, two people are murdered, three, really, if you count him, and I did the last one." He pointed at Jonathan's body. "God, how did it come to this? I must tell the police."

"Did you murder Colin?" she asked.

He paused. "You've got to understand. It seemed a good idea at the time. The situation was becoming untenable. We were all coming a bit unglued. Jonathan was all for us doing it together. But he did it himself, all by himself." He glanced at the still form. "If he weren't dead, he'd probably confess, too."

There was a long pause. Margot could feel her heart pounding in the silence.

"Do you think I'll go to prison?" he asked. "The murders were strictly unintended consequences. You must believe me. Madrid went berserk on me and then Jonathan just went crazy when Colin upped the ante again. He couldn't handle it anymore. You do believe me, don't you, Margot? I don't want to go to prison." He reached down, picking the cassette off the floor.

"Prison?" Margot caught the unnatural light in his eyes. "I'm sure you'll get an excellent lawyer. You'll probably get off."

"But you don't think I deserve to get off, do you? That's what you're thinking," he said. "How could I have known Jonathan would carry everything to such lengths? Believe me, Margot, I am not a barbarian. I didn't want anyone to *die*. I really didn't."

Margot stared at the man, the cassette still resting on his lap. She felt nothing, not pity, not fear.

"I'm going for help," she said. She looked over at the

crumpled body sprawled on the cement floor, then at the man still huddled in his wheelchair. She shook her head and walked away toward the stairs.

All this revenge and avenging and the three men couldn't even make their stupid, terrible, sickening crimes go off without a hitch. They remained clueless to the end.

Epilogue

"I'M REALLY SORRY ABOUT ROBERT, CARLOS. He was an innocent victim, a victim of those two murderous idiots with the Keystone Kop mentalities. Man, I can't believe those guys." Max took a bite of Carlos Estrella's legendary *Pasta del Estación*, a glass of Loretta Rose's Chardonnay of the Month in his hand. "None of them is really worth a damn. Both fools dancing around keeping their mediocre careers going, while they kept a half remembered scandal from ages ago under wraps. And then they kill off a brilliant producer..."

"Max," Margot said. "Don't start saying nice things about Colin Peabody now. He was part of the porn ring. He was blackmailing everyone. It's really all his fault what eventually occurred."

"Of course, you're right. But you gotta admit they're an incredible bunch of bozos. And then Ferrigan didn't even manage to kill off Keller when he bopped him on the head. If he'd killed him, maybe he could have lied his way out everything. What a waste of energy."

"He confessed to me," Margot said.

Max shook his head. "His word against yours, babe. Not much proof there."

"He tried to kill Jonathan."

"Sure and he was probably going to go for you next, but Keller will recover. His head is made of cement. The nice thing is that, among everything else, I betcha he's gonna charge his old buddy with attempted murder."

"But which of the murders did each of them do? I'm confused on who did what." This was Loretta Rose, still looking strained from not only losing her financial backer who was wheeled away through the wine bar in handcuffs, but from watching Jonathan Keller being put in a police ambulance, interrupting the cheery crowd tasting last night's Pinot Noir Library Selection.

Max shrugged. "Well, like Margot said, Elliot got Jonathan to help him take care of Robert. I guess Elliot thought initially that he could get Robert to keep quiet about their past forays into porn—you know, stress the fact his baby sister was a porn star, contrast that with his current star status, stuff like that. But Robert wouldn't go along."

"Bobby had strong family values," Carlos said.

"Right," Max said. "So Elliot was right about one thing, no matter how ancient, the scandal would have ruined him. God, look what happened to Roman Polanski. And then Jonathan got involved. And forget that Elliot can walk, he couldn't have maneuvered Robert's body the way it was maneuvered. But old Jonathan's strong as a horse. Now I'm not completely clear about Colin's demise. Both of those idiots had prime motive for doing away with Colin. No one enjoys paying blackmail for the rest of their lamentable lives and Elliot told Margot that Colin kept raising the premium. So I figure for the second time in their lives, the boys teamed up. But God, all those dummies had to do was pay up, shut up, keep quiet, and let their un-illustrious careers continue at the snail's pace they were on. But, typically, they couldn't leave bad enough alone."

"It's kind of funny in a horrible way. Jonathan Keller's one and only stint as first director and look where it led him."

Max shook his head. "Yeah, and he was always telling *me* how to do stuff. He was probably dying to tell me how good he was as a porn director. Hell, no one cared, I mean no one except your family, Carlos, of course. But those inept idiots weren't actually responsible for your poor sister's death. were they? She must have lied, or someone lied for her about her I.D. How the hell were those dolts supposed to know the truth, how underage she was?"

"Estrella family legend has it that Paloma was the supreme victim, not that we were ever encouraged to talk about what happened." Carlos sighed and Loretta Rose took his hand. "And Paloma was a victim, of course. She was just a kid. But she was an old, old, fourteen-year old kid. Our family, all of us, failed her. Then she took mama's stash of Valium. Mama has terrible guilt about that…and I think mama's guilt fueled this vengeance streak she's been on, too. Thinking back, I don't know if Paloma really realized what she was doing. Poor dove."

There was a pause as Loretta Rose and Margot sniffed noisily into hastily retrieved tissues.

"So you're kind of head of the family now, aren't you Carlos?" Max said.

Carlos laughed. "Sure, that's if you don't count Mama Louisa. Mama will always be in charge. And then, of course, there's Uncle Wayne…"

Margot and Loretta Rose looked up. "You mean Detective Wilson?" Margot said.

Carlos smiled broadly. "Yeah, however he fits in. I've never been totally sure exactly what his position is with the family. But maybe now that we're all grown up..."

"It might be time to *ask*, Carlos," Loretta Rose said. "It might be interesting to know."

"Good old Uncle Wayne..." Carlos said.

"Well, *whoever* he turns out to be, Robert should never have been killed. And Colin shouldn't have blackmailed his friends," Loretta Rose said, still angry.

"Colin Peabody, the great producer of porn. Jeeze. Man, the studio would have loved that. They would have axed him with a vengeance. Hell, they were going to, anyway, I think. Oh, meant to mention it, but I'm outta there after we finish *Extreme Cuisine*. No more studio for me."

Margot blinked. "You're out of Arcturus?"

"Sure. Gotta go while the going's good. They want big commercial stuff. I don't do big commercial. I'm weary of fighting their bottom line. But," Max smiled, "you know all that money from Colin? I don't mean the houses and stuff. We'll give all that to some good causes. But the money, the cold hard cash, undoubtedly from the unwilling pockets of Keller and Ferrigan and God knows who else...well, it's time to go independent, don't you think? First, we're gonna give you guys this old building," he said looking at Carlos and Loretta Rose. "Margot hates it—not your places, of course, but the rest of it. You've both lost your financial backer and this way you can work out the economic details by yourselves. Margot and I, well, we'll start our own company, too. You and me, babe."

Margot nodded, smiling. She realized she was thrilled at the idea. The next chapter in their lives would be filled with uncertainty, fraught with danger, packed with crises at every turn—all the things Max thrived on.

She reached for his hand across the table, her newly reset ruby glowing deep crimson under the soft, flattering lights of Café Estrellado. "It's time, Max, " she said. "It's time.

— THE END —

Check out these other fine titles by
Durban House at your local book store.

Exceptional Books
by
Exceptional Writers

FICTION

NONFICTION

FICTION

A COMMON GLORY   Robert Middlemiss
What happens when a Southern news reporter falls in love with a WWII jazz loving
English pilot and wants to take him home to her segregationist parents? It is in the
crucible of war that pilot and reporter draw close across their vulnerabilities and fears.
War, segregation, and the fear of death in lonely skies confront them as they clutch at
the first exquisite promptings of a passionate love.

BLUEWATER DOWN   Rick O'Reilly
Retired L.A. police lieutenant Jack Douglas wanted only one thing after years on the
bomb squad—the peace and serenity of sailing his yacht, Tally Ho. But Lisa enters
his carefully planned world, and even as he falls in love with her she draws him into
a violent matrix of murderers and terrorists bent on their destruction.

BY ROYAL DESIGN   Norbert Reich
Hitler's Third Reich was to last a thousand years but it collapsed in twelve. In Berlin,
in the belly of the dying Reich, seeds were sown for a new regime, one based on
aristocratic ruling classes whose time had come. Berlin's Charitee Hospital brought
several children into the world that night in 1944, setting into motion forces that
would ultimately bring two venerable Germanic families, the Hohenzollerns and the
Habsburgs to power.

THE COROT DECEPTION   J. Brooks Van Dyke
London artists are getting murdered. The killer leaves behind an odd signature.
And when Richard Watson, an artist, discovers the corpse of his gallery owner, he
investigates, pitting himself and his twin sister, Dr. Emma Watson against the ruthless
killer. Steeped in the principles of criminal detection they learned from Sherlock
Holmes, the twins search for clues in the Edwardian art world and posh estates of
1910 London.

CRY HAVOC   John Hamilton Lewis
The worst winter in over a hundred years grips the United States and most of the
western world. America's first lady president, Abigail Stewart, must deal with harsh
realities as crop failures, power blackouts, shortages of gasoline and heating oil push
the nation toward panic. But the extreme weather conditions are only a precursor
of problems to come as Prince Nasser, a wealthy Saudi prince, and a cleric plot to
destroy western economies.

DEADLY ILLUSIONS
Chester D. Campbell

A young woman, Molly Saint, hires Greg and Jill McKenzie to check her husband's background, then disappears. It starts them on a tangled trail of deceit, with Jill soon turning up a close family connection. The deeper the McKenzie's dig, the more deadly illusions they face. Nothing appears to be what it seemed at first as the fear for Molly's life grows.

EXTREME CUISINE
Kit Sloane

Film editor Margot O'Banion and director Max Skull find a recipe for disaster behind the kitchen doors of a trendy Hollywood restaurant. Readers of discriminating taste are cordially invited to witness the preparation and presentation of fine fare as deadly drama. As Max points out, dinner at these places "provides an evening of theater and you get to eat it!" Betrayal, revenge, and perhaps something even more unsavory, are on the menu tonight.

THE GARDEN OF EVIL
Chris Holmes

A brilliant but bitter sociopath has attacked the city's food supply; five people are dead, twenty-six remain ill from the assault. Family physician, Gil Martin and his wife Tara, the county's Public Health Officer, discover the terrorist has found a way to incorporate the poison directly into the raw vegetables themselves. How is that possible? As the Martins get close to cracking the case, the terrorist focuses all his venom on getting them and their family. It's now a personal conflict—a mano-a-mano—between him and them.

KIRA'S DIARY
Edward T. Gushee

Beautiful, talented violinist, seventeen-year-old Kira Klein was destined to be assigned to Barracks 24. From the first day she is imprisoned in the Auschwitz brothel, Kira becomes the unwilling mistress of Raulf Becker, an SS lieutenant whose responsibility is overseeing the annihilation of the Jewish prisoners. Through the stench of death and despair emerges a rich love story, richly told with utter sensitivity, warmth and even humor.

THE LUKARILLA AFFAIR
Jerry Banks

Right from the start it was a legal slugfest. Three prominent men, a state senator, a corporate president, and the manager of a Los Angeles professional football team are charged with rape and sodomy by three minimum wage employees of a catering firm, Ginny, Peg and Tina. A courtroom gripper by Jerry Banks who had over forty years in the trade, and who tells it like it happens—fast and quick.

MURDER ON THE TRAP
J. Preston Smith

Life has been pretty good to Bon Sandifer. After his tour in Vietnam he marries his childhood sweetheart, is a successful private investigator, and rides his

Harley=Davidson motorcycle. Then the murders begin on Curly Trap Road. His wife Shelly dies first. A fellow biker is crushed under a Caddie. And his brother is killed riding a Harley. When Sandifer remarries and finds happiness with his deaf biker bride, the murderous web tightens and he grapples with skeptical detectives and old Vietnam memories.

PHARAOH'S FRIEND
Nancy Yawitz Linkous

When Egyptian myth permeates the present, beliefs are tested and lives are changed. My Worth vacations in Egypt to soothe the pain over her daughter's death. She dreams of a cat whose duty is to transport souls to the afterlife. And then a real cat, four hundred and twenty pounds of strength and sinew, appears at an archeological dig. Those that cross its path are drawn into intrigue and murder that is all too real.

SPRING, 2005

NONFICTION

I ACCUSE: JIMMY CARTER
Philip Pilevsky
AND THE RISE OF MILITANT ISLAM

Philip Pilevsky makes a compelling argument that President Jimmy Carter's failure to support the Shah of Iran led to the 1979 revolution led by Ayatollah Ruhollah Komeini. That revolution legitimized and provided a base of operations for militant Islamists across the Middle East. By allowing the Khomeini revolution to succeed, Carter traded an aging, accommodating shah for a militant theocrat who attacked the American Embassy and held the staff workers hostage. In the twenty-four years since the Khomenini revolution, radical Islamists, indoctrinated in Iran have grown ever bolder in attacking the West and more sophisticated in their tactics of destruction.

MOTHERS SPEAK: FOR LOVE OF FAMILY
Rosalie Fuscaldo Gaziano

In a world of turbulent change, the need to connect, to love and be loved is greater and more poignant than ever. Women cry out for simple, direct answers to the question, "How can I make family life work in these challenging times?" This book offers hope to all who are struggling to balance the demands of work and family and to cope with ambiguity, isolation, or abandonment. The author gives strong evidence that the family unit is still the best way to connect and bear enduring fruit.

THE PASSION OF AYN RAND'S CRITICS
James S. Valliant

For years, best-selling novelist and controversial philosopher Ayn Rand has been the victim of posthumous portrayals of her life and character taken from the pages of the biographies by Nathaniel Branden and Barbara Branden. Now, for the first time, Rand's own never-before-seen-journal entries on the Brandens, and the first in-depth analysis of the Brandens' works, reveal the profoundly inaccurate and unjust depiction of their former mentor.

SEX, LIES & PI's   Ali Wirsche & Marnie Milot
The ultimate guide to find out if your lover, husband, or wife is having an affair. Follow Ali and Marnie, two seasoned private investigators, as they spy on brazen cheaters and find out what sweet revenge awaits. Learn 110 ways to be your own detective. Laced with startling stories, Sex, Lies & PI's is riveting and often hilarious.

WHAT MAKES A MARRIAGE WORK   Malcolm D. Mahr
Your hear the phrase "marry and settle down," which implies life becomes more serene and peaceful after marriage. This simply isn't so. Living together is one long series of experiments in accommodation. What Makes A Marriage Work? is a hilarious yet perceptive collection of fifty insights reflecting one couple's searching, experimenting, screaming, pouting, nagging, whining, moping, blaming, and other dysfunctional behaviors that helped them successfully navigate the turbulent sea of matrimony for over fifty years. (Featuring 34 New Yorker cartoons of wit and wisdom.)